MONKEY BUSINESS

THE ERICA JEWELL SERIES - BOOK 2

KATHRYN LEDSON

PILYARA PRESS

ISBN: 978-1-925827-16-3
Cover Art by Kellie Dennis at Book Cover By Design

Pilyara Press
Melbourne

For Annette

ALSO BY KATHRYN LEDSON

Rough Diamond (The Erica Jewell Series - Book 1)

COMING SOON

Grand Slam (The Erica Jewell series - Book 3)

A tap on the window snapped me awake and I sat up, listening. Had I dreamed it? My bedside clock said three a.m.

'Hello?' I said, croaky voiced.

'It's me.'

'Oh!'

I jumped up, flicked on the lamp, called out, 'What are you doing here?', as I rushed to the mirror. This wasn't what I expected, this man at my bedroom window. One who was supposed to be on a plane or going somewhere, not standing in my front garden.

'I, ah, forgot something,' he said.

'What did you forget?' I shoved the framed photo of the two of us into the bedside drawer.

'Can I come in or will we just chat through the window?'

I pushed my fingers through tangled hair and blew into my cupped hand, checking my breath. When I opened the front door, Jack Jones was standing there with a sheepish yet still-perfect face. He was wearing camouflage army pants and a snug black T-shirt. His hair was scruffy. He'd been sleeping.

I looked past him to the four-wheel-drive parked at the kerb, Joe's silhouette behind the wheel.

'What's Joe doing?' I said.

'Waiting for me. Can I come in?'

I swung the door wider and he stepped inside my house.

I said, 'I thought you were going away.'

'I am. Tonight.'

'It's now morning.' In the dim light we looked at each other. He towered over me, even more than usual in his army boots. 'So,' I said, 'what did you forget?'

'You left this at my house. I forgot to give it to you last night.'

He held out a cheap, plastic hair comb. I took it. Yes, I may well have left it at Jack's house last time I was there, or when I was living there a few months ago, hiding from bad guys with guns. Back in the good old days when life was, well, life-threatening.

'I can probably afford a new one,' I said. 'They're about fifty cents.'

'I thought it might be a special one.'

I turned it over, inspected it. 'No. It's not special, but thanks anyway.'

'Okay,' he said. 'Well, I'll go.'

'Alright. Um. Thank you?'

We stared at each other a few moments more. What else did he want? Maybe to ask me to wait for him, like men used to do before they went off to war. That'd be nice. And I'd wait, of course. But more likely, he wanted to ask me to put his bins out.

He sighed. 'And something else.'

'What?'

'I didn't kiss you enough.' He put his arms around me and I leaned into him.

'If you insist.' I could take as much kissing from Jack Jones as he cared to dish out. It was a soft, tender kiss. Last night he'd come to find me at the pub and told me he was going away. He'd kissed me very nicely, but wouldn't say where he was going.

I tugged at his hand, stepping back into my bedroom, away from the open front door.

He said, 'I can't stay.'

'A few minutes?'

'Alright.'

I lay on the bed, pulling him down next to me. He resisted but only slightly. Willing and reserved at the same time. Probably trying to work out how he could love me without me catching on that he might actually love me. But anyway, he couldn't stay. That was okay. This was better than nothing. Maybe. He kissed me again. Still soft but lingering. Nope. I wanted him to leave. This was going to be painful. I put a hand on his chest.

'Talk to me,' I said.

'What about?'

'Well, where are you going in the middle of the night dressed like G.I. Jack? Am I allowed to know?'

He lay on his side, head propped on his hand, and brushed my cheek with his thumb. 'No.'

'Is it a secret?'

'Yes.'

'Is it dangerous?'

He gazed at me. Jack's eyes have a way of revealing his mood and they were currently showing concern. For what, I didn't know.

I pressed, 'What do you have to do?'

He hesitated. 'There's a guy . . . causing trouble. Big trouble.'

'What sort of trouble?'

He shook his head.

'But why you?' I said. 'Why do *you* have to go?'

He smiled. 'Because, baby, I'm the best. Didn't you know?' He gave me a wink.

Yes, I knew that. He's the best in the business. The best person for anyone needing a big, tough soldier to sort out troublemakers in dangerous places. Or a hired gun to secretly deal with local bad guys, terrorists even. Or someone to rescue an office worker who might get herself kidnapped in a nice safe place like Melbourne or Sydney. And then make love to her in a flash hotel and break her heart by going off on a dangerous mission, which is probably just a cover for the mercenary's commitment issues.

Jack kissed me again, much deeper. He ran his hand over my back and pulled me closer. I wallowed in the feel of him – the warm length of his body. His hard body. Goodness. Joe honked the horn. One short toot the neighbours probably didn't even hear. Joe's so polite.

CHAPTER 1

*A*h, autumn in Melbourne. When we farewell the sleepless, sweaty nights of summer and welcome the frost, snuggle up on a soft sofa with hot chocolate or even better, a nip of ancient cognac served in crystal, all before a roaring fire in the posh Brighton home of a wet-your-pants hunk of a mercenary.

That would have been nice but unfortunately not where I was right now, and even though said handsome tough guy was sitting next to me, I didn't feel I could do with him what I wanted.

Jack smiled. Actually, it was more of a smirk. 'Hot pie?' he said.

'Very funny.'

'I'm just asking if you want a pie.'

'No, you're not. You're being a smart-arse because the Mag*pies* are winning.'

'Pies are on fire.'

'They're not on fire,' I said. 'They're only thirty-eight points ahead.'

The crowd roared and I looked to see what was happening. A Richmond player handpassed the ball . . . straight to a Collingwood player.

'Come on, Tigers!' shouted Steve. 'Jesus Christ, what are they *doing*?'

I'd lost interest. Richmond had been brilliant last year; such a welcome change and everyone predicted another mighty season for them. But so far, nothing but disappointment, despite Steve and me willing them on, forever hopeful. In fact, we'd stuck with them since we were kids, but they hadn't won a grand final since 1980. Not that either of us remembered it, being one-year-olds at the time.

Steve shook his head, disgusted.

I shivered, blowing onto my cold hand, the one that wasn't holding the plastic cup of beer. Jack took that cold hand and rubbed it between his palms. Heat radiated from my stomach and I was instantly warm. Hot, actually.

'Tell me again,' I yelled over the roar of the crowd, 'why we're not sitting up there in the nice, warm members' area? Or in the Dega Oil box drinking free wine. From real glass.'

Jack said, 'It's better here. In with the action.'

'But you're an MCC member. You love swanning around in posh places.'

'I don't *swan*, Erica. And I only like the Melbourne Cricket Club during cricket season.' He said to Steve, 'Another beer?'

'Yeah. Make it a double,' Steve mumbled into his hands.

'Same again, girls?'

'I think I'll have champagne,' said Lucy. 'Celebrate another Collingwood win.' She and Jack high-fived.

'They haven't won yet,' I countered, not very convincingly. 'I'll have champagne, too.'

'Sparkling wine,' Jack corrected, 'but I'm sure even that's an insult to sparkling wine.'

He stood and made his way along the aisle past other Collingwood supporters. As usual, women gazed up at him, open-mouthed with shock at his gorgeousness.

Lucy scooted across to Jack's seat and nudged me with her shoulder. 'Having fun?'

'Why do I have to sit with all the Collingwood supporters?' I mumbled. 'How come I'm not up there?' I looked at the Dega Oil box, where I could see my Richmond-supporting workmates *swan-*

ning around in warmth and happiness. With nice wine. In proper glasses.

Lucy said, 'How did Jack's mission go? I wasn't sure if I should ask.'

I shrugged. 'He just said it isn't finished yet. I don't think he's allowed to say.'

'What does that mean? Not finished?'

Another shrug. 'I guess it means he'll be going away again.'

Jack had been away for two weeks on some secret thing, and then called me out of the blue, saying he was back and suggesting we go to the footy. I'd asked at work about tickets to the corporate box, which were available, but Jack said he likes mucking in with the plebs. He didn't actually say plebs. Or mucking in.

I peered around Lucy at Steve. He was sitting there with his head in his hands. Luce reached across and gave his leg a pat. 'Cheer up, my darling. There's always next year.'

He shook his head and groaned.

As Jack made his way back to us, women stood, pretending to make space for him to pass, but really just wanting his attention. He smiled into their faces, oblivious to their underlying desire. Or maybe he *was* aware of it and just thought that's how all women felt about all men. Lustful. I took the two champagnes and handed one to Lucy.

'Thanks,' we said in unison.

He screwed up his nose. 'Don't know how you can drink that rubbish.'

'See?' I said. 'You're a snob.'

Lucy stayed in Jack's seat and Jack sat in hers. Luce shouldered me again and gave me a wink.

I said, quietly, 'Thanks for coming tonight.'

'I love watching my boys kick butt.'

For some reason I'd been overwhelmed with shyness at the thought of seeing Jack, and had asked Steve and Lucy to come along. They both knew about Jack's secret life, and mine, and this made it easier when socialising and answering the inevitable, 'How was your week? Work? What did you get up to?' especially when Jack's response could be, 'Oh, killed a couple of bad guys . . . '

The match and pain finally over – the Melbourne Cricket Ground more like the killing fields than a football oval – we all headed for my house, where Jack and Steve had left their cars. Steve and Lucy held hands, I walked next to Luce, and Jack walked with Steve as they talked about the game. Steve was frustrated as usual and wondering where it all went wrong. Jack was kind about it, saying that Collingwood seemed to be especially brilliant tonight, that they would've beaten any team.

I wondered if I should walk next to Jack and hold his hand. It's pretty intimate, hand holding. In a way, it's more intimate than sex, which is something I had actually done with Jack, a few weeks ago, in Sydney. But only once. Well, more than once but it was all on the one night. Couples hold hands, and we weren't a couple. I stuffed my hands into my coat pockets.

We stopped at my local, the London Tavern in Lennox Street, Richmond, a popular drinking hole before and after games at the MCG. There was a big crowd in the pub and, as we pushed through to the bar, Jack reached for my hand and I gave it to him.

CHAPTER 2

The next morning was agonising in every possible way. Thinking about the past was distressing, the current moment painful, and the future disastrous. The night before, Jack, Steve and Lucy had walked me home from the pub, where the happy couple then waved and drove off, but not before Steve asked Jack if he was interested in playing squash on Tuesday nights, to which Jack said he was but couldn't commit to every week. I'd asked Jack if he wanted to come in for coffee, to which he responded by checking his watch and saying he had an early start, kissing my cheek and driving away without making any plans for more time with *me*.

And now this moment sucked because there was just me, alone in my house, apart from my cat.

And thinking about the future caused general panic about everything. Not least the fact that it was Saturday morning and I had not a single plan for the weekend.

On the pillow next to me Axle was suddenly awake. He pounced on my stomach so abruptly and with such fierceness I jumped and squealed, even though I'm always expecting it. Then he darted away, changed personality, and returned purring softly and bumping my hand gently with his head. Breakfast time, and that too was something

I needed to be ready for because if I'm not quick enough, he might decide to go hunt his own and leave some for me. Something headless or a nice piece of offal, for example.

I rolled out of bed, stretched, yawned, pushed fingers through my weighty curls to untangle them. I shivered and pulled on my bright pink Ugg boots, a present from Lucy and much nicer than the Woolworths nana slippers Mum had given me, which I couldn't take to the op shop because Mum always looked for them when she called in. It was a cold morning but the sun was shining and it was already a gorgeous day. I thought how nice it would be to go for a walk in the Botanic Gardens with a handsome guy, or maybe a bike ride along the Yarra River. Brunch on Swan Street, where I first met Jack. Well, where I first met him after the *initial* meeting, when he was in disguise and bleeding to death in my front garden. I hadn't recognised him when he'd come into that cafe and sat opposite me two weeks later. He'd wanted his gun back. It was in my laundry hamper. Now I have my own gun in my laundry hamper. At least, I assume it's still there. I never touch the bottom of the pile because I'm scared of it – the gun, not the dirty laundry.

I had a shower, dressed and headed for the kitchen. My house is pretty basic: a small, semi-detached Victorian, only five metres wide, with a tiny courtyard garden at the front and a long passageway that runs from the front door past my bedroom, the spare bedroom and the bathroom, which doubles as the laundry. There's an open kitchen/living room at the back that looks out through French doors to a miniature backyard and carport. My house was in desperate need of renovating, which I'd been considering.

Axle crouched at the French doors, tail twitching, his eye on something scuttling around out there. Hopefully something that would stay out there or preferably scuttle next door and get eaten by *their* cat.

'Here, baby.' I took his food from the fridge and scooped some into his bowl. Axle trotted across the room, leaped onto the bench and scoffed it down. The eating-from-the-bench habit was something he picked up at Jack's house when we were staying there. Everyone is spoiled at Jack's house.

My landline rang and I answered it.

'Good morning,' said Jack.

'Oh! Hi! Surprise!'

'What's the surprise?'

'Well, that you're calling me.'

'Why are you surprised?'

'Well . . . because I just saw you last night. Don't want to get sick of each other.' I laughed in an overacting kind of way and felt like an idiot.

And Jack, being considerate, respectful, and well-mannered, changed the subject. 'Have you got any plans today?'

'Yes, heaps. In fact, I'm exhausted thinking about everything I've got to do today.'

'Shame,' he said. 'It's a beautiful day.'

'What were you thinking?' I asked quickly. 'I mean, they're not so important I can't shuffle them around, fit in something else.'

'I thought we could have a picnic at the zoo.'

'I *love* the zoo.'

'But it'd be all afternoon, and if you don't have time for that —'

'It's fine. I can fit it in.'

'We can go another time —'

'No, let's go today.'

'Next week maybe —'

'Let's go to the goddamn zoo!'

He chuckled. 'I'll pick you up.'

'What should I bring?' I said. 'I need to go shopping.'

'I've got it all. Joe's re-stocked the cupboards.'

'So . . . Joe's back, too? From wherever you guys went.'

'He is.'

'Don't suppose you could survive long without Joe.'

He tried to sound annoyed but I could tell he was smiling. 'I'm perfectly capable of looking after myself, Erica. I'm a big boy. And military trained, remember.'

'Soldiers don't have to cook for themselves. Unless they're in the jungle, but even then I suppose you just eat worms and poison berries.'

'I'll pick you up at twelve,' he said, the only possible response to the rubbish I was talking.

'See you then,' I said, hung up and danced around on the spot.

IT TOOK me ages to find something to wear that didn't look like I'd spent any time on it. I finally settled on my old jeans because my bum looked nice in them, a T-shirt that clung in all the right spots and was just the right length, even though it was old and worn, and my comfy old sneakers because I thought we'd be doing a bit of walking. And no make-up. I checked the mirror. I looked like a homeless person. It took me two minutes to change into something nice.

Jack knocked on the door at quarter to twelve. Fifteen minutes early, but I was expecting it because he's always early. Usually half an hour. I suspected this annoying habit developed after he was late for breakfast with his parents and wife in New York on September 11, 2001. They were waiting for him at the top of the World Trade Centre. Personally, I was glad he wasn't on time for that particular appointment.

'You look nice,' he said.

'This old thing?'

He stepped inside and kissed my cheek.

I said, 'Do you want coffee before we go?'

'You make horrible instant coffee.'

'Well, I've got an expensive coffee machine some guy gave me for Christmas.'

'Some guy?'

'A pretty cute one. But I don't know how to use it, the machine.'

'I showed you how to use it the day I gave it to you. And several times since.'

Axle galloped up the passageway from the living room. 'Shit,' said Jack and stepped back. Axle loves Jack, but in a weird kind of way. He launched himself at Jack's leg and hung off his thigh like a koala. 'Jesus, that hurts. His claws are getting sharper. And longer.'

'You need to catch him before he attaches,' I said, pulling gently at Axle's little paws and cooing, coaxing him.

'You make him sound like a leech.'

Axle released and darted under my bed, chasing some imaginary mouse. Well, I hoped it was imaginary.

I said, 'Maybe we should just get going.'

'Good idea,' Jack said, rubbing his leg.

We drove in Jack's lovely old convertible Mustang. A 1967 model, he'd told me the only other time we'd driven in it, last Christmas Day. My car's almost as old, but not a classic. I don't think Mazda makes classics. And Jack's doesn't have rust. He's got a garage full of cars and motorbikes but I like the Mustang best.

As we skirted the city, he said loudly, so I could hear him over the wind, road noise and radio, 'Are you still thinking about an investment property?'

Before Jack had left on his mission, I'd asked him to advise me on buying another property, but now I wasn't so sure.

'I think I'll renovate instead,' I said. 'Good idea?'

He nodded. 'Can't go wrong.'

But I really wanted to ask about the mission. It was hard to talk though, with all the noise, and it didn't seem appropriate to shout out, 'So, did you kill anyone?' Instead I asked if he wanted to eat straight away or have a walk around when we got there.

'Walk,' he said.

We parked and as we headed for the zoo entrance, I said, 'Will you have to go away again?' He didn't respond and he was carrying all the picnic things, so I said, 'Why don't you let me take some of that?'

'I'm fine,' he said.

'Here.' I took the picnic rug from under his arm so now he just had a basket and small esky to carry.

'Thanks,' he said.

'Give me the basket.' I tried to take it.

'No, I'm fine.'

'Really, I want to help.' I pulled at the basket and it fell on the ground. A packet of biscuits rolled out. 'Sorry.' As I gathered up the basket, without looking at him, I said, 'You didn't answer my question.'

'Yes, I will.'

'Yes, you'll answer my question or yes, you'll be going away again?' I stood straight and we looked at each other.

'Going away.'

'Oh. Right.'

We stood in a short queue behind some mums and their kids. The mums were trying to discreetly check out Jack. I've noticed that when women perv at him, they also look me up and down and I know what they're thinking. *She's not good enough.*

'I'll pay,' I said, reaching for my purse.

'No, I've got it.' He took his wallet from his back pocket.

'But you always pay.'

'And I always will.'

I *LOVE* MONKEYS. They're so funny and the spider ones remind me of Axle. We watched them for ages and I chortled at the constant parade of mischief. When I glanced at Jack, he was watching me, not the monkeys, with a smile. He held out his hand, I took it and we walked, and stood in front of the baboons with their pink bums. One picked a flea from another and ate it. I can understand why Darwin's theory holds water.

Jack turned his back on the baboons and leaned against the glass wall, arms folded across his chest. 'I've got a favour to ask.' He glanced around and so did I. We were alone.

'Okay.'

'I can't tell you about this mission, but I need your help with it.'

I didn't think he was happy about having to ask me whatever he was about to ask, and that made me nervous because Jack and I work secretly for an organisation of vigilantes called 'the Team'. Jack's job is to quietly, illegally, go about eradicating nasty types from Melbourne's streets. And my job is to take Jack's orders if and when he has any. But I didn't think this current mission was based in Melbourne, and I also hadn't realised it was a Team assignment. Jack is a consultant for the federal police and armed forces, too.

'What's wrong?' I said.

'Nothing,' he said, too quickly, and adjusted his sunglasses. He looked at his feet. 'There's a guy I need you to watch.'

He glanced at me and I nodded for him to continue.

'My team for this job isn't ideal.' He paused. 'The reason I'm asking you is because I trust you.'

'*What* are you asking me?' This was serious shit. Jack didn't need anyone for anything. Except Joe to cook his dinner and organise the cleaning lady.

'Joe's on my team – obviously I trust him – and one of the others I selected because of his experience, but the fourth guy I don't know well enough. I think he uses drugs, and I can't have that.'

'Right.'

'There's a pub he likes in Richmond, near your house. Would you go there? Watch him and report back?'

'Sure.'

'Thanks.'

'Can I take Lucy?'

He looked away, considering it. 'Yes. Take Lucy. No details, though.'

'No details.' I nodded once, serious. 'When do you want me to go?'

'Tonight.'

CHAPTER 3

Okay, so I told Lucy I was on a case for the Team and, yes, that was more than I'd intended saying, but it was easier if she knew I had something important to do. Otherwise she'd make me get drunk and dance. But Lucy is also sensible and trustworthy – she saved Jack's life after all – so when she suggested we go in disguise, because it was an undercover thing, I agreed straight away. Lucy arrived at my place looking exactly like Lucy.

'I thought you wanted to go in disguise,' I said.

'I *am* in disguise. Do you ever see me in anything other than a nurse's uniform?'

Good point. 'What have you got for me?' I indicated the bag she was carrying.

'This!' She whipped a wig from the bag. A straight, shoulder-length, blonde one. It couldn't have been more different to my unmanageable brunette mane.

'Why do you own a wig?' I said.

'Remember when I had that nightmare haircut? I wore this until it grew out.'

'That's right. I remember.'

'It's a good wig.'

And so it was. We looked like the Bobbsey Twins except I was a lot taller. I liked myself as a blonde.

THE PLAN WAS that Jack would be around. He was going to park somewhere nearby and we'd be in touch by phone. He was worried about me, I could tell, and I thought that was sweet.

There was a long queue at the club. I shivered, hopping from foot to foot, rubbing my bare arms. I was dressed like a hooker because from what I'd seen – usually driving past on my way home from a movie or dinner – that's how you're supposed to dress for a place like this. I wore a skirt that sat just under my bum, a strappy top and frighteningly high heels. Anyway, I knew I was wearing the right thing because every other girl in the line was dressed the same. Although mostly they looked a lot younger than me.

My phone buzzed in my bag. A message from Jack: *Are you there yet? I've been looking for you.*

I glanced around. Couldn't see him. I messaged back: *In the q.*

Where?

Nr the back. I'm blonde! I smiled when I thought about him reading that. Where was he? Sitting in a car somewhere with binoculars?

Walk to the front of the queue, tell security your first names and he'll let you in.

I told Lucy and as we walked, I messaged: *Ur sposed 2 abrev8.* I gave the guy our names and he let us in.

Jack replied: *We've had this conversation. I refuse. And you look . . . Jesus, be careful.*

Now that made me smile. The zoo had been a fizzer. Not in a zoo sense but in a romantic sense. After our conversation beside the monkey den, with Jack showing me photos of the guy in question, we'd had our picnic, which potentially could have led to something smoochy and nice, but all I could think about was my assignment, and I'd found I was checking my watch all the time, knowing I needed to call Lucy and go shopping for something to wear.

Inside the club we elbowed our way through the crowd and my

phone vibrated again. Another message from Jack, this time with a photo attached: *He's just arrived.*

Okay, so now I knew what the guy was wearing. I looked around but didn't see him.

Lucy yelled in my ear, 'Let's have champagne!'

I yelled back, 'I can't. It'll make me drunk and I need to be alert.'

'Spoilsport.'

'I'll have beer,' I said. 'Jack's buying our drinks, by the way.'

'Well, in that case I'll have real champagne!'

'He'd expect no less.' I handed her a fifty. Jack had given me three hundred dollars. I don't know what the hell he thought I'd be doing with all that money.

While Lucy was at the bar, I saw the guy. He wasn't hard to spot with his carrot-coloured hair. He was talking to some other guy – a pretty cute dark-haired one – across the room. Lucy returned with my beer and I sipped on it, watching my target.

IT DIDN'T TAKE LONG for Carrot Top to find the guy I assumed was his dealer. Even from a distance their conversation looked shady, with my guy checking something in the other guy's hand and then giving him money in exchange for something.

Lucy was talking to someone next to me. I was surprised to see the cute dark-haired guy cosying up to her. She was laughing with him but not in a flirty way. I knew Lucy – she'd give him a few minutes and send him on his way well before he got any ideas. I looked for my guy again but he'd disappeared. I said to Luce, 'I'll be back in a minute.'

She nodded and I pushed through the crowd (God, it was hard work. Why do people think this is fun?) to where I'd seen him a minute earlier. Some kid slobbered in my ear, 'Best lookin' old chick here,' and I brushed him off, wiping the drool from my shoulder. Old chick! Hmph.

I spotted my guy again, heading for the back of the room where he disappeared through a set of double doors. It took me a couple more minutes to reach those doors, which were ajar. I peered into the dimly lit VIP area and saw the redhead sitting on a couch, laughing with a bunch of people. He rolled what looked like a fifty-dollar note, leaned forward, head right down, then sat up again and wiped his nose. Snorting coke? I had no idea but supposed it wasn't self-raising flour. This was evidence I needed to pass on to Jack. I headed back to where Lucy was still talking to the cute guy. As I approached, I could see she was getting agitated and trying to brush him off. In an instant his laughter turned to a snarl; he grabbed Lucy's breast and twisted. I barged through the crowd. Lucy punched the guy's chest and he raised his fist. I rushed in and pushed him; he shoved me and I fell backwards, landing hard on my bum. A young guy stepped in but the bastard punched him right in the face. The kid hit the floor and didn't move. Blood poured from his nose. Someone stood on my hand. Lucy was crouching over the unconscious guy.

'Let's get out of here,' I shouted to Luce, struggling to my feet.

Security guards surrounded the unconscious guy. Lucy said to them, 'He needs an ambulance. He was just trying to help us.' I looked for the culprit but he'd disappeared.

We stumbled out of the nightclub onto the street. I was worried about the unconscious guy – I didn't think the security guards would look after him. Lucy was calling an ambulance and I called Jack.

'Something happened.' I said. 'We had to leave.'

'I'm coming. Where are you?'

Jack pulled up ten seconds later and we scrambled into the back of his car. As he sped away from the kerb he said, 'What happened?' His anxious eyes were watching me in the rear-view mirror. I think I was in shock. Did this kind of thing go on every night in these places?

'For fuck's sake,' said Lucy, finding her voice. She rubbed her breast where the guy had grabbed her.

I squeezed her hand. 'Sorry, hon.'

'It's not your fault. That guy . . . what a psycho!'

Jack kept glancing at us in the mirror. Not questioning, giving us time to recover. We pulled up in front of my house and he helped us from the car.

Lucy said, 'I'm just going to head home.'
Jack said, 'I'll drive you.'
She nodded. 'Thanks.'
He said to me, 'I'll come straight back. You're okay?'
'Yes.'

BY THE TIME Jack arrived I'd transformed into my usual scruffy self. Tracky daks, Ugg boots and no wig. When I opened the door to let him in, the tears finally came.

He held me and said softly, 'Lucy told me what happened.'

'Is she okay?'

'Yes. Steve was there.'

'That guy . . . and I'm worried about the kid who tried to help us. I think that man killed him!'

Jack walked me down the passage to the living room. 'I just dropped by the club,' he said. 'He was alright. The ambulance was there.'

'Really?'

He nodded. 'I spoke to him. He was angry, but fine.'

'Okay.' I took a great shuddering breath and sat on the sofa.

Jack asked if I wanted a drink.

I nodded. 'Cup of tea.'

He went to the kitchen and put the kettle on.

'I want English Breakfast,' I called out.

'Alright.'

'With milk but don't put the milk in straight away.'

'Okay.'

'Let it brew for a while but don't jiggle the bag. Not too much milk. I don't like it milky. And one sugar but just a level spoonful . . . hold on, what mug are you using?'

'Maybe you should make it.'

I went to the kitchen. Jack dusted off the coffee machine. I poured boiling water into my mug and leaned against the bench, sniffing and sighing. I held up my hand. 'Someone stood on it,' I said, my bottom lip trembling.

Jack took my hand and kissed each finger in turn, the back of it three times, and my palm. 'Better?'

'Yes.'

He pulled me against him, arms tight around me. 'I'm sorry I asked you to go there.'

'That kind of thing must go on all the time in places like that.'

'I suppose. But I didn't think you'd be in any real danger. I would never —'

'I know,' I said, feeling suddenly guilty about being such a sooky-la-la. I pushed him back so he could see my face. 'I'm fine, really.' I gave him a little smile. 'I bet you want to know about your guy.'

'When you're ready.'

WE SAT next to each other on the sofa and I told Jack exactly what I'd seen the redhead doing.

He nodded. 'That's important information. I can't have him on my team.'

'So, it was worth all my pain? The pain of being in that horrible place?' I smiled so he knew I didn't mean it. Even though I did.

'Nothing is worth your pain.' He pushed a curl behind my ear.

I set down my tea, turned and lay across his lap. He cradled me and I stroked his hair and he smiled gently down at me.

I said, 'Give me that delicious mouth.'

He stiffened and his smile vanished. I knew he was having stupid concerns about getting too involved but I wasn't going to let that stop me. With my hand behind his head I tried to pull his face down to mine. It was like trying to move a marble statue and I had to lift myself up to force him to kiss me. But once he decided to go with it – groaning with pleasure or pain, I wasn't sure – his body relaxed; he held me against him, kissing me deep and long. He whispered against my lips, 'God, you looked so hot tonight. You can't imagine how I panicked when I saw you.'

'You prefer blondes?'

'No, I prefer what's under what little you were wearing.'

'It's the same as what's under what I'm wearing now.'

'And therein lies the problem . . .'

An hour later we were in my bed with my head on his shoulder, finger twirling his chest hair. From the sofa he'd swept me up and rushed me to the bedroom, then slowed everything down as we redis-covered each other.

'I wasn't going to let this happen again,' he said.

I looked up at his perfect face, shadowed by the lamp at his side.

'Why? It's so nice.'

'It's *very* nice, but —'

'I know, I know, you can't get involved.'

'Tonight was agony for me, Erica. Even just sending you into that place —'

'Oh, pooh, it was nothing.'

'I'm dangerous. Unreliable. My life is complicated.'

Axle appeared and sat on Jack's stomach. Sleek and black like a tiny panther, green eyes accusing and jealous, pink tongue poking slightly out of his mouth. I think the permanent tongue-poking was caused by a car accident before I got him at the shelter.

I said, 'You're in his spot.'

'He doesn't need half a queen-size bed.'

'He loves you, you know.'

'Well, if he starts clawing me he'll be locked in the bathroom.'

I kissed Jack's shoulder. 'I'll lock him in the bathroom now if you want.' I nipped Jack's earlobe, ran my tongue very lightly along his jaw and gently bit his chin. My hand wandered under the doona as his breathing picked up speed. 'I mean, I know you think we shouldn't, but we're here now, and we're not wearing anything, may as well —'

Jack was suddenly upright, throwing the doona, sending Axle scampering and me squealing. He straddled me, pinned my hands above my head, said, '*You're* the dangerous one, you know that?'

I smiled.

. . .

IN THE MORNING I was hoping for another day spent together, this time without the work issues. I was still thinking about strolls along the river or in the Botanic Gardens, another picnic even, but Jack said, standing there in the kitchen with water dripping from his hair and rolling off his magnificent shoulders, over those powerful biceps, that chest, getting caught in the line of hair that ran south from his navel and disappeared under the towel that sat so very low on his hips, 'I'm sorry. I can't stick around.'

'Hmm?' I forced my gaze north. 'What did you say?'

He smiled. 'I have to go.'

'That's okay.' It wasn't really.

'I need to do something with the information you gave me, make it worth your pain.'

'Work calls,' I said.

'It does.'

He hesitated, eyes flicking over me, caught between two cravings, I knew – the one to stay a little longer and the other more sensible option. I took advantage of that hesitation, snagging the towel, which fell away, and it was another hour before he walked out my front door.

CHAPTER 4

The next day I wore a smug smile all the way to work, thinking about Jack naked. The nasty business at the nightclub was now, happily, a blur. I'd called Lucy on Sunday morning and it seemed Steve had made it all better for her the way Jack had made it better for me, although she said Steve wanted to go to that nightclub and find the guy and kill him.

When I reached my desk I tried to be as quiet as possible so my boss Rosalind wouldn't hear me. It's not that I was trying to avoid work – not at all – I just wanted to avoid *her*.

My phone rang. It was Rosalind, even though her office is only three metres from my desk. I peered over the partition to see if Marcus, Rosalind's PA, was in yet and then remembered he was taking about six years worth of annual leave. Rosalind doesn't think it's necessary for Marcus to be replaced when there's 'an entire team of people who can share his responsibilities'. Rosalind doesn't seem to think *she* should be involved in that sharing.

'I don't seem to have coffee yet,' she said, amazed at the very possibility that someone had not yet delivered her coffee.

'Good morning, Rosalind. How do you like your coffee?' I asked, just to be annoying because of course everyone in the media and investor relations department knows how she takes it.

'White with one sugar.'

'I'll get it for you if you like.'

'That's why I'm calling you, Erica. To remind you about my coffee.'

'Of course.'

I hung up but my phone rang again straight away. It was Celia, John Degraves' PA, saying that JD wanted an update on the annual report.

'Should I bring it up?' I asked her.

'Yes, he wants to see you.'

I took tremendous juvenile delight in telling Rosalind I had to go see JD, the big boss, and asked if I could show her where the kitchen was. She said she'd get someone else, and that was satisfying, too.

I pulled my annual report work-in-progress folder from my drawer and headed for the lifts, pushing the button for the sixty-fifth floor, the Grand Poobah's den.

Before I joined the Team, John Degraves didn't even know my name. Well, he did, but had no real reason to remember it. That was until he decided to recruit me. JD is not only the CEO of Dega Oil, he's also the brains and money behind the Team, having decided a few years ago that Australia's defence forces needed help, especially its anti-terrorism department. So he recruited Jack Jones – ex-SAS, special ops or something – still hurting and vengeful after the loss of his wife and parents in New York on September 11. And Jack recruits all the other Team members – some ex-military people for the scary business and some civilians, like me, to help out with other stuff. It was JD's idea to get me because, at the time, it appeared I was pretty much available at the drop of a hat, had no social life, few friends, hardly went anywhere except to work and my parents', and would probably do anything for money. Oh, and that I seemed trustworthy. And there was the minor fact that the Team had targeted my ex-husband, who was, and probably still is, a scumbag and the reason I was in such serious debt (which is no longer a problem, thanks to the Team's generous hourly rate).

I walked across the cavernous foyer of the executive floor, trying not to make footprints in the thick rugs or dints in the soft parquetry with my heels. Celia sent me straight in to JD's office. He looked up from his desk and indicated the seat opposite, which I took.

He smiled broadly. 'It's a beautiful day,' he said.

I glanced out the window, nodded. 'Yes, it is.'

JD's got a reputation in business for being pretty laid-back and easy to get along with. Originally, this made it hard for me to understand how he could have even considered employing a bunch of mercenaries to do secret nasty things. But he's also a corporate leader, one of the most admired in Australia, and I guess you need to be pretty tough to survive in that world.

I opened my file and showed him where we were up to with the annual report, but he didn't seem all that interested. He knew we were doing a good job on it. Or rather, *I* was doing a good job and Rosalind was taking the credit.

He said, suddenly, 'My wife and I are having a small cocktail party on Saturday night. We wondered if you'd like to join us.'

I blinked at him.

He said, 'There'll be people there you know.'

'Rosalind?' I said before I could stop myself, knowing that if she were going I'd rather spend the evening with my mother. Maybe.

He smiled. 'No. It's a work-related function, but not Dega.'

'Oh.' It was a Team cocktail party. Which meant Jack would be there. 'I'd love to. Thanks, Mr Degraves.'

'Very good,' he said. 'Six-thirty. You remember our address?' Yes, I remembered where John Degraves lives in one of Toorak's poshest streets. How could I forget last New Year's Eve and all the cars that blew up in front of his house?

I WAITED until after work before I called Jack, in case someone overheard me. Most people at work think I've got a new boyfriend, which is kind of what we want so people don't wonder about my real relationship with Jack Jones, which is a work one, of course. Although I quite like the occasional extracurricular activities. I called him as I drove. I don't have Bluetooth in my old car but I put my mobile on speaker and rested it on my lap.

'Hey,' he said.

'You haven't called! When am I going to see you?'

There was a brief silence, then, 'I —'

'I'm *joking*, Jack. Don't worry, I'm not going to get all clingy and demanding just because we had magnificent sex.' I sighed, remembering it.

'It was.' I could hear his smile.

'I'm not even going to invite you to my parents' for dinner tonight.'

'I wouldn't mind dinner at your parents'.'

'I'll assume you're either joking or have some form of mental deficiency.'

He laughed again. Jack had in fact been to my parents' house for dinner and hadn't seemed to mind, which is the only thing about Jack Jones I find suspicious. That and the fact that he goes for Collingwood.

'Actually,' I said, 'I just wanted to tell you that JD's invited me to his cocktail party on Saturday night.'

He made a hissing noise.

I said, 'Didn't you know he was inviting me?'

'No,' he said, clearly unhappy.

'You don't want me there?'

He hesitated. 'It's not that I don't want you there. It's the reason he's invited you that annoys me.'

'What's the reason? Apart from the fact that he might enjoy my fabulous company and witty repartee.'

'No doubt.' But that's all he said and I waited through a long period of silence.

'Sorry,' I said, 'too many questions.'

Jack said, 'Look, I'm going to talk to Degraves. Don't be surprised if you're uninvited.'

I couldn't help feeling a bit hurt by that but I was trying not to. Jack must have sensed it, probably because of the deafening silence from my end, and he said, 'I don't want you any closer to this than you need to be. I already regret involving you.'

We said goodbye and hung up, and I continued on to my regular Monday dinner with my folks. As I whizzed by Chadstone Shopping Centre I felt a deep and sudden yearning for the good old days, when life's agonising moments meant trying to find a parking spot there on Christmas Eve.

I sat in my car out the front of Mum and Dad's cream brick, 1950s house. I could see Mum in her bedroom, fluffing the curtains. My old room was the next window along, with its frilly pink curtains that were a present for my fifth birthday. I thought with a big sigh how nice it would be to return to my childhood days when everything was pink and frilly. Nah. Because that would mean I'd have to do everything again, including living with my mother until I moved out with my crappy husband. But if I knew what was coming, I could have not been at that bar the night I met my ex, and I could have definitely been at the pub instead of finding Jack Jones half-dead in my front garden. Except then I wouldn't have met him. Or I still would have met him, but he might've been dead by the time I got home.

They parted suddenly, the curtains, and Mum stared out at me. She gestured wildly for me to come inside. I gave her a wave. She stood there, hands on hips, mouth pursed, probably wondering why I was still sitting in my car, not knowing that I always do this, mentally prepare myself for a visit with her. She crossed herself – I could see her lips moving and her eyes rolling heavenward – and walked away. Poor Mum. Traumatised by her own wicked mother's indiscretions. My gran who had a one-night stand in Italy with a swarthy local and that fling produced Mum. Scandalised before she was even born. She's tried to make up for it since by living like a nun (apart from two times – I have a brother).

I got out of the car.

'Hi, Dad,' I said as I walked in.

He peered at me over the top of his glasses. Grunted. Turned back to the telly.

I found Mum in the kitchen, got a glass of cordial from the fridge and asked if I could help. She shooed me away because, according to her, I'm useless in every kind of domestic activity. She's probably right. I sat at the breakfast bar on an orange vinyl stool that swivelled of its own accord, and watched Mum doing what *all* women should be able to do and do well: cook for a man.

'Has my order come in yet?' she asked.

'What order?'

'Didn't you go to a Tupperware party?'

'Lucy's? That's next week.'

'It won't be the same as the good old Tupperware, you know, but I do need some things,' she said. 'Don't forget to tell them I need a new lid for my flour container. It's got a crack!' She pulled it from the cupboard and showed me again. 'Make sure they know it's the self-raising one.'

'It's pretty old, Mum.'

'But they have a lifetime warranty. If it's the same girl who sold it to me, she might remember.'

'I've got your order. I'll make sure they replace it.' The *girl* who sold it to her was probably in a nursing home by now or six feet under.

'How was work?' Mum asked, bustling about. 'Did you type any letters today?'

I sighed and swivelled to the right, hanging on to the laminated bench. 'I'm media relations, Mum, not a secretary. Besides, everyone does their own typing these days.' (Except Rosalind.)

Mum was a secretary before she had her annoying, disappointing babies. She can't imagine a woman doing anything in an office other than typing on a clackety old typewriter or making coffee for a man.

'Surely not men.'

'Yes, even men.'

Mum was bending low, rifling around in her Tupperware cupboard, and things tumbled out, all over the floor.

'What are you looking for?' I said.

'The beetroot one. Your father opened a new can and just left it there in the fridge with no lid, for all the world to see.' She pulled out the containers she never uses to reach the useful ones at the back.

I said, 'Why don't you keep those ones at the front?'

'They fit better this way.'

'You really need a new kitchen with more storage space, Mum. Or you need to declutter. I'll help if you want.' I could get her hand-me-downs.

'No, dear. I like it as it is.' She put a box on the bench and I pulled it close, opening the lid. Inside was a lettuce crisper.

'Have you got two of these?' I said, lifting it out. I was sure I'd seen one in the fridge.

'Yes,' she said, taking the crisper, returning it to its box. 'I keep a spare, just in case. And it seems I might need it, too, if things keep going the way they are.'

'What do you mean?'

'Haven't you heard?'

'Heard what?'

She banged the beetroot container down on the bench and glared at the back door. 'There's a thief in the neighbourhood,' she said, 'stealing Tupperware!'

This was rich, even for my mother. But still I didn't laugh because she looked so serious.

'Why would someone steal Tupperware?'

'Because they just don't make it like they used to! You can't get these things any more.' She waved her hand at the ancient collection, scattered across the floor and benchtops. She turned and narrowed her eyes at me. 'Someone's stolen the spike out of my lettuce crisper.'

'It wasn't me!'

'Well.' She returned to her bustling, pretending to believe I hadn't stolen the spike. 'Mary and Janice have both had some things stolen. And what's-her-name.'

'Maybe I could look after the spare lettuce crisper?' I said. 'I could protect it for you.'

Mum snatched up the box. 'This one is special.' She regarded the box lovingly, arms outstretched. 'It's a limited-edition crisper. And besides, it was a gift from a friend. A shower tea gift.'

'*Shower tea*? How old is it, for God's sake?'

'Blasphemy!' Mum tsked. 'I really think you should go to confession, Erica. I'm sure you have impure thoughts.' She gave me a look.

'For God's sake,' I muttered.

'There, you see! Blasphemy comes out of your mouth as quickly as Jack Robinson.'

I WOLFED down my stew and mash, shovelled in the peas.

Mum wasn't pleased. 'Your bottom seems to be getting bigger,' she said and reached for something on the buffet next to the dining table. An iPad.

I gaped at my mother as she flipped open the cover and tapped the screen. It was a newer model than mine.

'Where did you get *that*?' I said, with sudden, unbidden envy.

'Your brother gave it to me. An early Mother's Day present.' She looked at me over the top of her glasses – it was a you'd-better-come-up-with-something-pretty-special look. Damn my brother to hell.

My mobile rang and I plucked it from my bag. It was Mum, wanting to Facetime. I sighed and answered, and Mum's face loomed on my screen.

'Hold your phone closer, Erica. I can't see your face.'

I did it.

'You've got a pimple!' she shouted.

I hung up. 'Why did Nick give you an iPad?'

'Because he loves his mother.' There was that look again. And then, 'It's amazing! This iPad knows everything. I just gooble a question and it knows! Look at this.' She tapped and showed me the screen. 'Look how many wedding planners there are in Melbourne.'

Time to change the subject, or better still, leave the table. I stacked the dishwasher, Mum rearranged it all, then we sat on the sofa. There was a Steve Irwin special on. An old one, obviously, from before he died. Dad was in his chair, head thrown back, mouth hanging open with a snore whistling in and out of him. Mum knitted.

'I miss Steve Irwin,' said Mum. 'He was such a good husband. It's a shame you didn't meet him before that other woman. He might have liked you, you know,' she said, as though it might have been a real possibility. I had a fleeting image of myself – the only woman in a crowd of khaki-clad men – struggling with a section of anaconda, trying to smile for the cameras and look like I wasn't shitting myself.

I watched Mum's knitting needles fly. Knitting is another field of domesticity in which I suck.

'What are you making?' I said, feigning interest.

She held up the tiny blue thing. 'Baby booties.'

'Who had a baby?'

'They're for you, dear,' she said, without dropping a stitch or moving her eyes away from the television.

'Mum, I'm not planning on having babies for a while. I'm not even planning on getting married.'

'I'm using vigilisation,' she said.

'Visualisation?'

'Yes. I heard that you can get whatever you want if you vigilise it and act as though it's already true. I made some pink ones, too. I think when Jack comes back from his business trip he'll be looking to settle down. I can feel it in my waters.'

Mum desperately wants me to be decently married again. She loves Jack, not just because he's good-looking and appears to be interested in me, but because he's got lots of money, and is big and strong and capable of caring for her when she's old. I hadn't told her that he was already back from his 'business trip' and decided I probably wouldn't, especially if he was about to head off again.

'You should watch out, you know,' she said.

'Why?'

'Well, if you're going to let him run off here and there, he might meet someone else.'

I nodded. What to say? She was probably right.

'Where is his business trip?' she asked. 'I can't remember where you said.'

And because of all the lies I tell my mother, I couldn't remember either.

'Um, Europe?'

'I don't know how he can bear being in that godforsaken country.'

'Europe's not a country, Mum.'

'It's near Italy, isn't it?'

'Italy's *in* Europe.'

'Then it's godforsaken, is all I can say.'

'The Pope lives there.'

'He lives in a blessed place. Away from all the riff-raff.'

I muttered, 'You know, Jack might like Europe. He was born there, remember? He might not even come back.' Why was I having visions of Jack going away and never coming back? A lump formed in my throat and I could sense her staring at me.

'Whatever do you mean?' said Mum, but I was already leaving the room.

CHAPTER 5

I didn't see or hear from Jack for the next few days and I was shitty about that. I couldn't think of a really good reason to be shitty, so I decided that he should have let me know one way or the other about JD's cocktail party so I could make other plans if necessary. Other plans. Yeah, right. But when he finally called me on Thursday and said that he'd pick me up at six-fifteen for JD's party, I didn't even ask why I was still invited. I couldn't ask because I was smiling too much.

Of course I made an extra special effort. I bought underwear and a dress. Something understated. The dress had long sleeves and a scoop neck, sat just above the knee, was simple and black but with a narrow emerald-coloured belt and trim, to match my eyes. I'd straightened my hair, which made it longer and glossier; something I should do more often, I decided. And I wore high heels to boost my average height so I didn't look too short next to Jack. Ultimately, I wanted to look elegant and relaxed, like society cocktail parties were part of my regime, even though it took about four hours to get ready.

When Jack arrived at my house he wasn't smiling. He was polite, as always, holding the door for me as I climbed into his Merc. His telltale eyes were worried and angry.

In an attempt to make light conversation, I said, 'Did you play squash with Steve?'

'No. Maybe next week.'

'Right.'

I was silent for a while and so was he. Eventually I said, 'You're not happy.'

'No. Sorry.'

'It's okay.'

He nodded.

'Can I ask something?' I dared.

He gave me a sideways glance, but didn't say anything, so I took that to mean, 'sure, go ahead'.

'Why is it even an issue with this guy? I mean, don't you have final say on who you work with?'

He frowned slightly, and I had an impulse to tell him to forget it, that it was none of my business, but instead I held my breath and waited.

Finally, he said, 'I was asked to interview the guy, which I did, and he's qualified.'

'But you're not happy about what he gets up to after hours.'

'No.'

'And if you just refuse to take him?'

Jack swore softly at the car in front of us, which was travelling at a snail's pace. After a long time, he said, 'It's complicated.'

We arrived at JD's big house 'What do you want me to do tonight?' I said. We'd driven the last ten minutes in silence.

'Just enjoy yourself. I'll let you know when it's time to leave.' He looked at me. 'You don't have to leave with me if you don't want.'

'Of course I'll leave with you. Unless you don't want me to.'

He smiled, at last. 'We'll leave together.'

Goody gumdrops.

'You look beautiful, Erica,' he said out of the blue.

'This old thing?'

He gave my leg a squeeze and we got out of the car.

WHEN WE WALKED into JD's house a butler greeted us, offering to take bags, coats, whatever. To the left of the entry hall was a door that led to the library, I seemed to remember, and to the right was a vast ballroom where most people were mingling. It wasn't a 'small' function at all. I could see others at the far end of the room on the open terrace where there were overhead heaters and where soft lights lit the surrounding garden.

We made our way across the ballroom as John and Sue Degraves came to greet us.

'Hello! Hello!' said jolly JD, shaking Jack's hand vigorously, but not making eye contact with him. 'Come, let's have a drink.' He was already pulling Jack across the room.

Sue Degraves took my arm and we followed.

I said, 'Thanks for inviting me, Mrs Degraves.'

'For God's sake, call me Sue. I'm not stuffy like my husband and I certainly don't want to be reminded of my awful mother-in-law.' She laughed. 'Champagne?'

'Please.'

They led us to a heater on the terrace and a waiter brought us drinks. JD moved on, but Sue lingered, smiling at us, then she reached out with both hands and gripped our arms. 'You're such a *gorgeous* couple!'

My mouth fell open and Jack cleared his throat.

She said, looking up at him, 'I'm so happy for you, Jack.'

He did one of those mutter-mutter looking-away things.

'And you,' she said to me, 'are one lucky girl.'

I pushed my smile wide. 'Certainly am! Luckiest girl on the planet.'

Sue gave my arm a squeeze and left us. Jack was studying something on the ground. I nudged him and he looked at me, unsure.

'I notice she didn't say how lucky *you* are.'

He laughed, went to speak, changed his mind. But then his eyes narrowed as he focused on something over my shoulder. When I looked, I saw Mr Redhead-Drug-Addict having a fine old time with some people on the other side of the terrace. He raised his glass to Jack and threw his drink down in one go.

Jack sighed. 'I need to talk to Degraves.'

'Why do I feel like I know him, Jack? I mean, apart from last week.'

Jack ignored that but said, 'Will you be alright if I leave you here?'

'Oh. Sure.' I looked around. There were some faces I knew.

He headed back inside and I watched him approach JD. They walked to the front of the house and through the library door.

I looked for Mr Drugs again, and that's when I noticed the other people standing around him. One of the men was smiling at me and, as our eyes met, he gave me a wink. I gasped and looked away. It was the violent dark-haired guy from the nightclub, I was sure of it. Had he recognised me? No, I'd been wearing a wig. Who was he and why was he here? Then I remembered that I'd first noticed him at the club *because* he was talking to the redhead. My heart pounded so hard I felt faint.

I walked quickly through the ballroom. I needed to tell Jack. Tell him what? In front of JD? I slowed as I approached the library. Couldn't barge on in there. I needed to wait. The door was slightly ajar. I glanced over my shoulder but the redhead and the violent guy were out of my line of sight.

Then I heard Jack's voice. 'I won't have him, John.'

JD said quietly (and I moved closer so I could hear), 'From what I understand, Berringer's recruiting more men every day. You'll need the manpower.'

Jack didn't say anything for a while – I could imagine him standing there all broody, hands on hips, looking at the floor. He finally spoke. 'This is a favour *you* owe, not me.'

JD said, 'Look, he's qualified and he respects you.' More silence. 'Come on, Jack. Just talk to him about your concerns.'

I heard shuffling and quickly dashed across the hallway, turned and pretended to be approaching as they came out. Jack saw me and frowned. JD smiled and held his arms wide.

'Ah, Erica!' he said, as though seeing me for the first time. 'So nice you could make it tonight.' He shook my hand.

'Thanks for the invitation, Mr Degraves.'

'Come, come,' he said. 'Let's all have a drink!'

JD tried to herd us back to the terrace, but Jack took my arm gently, holding me back, and said to JD, 'Give us a minute.'

JD's smile faded – his plan to force everyone to have fun foiled – and he nodded, then headed across the ballroom.

I turned to Jack. 'I need to tell you something.'

He looked into my face, concerned. I might have been a bit pale.

'What's wrong?' he said.

'Can we go in there?' I pointed at the library door.

'Alright . . .' He looked past me. 'Hold on ... G'day, Mick.'

For some reason, before I even looked, I knew I'd be meeting the violent guy, whose hand Jack was shaking in a friendly way. Internally, I shrank away from him, even though I knew he probably wouldn't recognise me. I looked at the floor.

'No surprise you'd be with a gorgeous woman, Jack.'

'Erica, this is Mick Jansen.'

I glanced at Mick Jansen, who was smiling at me, so innocent, warm and friendly that I wondered for a moment if I was wrong. That somehow this wasn't the same man who'd assaulted Lucy, me and that young guy at the club. But it *was* him.

I found I was holding my hand out for him to shake, but I couldn't look at him for long. Eventually he moved on and when I looked up at Jack, he was watching me carefully.

'Come in here,' he said, and I followed him into JD's library. He shut the door. 'You look like you've seen a ghost.'

'More like an abusive bastard.'

'What do you mean?'

'That man, the one you just introduced me to?'

'Mick Jansen.'

'He's the one who assaulted us at the nightclub.'

Jack's jaw dropped and he stared at me for a long time. 'You're sure about that.'

'Yes. No. I don't know.'

'You need to know.'

'I *was* sure, but then he was so . . . so *nice* just then. I first noticed him at the club because he was talking to the redhead guy.'

Jack stepped closer, gripped my arms, and I looked into his serious face.

I said, 'I'm sure.'

He nodded once; that's all he needed. He left the room and I stood there, shaking.

It was about fifteen minutes before Jack came looking for me. I stayed in the library, sitting on the edge of a chair, biting my nails, my foot jiggling up and down. I felt so jittery that when Jack walked in I nearly hit the roof.

'Let's go,' he said. 'I'm taking you home.'

He took my arm and led me to his car. As we drove away I noticed a smudge of dried blood on his knuckle. When I looked closely at his face, I saw a small graze on his cheek.

'Jack, you need to tell me what happened. I can't stand it.'

'Mick Jansen's no longer on my team.'

I gasped, shocked. 'He was on your team for this mission?'

He nodded.

'What will you do?'

Jack ignored that but said, 'He might think twice about who he picks on in nightclubs.'

'Did he admit it?'

'Not in so many words.'

'What did he say? Like, she was asking for it or something?'

Pause. 'Something like that.'

'Bloody hell. Why do men think like that?'

He shook his head. 'Not all men.'

'I know. Sorry.'

We were silent for a while and I considered how this might change things for Jack. The job he was assigned to do. Eventually, I asked, 'Will you cancel the mission?'

He gave me a long look. I was being too nosy. But I held my breath and waited. I wanted to hear it.

'No,' he said.

CHAPTER 6

*S*aturday night had most certainly *not* ended the way I'd hoped. Jack took me home, walked me to my front door, asked if I'd be alright, kissed my forehead and drove away. I didn't think he was going home. I was pretty sure he was going back to JD's.

So now it was Tuesday and Lucy was having her Tupperware party. I decided not to tell her about Mick Jansen. She needed to forget about that bastard. Besides, tonight would be girly and fun and we were both looking forward to it. I didn't know if Jack was playing squash with Steve because I hadn't heard from him since JD's party. But when I got to Lucy's, I asked innocently, 'Is Steve playing squash tonight?'

'You just want to know if he's playing with Jack.'

'Who?'

She laughed. 'Yes, he's playing squash and I think Jack was going.'

'Oh. Good for him. Who cares?'

She smiled and answered the door to the Tupperware lady, who asked for help with her boxes. It was hard to carry boxes with champagne in my hand. So I held the door for them instead.

Women piled into Lucy's little apartment. Giggling women who all wanted champagne. That was good. They'd spend more if they were drinking and I knew Lucy would get a nice present from Tupperware if people spent a lot.

LUCY WALKED PAST WITH A BOTTLE. I held out my glass.

'More champagne please! Oh, sorry, *sparkling wine,*' I said, mimicking Jack's deep voice. I gulped the drink down. I liked it. It was kind of sweet. I asked for more – how much had I already had? Maybe I shouldn't drive home.

The Tupperware presentation rolled on. There were so many things I wanted. I didn't really need anything because I had a cupboard full of cheap plastic containers from the supermarket at home. But Tupperware is the best, I knew, and lasts a lifetime. Just look at my mother's collection. It had to be a hundred years old. *Must remember Mum's order.* I picked up the brochure and flicked through it again. Whoops, knocked over my glass. All over my lap. Probably shouldn't have tried to balance my glass on my knee. Better get more *sparkling wine.* Lucy came past.

'More please!'

'Think you've had enough, hon.'

'Never enough!'

She laughed and poured me some more. 'You won't be driving home.'

'Bah.'

The Tupperware colours were so pretty. I liked all the pink things. They'll match my Ugg boots, I thought. I laughed when I saw some of the funny things in the kids' section. Monkeys! I love monkeys. I love spider monkeys. I love Axle. I looked closer. Not monkeys. Mickey Mouse. I hate mice.

I asked Lucy for another drink. She said I'd had enough. I got up to get my own – who did she think she was? I tripped on someone's something. Who left that there? I poured bubbles. Whoops. Spilled some. I poured more to make up for what I'd spilled. Lucy tried to take my glass. I was trying to get it to my mouth and she was pulling it away. The glass flew across the room. I sat on the floor.

Jack's face swam before me. What a nice dream. Not a dream! I think he was really there. Where? I looked around the room. Still at Lucy's, but everyone had gone. They'd been replaced by boys. Boys wearing singlet tops with nice muscles. The singlet tops didn't have nice muscles. The boys had nice muscles. How did they get here? Maybe aliens took all the ladies and left Steve and Jack in their place. How funny was that? I laughed and fell off the couch.

'Whoopsie!' I got on all fours.

'Let's get you home, missy,' said a familiar voice. 'Or should I say *messy*.'

Jack stood me up. I elbowed his chin as I flung my arms around his neck. He was frowning at me. Was he? I couldn't tell. He was too far away. No, he wasn't. His hands were on my waist, holding me up.

'Bloody hell, Erica. You're wasted.' Was that Steve?

'You're not my mother,' I said to Lucy, flopping toward her and poking her chest.

'I didn't say anything!' she said.

I stuck my nose in Jack's armpit. 'You shmell nice.'

'Right,' he said and threw me over his shoulder.

'Careful she doesn't throw up on you,' said Lucy.

I hung down Jack's back. Smacked his bottom. 'Nice bottom.'

'Say goodnight, Erica.'

There were two pairs of shoes looking at me. One big pair and one small pair. 'Night, Erica,' I said to them and the shoes got higher and higher until they disappeared at the top of some stairs.

THERE WAS Jack's face again, smudgy.

'Is it tomorrow?'

'No, I just put you to bed.'

'I'm a bit drunk.'

'A bit!' He laughed. 'What time do you need to get up? I'll set your alarm.'

'You're my malarm.'

He was smiling and then he wasn't smiling. 'I can't stay,' he said.

'But whyyyyyy?'

I yawned and he was talking. What did he say? I reached up and put my hand on his face. I poked his eye.

'Shorry.'

'I've set your alarm for seven. Remember your car's at Lucy's.' He leaned in and kissed my nose and my eyes, one, two, three. And my cheek. And my lips for a long time. He stroked my hair.

I closed my eyes. 'I luff you, Jack. Soooo much.'

CHAPTER 7

I walked into the bar of the London Tavern, full and noisy because it was trivia night. Wednesday Trivia was new in my life and I usually loved it, but of course I didn't feel like being there this time. It was better than being alone at my house, though. Alone with my thoughts and snippets of memory. I'm sure my memory bank erased all the good, funny, nice things I did and said and kept only the ridiculous, embarrassing ones.

Steve was grinning at me from the bar. He mouthed, *Champagne?*

Ugh. My hangover was horrible. I mouthed back, *Very funny.*

Beer?

What a day it had been at work, with Rosalind hovering and demanding. I gave Steve the thumbs up – yes to beer – and he pointed to where Lucy was sitting. As I approached, I saw with some horror my tiny friend lean across a table, poke the air, and shout up at some really big, angry-looking bloke, 'If you even *think* about taking that chair you'll be limping home!' Unsurprisingly, he returned the chair and skulked away. Lucy threw her arms around me. 'I'm *so* happy!' she said.

'Great! Why?'

'Because I've got three days off and we're going shopping.'

I sat heavily. 'I thought that wasn't for another couple of weeks.'

'I can be excited about it now, can't I?'

She scowled at my lack of enthusiasm. And I felt pleased, as I often do, that I wasn't a patient at the Epworth Hospital. I could well imagine Luce full of nurse attitude, storming into a patient's room when that patient wasn't doing what he or she was supposed to be doing. Like sleeping or getting better or something. In fact, I have an agreement with the Law of Attraction: I'll try very hard not to get hurt on the proviso that if I do, I get sent to the Alfred Hospital.

'Have you got a hangover?' she said.

'Yeah.'

'Did you notice we brought your car home?'

'No, I didn't. Thanks.'

'Why are you looking so miserable?' she demanded. 'You're supposed to be happy.'

'I know.' I sighed. 'Why am I supposed to be happy, by the way?'

'Because it's trivia night and we're hanging out.'

'I know. Sorry.'

I watched Steve approach, smiling as usual. He towered over most people in the room. Six foot four, same as Jack. Sigh.

Steve pushed my beer across the table and gave Lucy a glass of red wine. 'Hey, buddy,' he said to me.

'Hi.' More sighs.

He said to Lucy, glancing over his shoulder at the big angry bloke who was lucky not to be limping home and who was giving us dirty looks, 'Geez, Luce, pick on someone your own size.'

She blew Steve a kiss.

I said, 'I agree. I'm still a bit antsy about that night.'

She said, 'You haven't told me why you're looking so miserable.'

I shrugged, my mouth turned down. It was hard to talk over the noise in the room. They leaned in. I said, 'I think I told Jack I love him, and now he seems to have disappeared.'

CHAPTER 8

*T*wo-and-a-bit weeks later …

MY HAIR SUCKS and I want to chop it all off. I need to blow-dry it to make it straight but blow-drying hurts my arm muscles and makes me sweat. And the sweat makes my hair frizz. It's a no-win situation.

I stood in front of the bathroom mirror, frowning at my hair, munching Vegemite toast, and an image of Jack, naked, popped into my head. I realised I hadn't given him a single moment's thought yet today. Which was miraculous. Usually, I woke to delicious memories of him and his sexy bod and that's me for the rest of the day. Sometimes I *can't* think about him because it might cause me to lose my job or get run over.

I've chosen denial over the likely reality, in relation to Jack, I mean. This way, I can pretend Jack's away on business and that, when he comes home, we'll resume our working relationship with hopefully the occasional 'social' time together. And denial stops all the pain. More people should try it.

Admittedly, I hadn't heard a word from him since he left and reality-check type thoughts like that made my stomach squirm. Where do they come from? Those thoughts? Like the ones I keep having about the Tupperware night. As soon as I'd woken the next morning I knew something had changed. I'd lain there in bed, going over and over the night before in my mind, horrified by my behaviour and making a mental note to email all the ladies at the Tupperware party and apologise.

But mostly what I remembered about that night was telling Jack I loved him. And now he's run away. He didn't just not answer my calls, no. He's too mature and decent for that. His phone was switched off. I'd wanted to tell him I was sorry, that I'm an idiot, and to please ignore my carrying on. I'd driven by his house, rung the doorbell, and even though he could have been inside, hiding from me, I knew he wasn't there. No one was there. The house *felt* empty. And not just empty because they might have been at the supermarket, it was long-term empty. I suspected he'd gone on his mission, and God knows how long that would keep him away.

Meantime, I just had to be brave and wait for him to come back. But even when he finally did return, he might not call me. He doesn't want girls falling in love with him. He's too nice to string someone along when there's no possibility of a future with him. He'd remove himself from her life before he'd do that. Finally and forever.

Axle strolled into the bathroom and wound around my legs, purring like a chainsaw, and this interrupted my unhelpful thought processes. I moved to the kitchen and dug around in the fridge for Axle's food, scooping it into his bowl, more snapshot images of Jack appearing, horror thoughts of all kinds about Jack not being here and maybe even *never* coming home. Damn you, denial! Where have you gone? I shook my head to get rid of the growing anxiety.

'Stop it!' I said out loud. It was Friday, and I'd been looking forward to spending the weekend with Lucy while Steve was busy with his kids. I tried to focus on the fun we'd have tonight at the pub and a weekend of hanging out together – shopping and lunch on Bridge Road, movies and pizza, my favourite things in the world apart from being anywhere with Jack Jones.

CHAPTER 9

*M*y mobile rang, waking me up, pissing me off. Where was my phone? I got out of bed, staggered around, tried to work out where the ringing was coming from. Kitchen? Who'd call me at seven a.m. on a Sunday morning anyway? Oh! Maybe it was Jack! I ran down the passage and snatched up my phone.

'Hello?'

'Erica!'

'Jack!'

The line was breaking up.

'. . . need you to . . .'

Not Jack.

'. . . tell J.D . . .'

'Joe? Joe, is that you?' There was a terrible noise in the background.

'. . . M.I.A. . . .'

I could barely hear him. 'What? Who's M.I— *what?*'

The line dropped out and I redialled. But that stupid recorded woman told me the phone was 'either switched off or out of mobile range'. I dialled Jack's number for the four-hundredth time since he'd left. Same infuriating message.

Axle clawed my bare foot. 'Ow!' He galloped across the living room and I followed, letting him out, staring at my phone.

That was definitely Joe on the phone and I thought he said Jack was M.I.A. And all I could hear was my mother's voice telling me about her favourite cousin who went M.I.A. in Vietnam. How sad she'd been and how awful it was that he was never found.

I went to the dining table, needing a seat, wracking my brain for some innocent meaning behind Joe's words. Maybe he meant a different M.I.A. Of course! Maybe there's a hotel called M.I.A. somewhere? I rushed to my bedroom, opened my laptop and googled 'M.I.A.'. Migration Institute of Australia and Malaysian Institute of Accountants came up. I remembered that Jack owns businesses and either option was preferable to the obvious. Denial tried hard. What else? I scrolled down. Miami International Airport. Maybe he was in Miami. I wanted it badly. I scanned and scrolled. What else, what else? But as I scrolled, I could sense denial dissolving like an Aspro. Common sense kicked in and smacked me around the head. I tried to stand but slumped to the floor instead, my back against my bed.

Jack was Missing In Action. No doubt about it.

I HAD JOHN DEGRAVES' secret business card in my hand, still stained with Jack's blood from that romantic first meeting. The card had just a number on it, gold-embossed; no name.

I took a deep breath and dialled, but hung up before the phone started ringing. I needed more courage for this. JD didn't know I knew anything about Jack's mission. Would it hurt Jack if JD knew? But what did I know? Nothing, really. It was a mission of four men, but Jack had sacked two of those men and I had no idea if he and Joe had gone ahead, just the two of them, or if Jack had recruited others. And if he hadn't, how could he and Joe achieve whatever they were meant to achieve with just the two of them?

I made another cup of tea. Axle crawled onto my lap and head-butted my hand. He clawed my lap and purred so loudly I couldn't hear myself think. I put him outside.

JD didn't answer and there was no voicemail. I followed the prompts to send my number, hung up and waited. Calling JD's secret mobile was a bit like calling the bat phone. It was used for Team business – emergencies only – so I thought it wouldn't be long before he called back. But he didn't. After an hour I sent a text – *Pls call Erica. Urgent.* I waited. And waited. Another hour. I needed to get ready to meet Lucy for breakfast. But should I be going for breakfast if Jack's missing in action? What else should I be doing?

I opened the fridge door and stood there, not really seeing anything. Would JD do something? *I* needed to do something. What? Axle wanted to come in, Lucy was meeting me for breakfast at ten. Washing needed doing. The bathroom needed cleaning. Jack would be alright. Surely he would. This is what he's good at, whatever he's doing. Maybe he ended up taking the redhead and Mick Jansen, after all. No, definitely not Mick Jansen.

Another cup of tea and I turned on the TV, sitting on the sofa, flicking around the stations to see if there was anything on the news. On Channel 9 racial violence had turned Sydney into something unrecognisable. On CNN bullets rained down on American soldiers somewhere and I watched hard to see where it was and if anything rang a bell. Somewhere in the Middle East. Not where Jack would be. No. His mission was secret and this didn't look very secret. Channel 7 reported on the recent flood of house break-ins. Great to know when you live alone. I flicked over to Foxtel. On *Bewitched*, Samantha kissed Darren goodbye as he left for work. Lucky Samantha – at least Darren would be coming home. I turned off the telly and put my face in my hands.

CHAPTER 10

I met Lucy on Bridge Road. The plan was to have breakfast and then head to Lucy's to watch movies all day. Yesterday we'd scoured our favourite shops. We went to Ikea because Lucy loves it. I hate it. Well, I don't hate it but I can't *see* anything in there. My brain can't process all the shapes and colours. I can't see the difference between a bedroom and a living room. I get lost and panic that I won't find my way out. I like Freedom Furniture, where all the blue cushions are together, all the pink ones, with clearly defined, colour-coded rooms. Jack wouldn't go to either store. He probably goes to Italy to buy his furniture.

I pushed my breakfast aside.

'So I'm thinking about getting it all cut off,' said Lucy.

'What?'

'Are you listening to me? I said I'm thinking about getting my hair cut. Something radical.'

'You tried that and hated it.'

'I know.'

Lucy ate. I didn't.

'There's nothing else you can do, you know,' she said between mouthfuls of omelette.

'About what?'

She sighed. 'Jack. JD will call when he gets the message.'

After breakfast I followed Lucy in my car to Hawthorn and we climbed the one flight to her apartment. Empty champagne bottles sat on the kitchen bench.

'Are those bottles still there from your Tupperware party?' The memory of it made me feel sick.

'I've worked every day and night since. I'm thinking about getting a cleaning lady.'

'Why don't we just take the bottles downstairs now?'

'Nah.'

I sat at her kitchen counter. 'Has my stuff come in yet?' I said.

'Your Tupperware? Not yet. One of your things is on back order. I'll let you know.'

'I forgot to order stuff for Mum.'

'Really? What did she want? I could probably add it.'

'I can't find her list.'

'Call and ask her now,' said Luce.

'You call her.'

'I'm not calling her.'

'Maybe she'll forget,' I said. 'You know, I don't even remember what I ordered for myself.'

'You ordered a lot of fabulous things and I'm getting a fantastic gift from Tupperware because of it.'

I blew out a big sigh.

'Tea or coffee?' she said, walking into the kitchen.

'I need more coffee.'

Lucy put some cake on a plate.

'Luce, I think something really awful has happened to Jack.'

She gazed at me. I knew she probably wanted to say something like he's not good for me anyway, but she didn't, and I was thankful for that. Lucy wasn't a huge fan of Jack – even though he's a Collingwood supporter – because she thinks he'll hurt me. And because I tend to end up in grave danger when he's around.

'Let's sit,' she said, and we propped on her sofa with coffee, cake and chocolate.

I told Lucy again what Joe said on the phone.

'So, what do you think's happened to him?'

I shrugged. 'Just before he went away the first time, Jack told me there was a guy causing big trouble somewhere.'

'But you don't know where that is.'

I shook my head. 'All I know is that it's something to do with the Team. At least, I assume it is because JD's involved.'

'Well, I think you should handball this to JD and forget it.' She picked up a magazine. 'We'd better read our stars.' She scanned the page. 'Sooo . . . This is mine. Taurus: Here's hoping your boss is understanding when an unexpected event requires your urgent attention . . . blah blah blah. Same as usual. Let's do yours. Libra: An unplanned trip to a remote place sees the blossoming of new friendships, potential danger and possibly a romance revisited . . . Nothing special. Let's watch movies.'

Well, there you go. If there's a problem, check your horoscope, and if that doesn't help, eat cake and watch a movie. Lucy loaded *Romancing the Stone* with Kathleen Turner and Michael Douglas before he had a mid-life crisis and married someone too young.

But after *Romancing the Stone*, I felt even more miserable. I doubted very much that Jack would come back from wherever he was and drive up my street in a yacht. Especially as I'd done nothing to help save him. All kinds of horrible things were going through my mind. What if he was lying at the bottom of a hole or well somewhere, and Joe had walked past him a hundred times without seeing him? I'd find him. If I were there, I'd *sense* him. I know I would.

Lucy put on *Tomb Raider* next with Angelina as Lara Croft. At the beginning Lara beats up the scariest mother of a robot, then she beats up a bunch of bad guys in her garage and she's wearing pyjamas and riding a motorbike. There's no weapon she can't use, no car she can't drive, no skill she doesn't have, no thing she's afraid of. And she's got fabulous hair. I'm a bit jealous, actually. And she's a good actress, too. I remember reading an interview with some actress once and when she was asked how she managed to be so good at it – acting – she said, 'I don't just act, I *become* the character.' I try that sometimes at Mum's. I try to *become* the kind of daughter she'd like to have, instead of just acting it, but it never works. Probably because I don't actually want to be a person who panders to men and goes to confession. Not that Jack is a man you could pander to, anyway. Besides, with his lifestyle, he probably won't even live long enough to be pandered to. I wish I could have the chance to pander to him.

I was trying so hard not to cry that the tears couldn't help but come. And I tried not to let Lucy see, but of course that made me do stupid things to cover up, like dragging my hair in front of my face and pretending to look for nits.

'Erica, what are you doing?'

I started sobbing. My shoulders shook and I sat there hiccupping, my hair a heavy curtain over my face. 'I'm … upset … about … Jack.'

Lucy muted the TV and scuttled along the sofa, pushing my hair back and putting her arm around me. 'Don't worry, hon. He'll be alright. He's so bloody tough. And good-looking.'

'I don't think his looks will help him where he is now, Luce.'

She shrugged. 'Well, what can you do? You'll just have to hang in there and wait. Women have done it all throughout history. Waited for their men to come home from war.'

I took a great shuddering breath. War. The word made me shiver. Was Jack in some kind of secret war? I wiped my tears and watched Lara. She was flying into a jungle in her jeep, which was dropped from a helicopter with her behind the wheel, and as soon as it hit the ground, she hit the accelerator. Lara wasn't waiting around for anyone.

CHAPTER 11

J didn't remember much of my trip to work, which must have involved the usual walk to Richmond Station, a squashed train ride one stop to Flinders Street, and the walk to the footbridge where I now stood, holding the handrail for support as my gaze ran up the flashy length of the Dega Oil building across the river. I stared at the windows at the very top. I still hadn't heard back from John Degraves. I didn't have his home phone number and no way of getting it, except by calling Celia or Rosalind, and there was no chance either would hand it over without good reason. Which I simply didn't have.

I SAT AT MY DESK. 7:45 a.m. Way too early for me, but at least Rosalind wasn't in yet. The thought of facing her when my life wasn't otherwise perfect was more than I could bear. I dialled JD's office. My call went to voicemail so I left a message for Celia and waited, sitting at my desk, chewing my nails, flicking through but not seeing the stuff in my inbox. I was about to upset three important people: the big boss's PA, who I was going to lie to, the big boss, who I was going to talk to about unmentionable things, and

56

my boss, who wouldn't like me approaching JD without her permission.

I willed Celia to call me, wondering what I could say to get an immediate meeting with JD. I waited until 8:15, when I couldn't stand it any longer. I left my desk, rounded the corner and walked into Rosalind. I mean, straight into her. She'd been holding a coffee, and now she was wearing it. We gaped at each other, both frozen in disbelief. Why did she have coffee? She never gets her own coffee!

I found my voice. 'Oh my God.'

Her face was turning red. 'Is that all you can say?' she squeaked. '*Oh my God?* How about, I'm so sorry, Rosalind, for ruining your suit!'

'I'm sorry.' Oh, geez. How to wind back time? How to do that again, but walk in the other direction? I needed a new job. I needed a holiday.

Rosalind pushed her now-empty mug into my chest and stormed to her office, throwing over her shoulder, 'Obviously, I'll need another coffee.'

The phone on my desk rang. Celia? I headed for it, but Rosalind appeared at her office door, '*Now* would be nice!'

She stood there, arms crossed, glaring until I turned and headed for the kitchen.

Fresh coffee in hand, I crept into Rosalind's office (her back was turned) and placed the coffee as quietly as I could on her desk. She spun around.

'And,' she hissed, 'what do you plan to do about my suit?'

'Um, of course I'll take it to the cleaners.'

'And what do you propose I wear while it's at the cleaners? Hmm?'

I dunno. She could change into her night gear; what do vampires wear? I said nothing.

She thrust a credit card at me. 'You'll need to get me a new one. Frederick at Hugo Boss knows what I like. The store at Crown.'

I HEADED for the front doors of the building – I truly meant to go straight to Hugo Boss, but when I saw the door open to the executive lift, I stepped inside, holding my breath, and pushed the button for the top floor. It whizzed me straight there.

As I walked across the foyer I could see Celia talking on the phone. She saw me and frowned.

When I reached her desk she said, 'I left you a message.'

'What did you say?'

'I asked why you want to meet with JD.'

I glanced at his office door, which was closed. 'Can I see him now?' I added quickly, 'It's really personal, Cee. He won't mind, I'm sure, but . . . I can't say.'

'Is it about Rosalind?'

I screwed up my nose, which could have meant anything. She hesitated, watching me, and I could feel a hot blush crawl up my neck. I'm such a bad liar – except to my mother.

Finally, she rolled back her chair, went and tapped quietly on JD's door. She disappeared into his office. I waited. It was interminable. She came out and said, 'It's your lucky day, Erica. You can go on in.'

'Thanks, Celia. Sorry about this.' I hesitated in JD's doorway and peered in. There he was at his desk, his head bent over some papers. He had a small bald patch I'd never noticed before. The heat was working its way up my neck to my ears.

John Degraves looked up and regarded me for a few seconds before beckoning me forward, asking me to close the door. I sat opposite him at his vast desk and he looked at me over the top of his glasses. His voice was hard when he said, 'This has something to do with your role here, I trust, Erica?' Daring me to answer differently.

I swallowed. 'Not exactly, Mr Degraves.'

He managed to look even less happy.

I said, 'I tried to call you —'

'I'm aware of that.'

I stared at him. He waited. I leaned in and said in a whisper, 'I got a call from Joe. He said Jack is missing in action.' I sat back and waited for his reaction. There was none. Just staring. Glaring, actually.

I looked away, then back at him. Eventually, I felt I had no option but to leave. So I stood, ready to mutter an apology, but he said, 'What were you hoping to achieve by coming to see me?'

I sat quickly. 'Maybe … can you send someone?'

'To Saint Sebastian? Who did you have in mind? You?'

His abruptness shocked me, as did the fact that he just told me where Jack was. I stammered, 'I … I don't know. I just thought —'

'What makes you think this has anything to do with me?'

'Joe said —'

'It's none of your business,' he said, angry.

My mouth opened but nothing came out. I hung my head.

His chair squeaked as he sat back and tsked, just like my mother does when she's cross with me, and this was somehow comforting. 'Joe had no right or authority to call you. He shouldn't even be calling me.'

I nodded, my head bowed, and wiped away a tear.

He continued, 'It's over. I'm not happy about losing an elite operative like Jones, but there's nothing I can do.'

I looked up quickly. Elite operative? Jack is more than an elite operative. For a start, he's a human being, and my friend, and a bit more than a friend. JD must have read something in my expression because he said, more softly, 'Jack was a good guy, Erica, but he knew what he was doing when he took this assignment.'

Was a good guy?

JD turned back to the papers on his desk, and I took that as my dismissal. But as I walked away, I could feel his eyes on my back. Outside his office, I staggered past Celia. She called out, 'Are you alright?', but I couldn't look at her. I ran for the elevator, pushing the button over and over until the lift arrived. When I got back to my floor, I went straight to the ladies, and stayed there for half an hour.

Now I really had to hurry. Rosalind would be expecting me back from shopping and I hadn't even left the building. I needed to pull myself together, focus. It's over, JD had said. Well, as far as I was concerned, it wasn't.

I rushed down the road to Crown and through the casino, which was already busy with gamblers at poker machines. I hurried past restaurants and shops and skidded to a halt in front of a travel agent's, where I scanned the posters in the window. There was a map of Indonesia with Bali highlighted; photos of blue sky, beaches, tanned people and local colour pinned to it. But I peered past those photos at the map itself, which included the top of Australia, East Timor, and a tiny island just south of Timor: Saint Sebastian. I stared at it, as though doing so might produce answers.

Inside the shop two staff members were sitting at their desks, chatting. The man looked up at me and smiled.

'I was thinking about a holiday in Saint Sebastian,' I said.

He stopped smiling. 'Why would you go there?'

I shrugged. 'I read an article about it somewhere.'

'What about Bali?' he said, addressing his computer. 'There are some fantastic deals right now.'

'Okay. Well, thanks. I'll think about it.'

While Rosalind was changing into her new suit, office door closed, I googled Saint Sebastian. It was a tiny oblong speck in the Timor Sea. Tiny, but with a big history. War ravaged from an Indonesian invasion in the '70s and troubled ever since. There was a substantial Australian military presence on Saint Sebastian for a while, and a small Australian military base remained. A couple of travel blogs popped up – backpackers diarising their trips. Because of its shape and because it's so densely green with jungle, Saint Sebastian was nicknamed 'Emerald Island', and this seemed to give a few unsuspecting travellers the idea that it might be a nice place to go, which apparently it isn't.

I wished I knew where Jack and Joe had been staying. Or maybe they were camping in the jungle or something? Saint Sebastian seemed to be more jungle than city. Maybe it was like being in Bali. Kind of third worldly but touristy at the same time. Where was Jack right *now*? I tested the unthinkable: was he dead, as JD thought? My heart and stomach switched places. No. That wasn't possible. I kept searching the net. No current news about fighting or war or anything on the island. So, why did Jack go there? I wished I'd pushed him for more information.

For the rest of the day, Rosalind kept catching me staring off into space. During those staring moments I was mostly trying to convince myself that there was nothing to be done about Jack, that it wasn't my business, that he knew what he was doing, that he probably didn't even want me in his life. Intermittently, I'd try both Jack's and Joe's mobiles, but they were still switched off.

CHAPTER 12

I lay in bed at one a.m. staring at the ceiling. When my alarm went off at seven, I was still staring at the ceiling. I got up and left a message on Rosalind's office phone, saying that I was sick and wouldn't be coming to work. I sat at my dining table with my laptop and looked up travel agents, scanning the options. I was really just sussing it out. I didn't actually intend to go there. Not really. Not consciously. But when I called the travel agent who 'specialises in unusual travel', he didn't think going to Saint Sebastian sounded so strange. 'Adventurous backpackers go there all the time,' he said. He gave me the prices and times, leaving the very next day, and there was something about the way he said, 'Shall I go ahead and book?' that made me say 'Yes'.

I sat in shock while the travel guy ran through the details and I gave him my credit card details, sounding like a robot. He said, 'You should take malaria tablets.'

After the call, I sat staring out the window, thinking about deadly mosquitoes. I did that for about an hour, and decided to call Lucy. It wouldn't be a pleasant conversation, I knew that, but someone needed to know where I was going. Just in case. Lucy had threatened to tie me up and lock me in her bedroom when I'd suggested I might actually go to Saint Sebastian.

'It's not that bad, really,' I'd said when I called her the day before to tell her about my meeting with JD. 'It's got nice beaches.'

'It's an urban war zone, Erica. The place is run by gangs and corrupt politicians who'd love to sell you to a brothel. That's if you don't get taken by a crocodile or die from malaria first.'

'People go there for work. Australians live there! And I can take malaria tablets.' I wasn't sure what I could do about the crocs, but I'd worry about that when the time came.

In the end I'd promised to call the Australian government or military office or something instead. But this was a top-secret mission. What the hell was I going to say to some government department? And if it *was* something to do with the government and they happened to know what I was talking about, how would they react? Send some ASIO agent to shut me up?

I dialled Lucy's number. 'I've done it,' I said, when she answered. 'I've booked a flight to Saint Sebastian.'

'You are fucking joking.'

'I'm just going to suss it out. See if I can find out anything.'

'Erica —'

'I'm going, Luce, and the only reason I'm telling you is so someone else knows where I am. Just in case.'

There was a long silence. Then, Lucy was crying. 'You . . . you might get killed.'

'I won't get killed,' I said, gently. 'And if I do, you have permission to kill me.'

She gave a brief laugh through her tears. 'I should come with you,' she said.

'Ha! You and me together; we'd find him in a flash.' In fact, I couldn't think of anyone I'd rather go to some scary place with, apart from Jack.

Next I called Rosalind again and told her I was having emotional issues and needed a few days off. I said John Degraves had authorised it. Which was a lie, of course, but I knew she wouldn't call Degraves about it in case it was something to do with her. She wanted to know why I was speaking directly to JD about anything and I said it was extremely personal. I knew how much she'd hate that, and that made me feel slightly better about everything else.

So now I had less than 24 hours to pack a bag, organise a babysitter for Axle, and get myself to the airport. I called my mother. I really would have liked to take a Valium before doing that, but I didn't have time.

'Hello, dear,' she said. 'Did you go to confession? I can make arrangements with Father.'

'Actually, Mum, I was hoping you could look after Axle for me.' I realised then that I needed to brighten my tone. 'I'm going on a holiday!'

'Where are you going?'

'Bali. I'm meeting Jack there.'

I cringed. In my worry about Jack and having to lie to my mother again – actually, that didn't bother me so much – I forgot how Mum was likely to react to my having an unchaperoned holiday with my supposed boyfriend.

There was the expected silence, and after a few moments, she said, 'Only hussies go on holiday with men who aren't their husbands.'

'Maybe in the '50s, Mum. Not these days.'

More silence.

I said, by way of distraction, 'I was thinking I could get you a nice present for Mother's Day while I'm there.'

'What did you have in mind?' She sounded mildly friendlier.

'Oh, I thought something locally made. Something special that Mary or Janice wouldn't have.'

Bingo.

'Really? Now that would be nice. Something special from Bali,' she mused, and added briskly, 'Well, I suppose you'll have separate rooms.'

'Of course, Mum.' Oh my God. If I was really meeting Jack in Bali, he'd be lucky to get to a room before I tore his clothes off.

'And you can go to confession when you come back.'

'When I come back.' When Hell freezes over.

'And, Erica, it might be wise to get some kind of commitment from Jack while you're there.'

'Good idea.'

'He'll be more likely to propose in a romantic environment like Bali.'

'Without a doubt.'

We hung up, still friends, and I stuffed my backpack with walking shoes and hiking clothes. I didn't want to end up like Kathleen Turner, trudging through a jungle with nothing but high heels and a wheelie suitcase. From my minimal research I knew there was civilisation in Saint Sebastian. Shops even. But there was jungle, too – lots of it. And I couldn't help but imagine Jack in camouflage, peering through giant palm fronds with black paint on his face.

I tipped my dirty clothes basket upside-down on my bed in case there was something I needed to wash and pack. But something else fell out that I'd forgotten about. My gun. The gun Jack had given me in case I needed to protect myself from knife-wielding bandits in my bedroom. I'd never used it except once at the shooting range, where Jack had told me I was a natural. Should I pack my illegal handgun and hope no one notices? I was on a roll, after all. Taking unlimited, unauthorised leave from work, heading for a dangerous country, lying to everyone – why not add another award-winning stupid decision to the list?

'Idiot,' I muttered and threw it back in the basket.

I packed my toiletries, sunscreen, some basic first-aid stuff and a compass that came for free with a pair of hiking pants. I packed a framed photo of Jack and me. It was taken at a dinner party I had last year to introduce my so-called new boyfriend to my mates. For the photo we'd leaned towards each other until we were cheek to cheek. Jack was so relaxed, so comfortable that evening. It was the first time he kissed me – but only because I made him do it. He's a good actor. Looking at that photo, anyone would think we were a regular couple. I chucked the pic in my bag. Thought about what else I could possibly need. Knives? Hand grenades? Nail scissors and an emery board, definitely. I made a mental note to buy mozzie repellent at the airport –

tropical strength. Then I emptied everything from my regular handbag into a black leather one that doubled as a small backpack. And the whole time I was packing, I felt like throwing up.

FIRST THING on Wednesday I called Kate and asked if I could pop by to see her. It was a tough decision because Kate is Joe's girlfriend – well, Jack and I reckon she is but they don't say and Jack seems to think it's none of my business, so I have to figure out what they're up to by being a stickybeak. Anyway, I didn't know what she knew about the boys' mission, but Kate is also the Team's doctor, and now my doctor, and it made sense that I got my malaria tablets from her. When I told her I was going to meet up with Jack she'd asked quietly, 'Do you know where they are?' I'd hesitated before saying I did and she said yes, she did, too, that she'd had a call from Joe but hadn't been able to reach him since. Then she'd started crying. I told her I was going to try to help Joe find Jack and she said she was terrified for them both. And now me. She could understand why I wanted to go (because Jack is my boyfriend even though Jack doesn't seem to be aware of that fact), but she didn't want me to because Saint Sebastian was such a dangerous place, she said.

After I left Kate's, I sent Jack and Joe a text saying that I was coming, and what time I arrived, but in my heart I knew they wouldn't see those messages.

CHAPTER 13

*A*fter three hours sweating my face off at Darwin airport, my hair was as frizzed out as it could possibly be. Except for the parts that were glued to my face and neck. Every time I unstuck my thighs from the hard plastic seat they made a loud sucking noise.

Finally, there was an announcement that all flights were cancelled until tomorrow due to the baggage-handlers' strike. The crowd made a collective groan. I took my place in line to find out what I needed to do, and after another hour I was told that I was lucky to get out of Melbourne. I didn't know if 'luck' was the right word when I could have been sitting in a pleasant 18 degrees with zero humidity. At home. In front of the telly.

I took my $12.50 accommodation voucher and caught a bus to the city. I'd checked accommodation options on my phone. Hotels in Darwin were really expensive. I sat behind the bus driver and asked him about a cheap place to stay. El Cheapo Backpackers in the centre of town, he told me. I thought of the five-star hotel I'd stayed at in Sydney with Jack, the first time we'd made love. And I thought of Jack in bed. In the shower. Naked. Kissing my neck. Moaning softly as he pulled me closer. Running his hands over my wet back and down, down, down . . . I sighed, really loudly, and the driver looked at me in the mirror. I know the Sydney trip had mostly been about attempted bombings, murder, kidnapping, etc, but it had been so romantic and lovely in that big suite.

The bus drove along a road that was lined on one side with nice hotels and on the other with a long, green park that overlooked the ocean. I wondered if there were any crocodiles down there, in the sea, and if they ever ventured up from the water and across the park and into the hotel swimming pools.

We kept stopping at those nice hotels where porters rushed to help with luggage and the driver smiled and waved. Then everyone was off the bus except me. Eventually we came to the bus terminal in the middle of town and the driver pointed towards a bunch of buildings.

'Go through there. The hostel is on the right,' he said. No helping with luggage. And no smiling and waving.

I DUMPED my stuff in the dorm room. I had no intention of hanging around the backpackers', but what to do? If Joe had gotten my text he might have gone to Seni airport to meet me. And if so, he would have discovered I wasn't coming until tomorrow. I had no idea how to contact him. He'd be there to meet me tomorrow, for sure. The fact that he hadn't returned my text was something I relegated to the denial department.

I showered, changed and headed out in search of a bar or pub that might give me icy cold beer. The mirror in my room confirmed my suspicions about my hair. The parts that weren't stuck to my face or frizzing out lay heavily against my back, causing a patch of sweat there.

The hostel was in the main street, where all the action was. Noisy bars and tanned people wearing bright colours and thongs spilling out of those bars. But I didn't feel like action, of course not. So I walked away, down side streets and between buildings, and found I was on the Esplanade, which I discovered was the name of the road with the nice hotels and park. I walked across the park, drawn to the sea, glancing around for crocodiles. There was a footpath that skirted the park, following the coastline, and a steep slope of treed terrain that ran down from the path to the water's edge. As I walked, I could see through the trees and across the ocean, catching glimpses of distant land. Maybe it was East Timor or even Saint Sebastian? I felt so close to danger, here in Darwin – and I don't mean the crocodiles. Just there across the water were countries with fighting and places that people wanted to risk their lives to escape from. Coming on rickety old boats, packed in like sardines. Was Jack just there? Across that sea?

I walked a bit further to a lookout point – a high one with a better view, where a circle of Aboriginal people sat. I climbed the steps warily, wondering if I was intruding, and nodded hello. One guy acknowledged me with a tilt of his beer can. The other three ignored me, their heads turned away, and I couldn't really blame them. If anyone had a right to have an issue with boat people, it was them.

I said to the man with the beer, 'Do you know what land that is?' I pointed.

He glanced at the others. One looked at me and rolled her eyes. 'That's Australia,' he said.

'Oh, I thought it was another country.'

They all laughed. 'Nah, that's Port Darwin, that sea.' He pointed to the right. 'Saint Sebastian's that way.'

'Okay, thank you.' I left them, wondering how the hell he knew I was looking for Saint Sebastian.

I HEADED BACK TO TOWN, thinking about that can of beer and how nice it'd be to have one. As I walked I pulled my hair up, twirled it into a bun and held it on top of my head. I fanned my neck. Walking down the street, I peered in shop windows, thinking about a gift for Mum. It would have to be something tropical. Something that looked like it came from Bali. Something that Mary or Janice wouldn't have. I continued down an arcade and stopped in front of a hairdressing salon.

'That's it,' I said to my reflection. 'I can't stand it.' I peered at the price list stuck to the door. I could get a cut – maybe even two or three inches off – for just $35. If Darwin was this humid, Saint Sebastian would be worse, for sure.

A face suddenly appeared in front of me on the other side of the glass door. *Erica Jewell?* it mouthed. I stared at the woman. Did I know her? She was holding a pair of scissors, snipping them in the air, a questioning look on her face. The door opened.

'Erica Jewell! Are you coming in or not?'

'Yvonne? Oh my God!' I would never have recognised her, but I knew that distinctive, husky voice instantly. My old university friend's hair used to be identical to mine and people thought we were related. But now hers was short and choppy, and pretty sexy, actually. She looked sensational, in fact, dressed in expensive-looking jeans and a singlet top, and strappy gold sandals. At uni she'd never worn make-up or waxed, but now she was fully made up and her armpits appeared to be hair-free. I couldn't stop looking at her, my mouth hanging open.

She laughed. 'I'm surprised you recognised me.'

'I didn't! Well, your voice . . . Do you work here?' I glanced past her into the salon.

'This is my business. Do you want to come in? I'm nearly finished here.'

'Oh, well, I was just going to find a pub or something.'

'Hey, how about I meet you for a drink?' She pointed towards the main street. 'There's a place just a few doors down. I'll only be twenty minutes or so.'

'Okay. Well, I'll see you then.'

I walked away, thinking how weird it was, Yvonne being a hairdresser, owning her own salon. I most definitely did not want Yvonne cutting my hair. Back at university I was always a bit scared of her and the things she did. Which was a lot of drugs, lots of activist-type stuff, sex with lots of people (gender not an issue) and some jail time for accidentally nearly killing a girl in a bar fight. She'd fancied me at one stage and told me so. I'd giggled and said something ridiculous because I was embarrassed and terrified. She didn't try again. And now she looked like Halle Berry.

I found the place Yvonne had mentioned, sat inside at the bar away from everyone else, and ordered a pint of beer. By the time Yvonne walked in, I'd finished that beer and she wanted to buy me another.

'Let's have champagne,' she said. 'Celebrate!' Yvonne and champagne seemed so wrong.

'Actually, I'm not good with champagne . . . maybe just one.'

Yvonne ordered. 'It's good to see you, Ruby,' she said. 'Remember we used to call you that?'

Vaguely. Something to do with my surname. 'Some people still do,' I lied.

She sat on the stool next to me. 'So, Ruby, what are you doing in Darwin?'

THREE HOURS LATER, I was still sitting on that stool, but now my head was resting on the bar next to several empty shot glasses. I would have been able to see all the way to the end of the bar if Yvonne's head wasn't in the way. She was resting her chin on her crossed arms. She was a good listener.

'And,' I said, 'I think he really luffs me.'

'He's an idiot if he doesn't,' said Yvonne.

I reached out and stroked her hair. 'I luff your hair. I want your hair.' I sighed. 'You used to luff me, Vonny.'

'I did indeed. Come on, Ruby, I can't leave you here with this lot.'

I peered through blurred vision at all the backpackers; they were making a lot of noise. There was one who was pretty cute.

'Let's get you home,' said Yvonne.

I thought she sounded a bit drunk. I hoped she'd be alright.

CHAPTER 14

I groaned, opened my eyes, squeezed them shut and prayed for a time warp to snatch me away, suck me up, whatever it is they do. Or a simple reversal of time. Twenty-four hours would be good. Take me back to Melbourne airport, where I would say to the check-in lady, 'No guarantee of flights leaving Darwin? No worries. I'll just stay here and carry on with my boring life.' Maybe the baggage-handlers' strike was a sign from the universe that I shouldn't be going to Saint Sebastian. The entire universe had set that up, just for me, and I'd rudely ignored it.

I sat up, groaning some more, and registered that I was on a sofa in an unfamiliar living room. I rubbed my eyes and, out of habit, pushed my hair out of my face. But something was different. Something was wrong. I ran my hands over my head. There was no hair to push! I bolted upright, standing, looking frantically for a mirror. Where the hell was I? Yvonne's house? I stumbled down a passageway, pushing doors open until I found a bathroom. I stood in front of the mirror. Oh, good God. My hair was short like Yvonne's, except I didn't look like Halle Berry. I looked like Anne Hathaway after she sold her hair in *Les Mis*. I burst into tears.

· · ·

After ten minutes of conversation with the toilet-roll holder, we decided it was a good thing. My hair had always been a nightmare. And anyway, it would grow back. But for now I could be nice and cool. My head felt lighter, in fact. And, I probably weighed less! That thought made me feel much better, but I didn't look in the mirror again. I found my way back to the living room and my things, which were neatly stacked on the dining table with a jar of hair product. There was also a note. *Hey Ruby, great to see you. I hope you're OK about the hair. You absolutely insisted! Here's a jar of wax. You'll need it. I had to go to work. Let yourself out. Yxx*

As I looked around, snippets of the previous evening dribbled through my memory bank. I'd told Yvonne all about Jack and my mother, and she'd finally half-walked, half-carried me out of the bar and taken me back to her place. And cut my hair.

There was a map drawn on the note to show me where I was and how to find the backpackers'. And under that: *My friend in Sebastian, as promised.* And a phone number and address. Yvonne had said something about living in Saint Sebastian? Actually, I didn't remember Yvonne getting to say much at all last night. I felt a slight pang of guilt. But only slight.

I glanced at my watch. *Oh shit!* My flight was in an hour and a half and I had to get to the backpackers' and get my stuff. I snatched up my bag and shot out of Yvonne's front door, letting it slam behind me, hoping I'd got everything, hoping her door had locked itself.

I raced down her driveway and stood on the street, my head swivelling from side to side, trying to work out which way to go. I had Yvonne's map in my hand; I headed for a main road where I started waving frantically at any car that passed, knowing that, without a doubt, I would hitch a ride with Jack the Ripper if necessary.

CHAPTER 15

I shoved my bag into the overhead locker and flopped onto my seat. I was sweaty, hung-over, thirsty and hungry. There'd been no time to shower or eat, after I'd finally managed to get a ride in an old Commodore with Beavis and Butthead, who'd sniggered all the way to the hostel. The only reason I made the plane was because it was delayed. There was a lot of police activity at the airport and I felt very glad I hadn't brought my gun. Imagine if Jack had come home to discover I'd been arrested trying to sneak a gun into Saint Sebastian – a gun that was registered to him. And because he'd just been there, the police would want to know, 'Why was Ms Jewell in possession of a gun registered to you, Mr Jones? And why was she trying to smuggle it into Saint Sebastian where you just happened to be? Hmmm?' He'd be pretty shitty with me if he survived some dangerous mission in Saint Sebastian, only to end up arrested in Melbourne.

The plane taxied away from the terminal but only for a hundred metres or so before it stopped. We sat there for 20 minutes and I watched through the window, past the guy sitting next to me, as a police van rumbled across the tarmac towards us.

I could sense the guy watching me. He was wearing a cowboy hat and I'd guessed he was American. 'You seem worried,' he said.

I sat back. 'No. I'm not worried. Why would I be worried?' Apart from about a million reasons.

'Well, the police are checkin' for stolen goods.'

He was watching me with his sparkly blue eyes, and he seemed almost amused. What was that accent? Texan?

He leaned towards me. 'You stolen somethin'?' Was he teasing me?

I smiled. 'No, have you?'

He waggled his eyebrows. 'Maybe.'

'Like what?'

He looked a bit like my pizza delivery guy, who looked a bit like Brad Pitt, but from a long time ago. When he did *Thelma and Louise*. The guy pushed his hat to the back of his head. 'Could be anything on a plane for Sebastian.'

I loved that accent. 'Are you from Texas?' I said.

He hesitated. Maybe I was being too nosy. But hang on, he just asked if I'd stolen something. Finally, he said, 'Sure am. Have you been?'

'To Texas?'

He nodded.

'No,' I said, 'never been to America. What part of Texas?'

'Dallas.'

'Dallas Cowboys!' I racked my brain for other things I knew about Dallas.

He grinned.

I said, 'So, why would a plane for Saint Sebastian have stolen goods onboard?'

He regarded me as though I was joking with him, and said, 'You tell me.'

'I really have no idea.'

'You don't know that Sebastian's the black-market capital of the universe?' he said.

Something to do with Jack? I gazed out the window for a few long seconds. I looked back at the guy. He was waiting for an answer.

'Um. No, I didn't,' I said. 'What sort of stolen stuff?'

He turned in his seat so he was facing me. God, he was good-looking. Blonde hair, and those blue eyes really did sparkle – a bit like Jack's, but Jack's are bottomless in their intensity and they tend not to sparkle so much when I'm being annoying.

'Well, let's see now,' he said. 'Everything, really, from rare Pokémon cards to vintage car parts. Current trend is Tupperware.'

I burst out laughing, thinking of my mother. 'That's ridiculous.'

'Is it?'

'Yes. Isn't it?'

'No, ma'am. Tupperware is hot property. Everyone wants the retro stuff. You just can't get it 'cause it's all stashed away in old ladies' cupboards.'

I stared at him, expecting him to laugh and tell me he was pulling my leg. But he didn't.

'What do you mean, retro?'

'Well, the original Tupperware they don't make no more. Like the lettuce container with the spike inside.'

'My mother has that stuff,' I mused. And what was it she'd said? That there was a Tupperware thief? I scoffed quietly.

'Oh?' said the man. 'What does your mom have? Probably worth a whole lotta dollars.'

'Well, she's got everything, really, from the seventies. Oh, and she's got a special edition lettuce crisper that's still in its box.'

I smiled at the guy and his face turned stony serious. He glanced around before whispering, 'She's got the special edition lettuce crisper? From 1976?'

'Yep,' I said, feeling suddenly very important. I didn't know if it was from 1976 but that sounded about right.

He whistled, low and long. Then he held out a hand and introduced himself. 'Dwayne Hitower, and I'd sure like to meet your mom.'

'Erica Jewell, and you're welcome to meet and keep my mother, if you want.'

He laughed and we shook hands. He had nice teeth. 'You don't happen to have some of that old Tupperware in your suitcase, do you?' He glanced out the window.

'No.' I said, 'How do you know all this about the Tupperware and stuff?'

But he didn't answer. Instead he leaned towards me again, fixed his sparkly eyes on mine, and said, 'First, Ms Jewell, you tell me something. What sends you to hell on earth?'

Flying into Seni, I wondered why Jack couldn't be a nice, ordinary kind of bloke like Dwayne instead of some gung-ho bloody tough guy. Although I didn't actually know what Dwayne did, or even why he was coming to Saint Sebastian, because every time I'd asked he changed the subject, questioning me instead about . . . everything.

I leaned across Dwayne – asleep with his hat tipped low over his face – and looked past my awful reflection at the scene below. Saint Sebastian really was very green. Densely so. Emerald Island. I bet there were a lot of snakes and other crawlies in that jungle. As we circled I had a good view of the airport, which seemed to be more civilised than I'd expected. Sprawling white buildings and a dozen or so planes, a few Qantas ones. The plane turned in a wide, sweeping arc and floated past those buildings on our final descent. Dwayne woke, yawned, gave me a smile and a wink, and watched out the window as we touched down. At the end of the runway we pivoted and headed for the terminals, and I saw a couple of heavy-looking aircraft sitting outside a hangar, their fat, grey bellies close to the ground.

'Hercules,' Dwayne informed me.

I nodded.

He said, 'Do they make you feel homesick?'

'No, why?'

'They're Australian.'

I squinted at the writing on them. *Royal Australian Air Force*. Is Jack here with the Air Force? I wondered. But if that's the case, what's JD's involvement? My heart started thumping. I sat back and fanned my face.

'You okay?' said Dwayne.

'Me? Yeah. Sure. Fine.'

INSIDE SENI AIRPORT I waited in line to pass through customs. There was no air conditioning; just ceiling fans swirling the wet air. Sweat prickled my scalp and my T-shirt clung to my back. The only thing I was remotely enjoying was my new haircut, as awful as it was.

Dwayne was well ahead of me. I'd avoided telling him about Jack. So Dwayne thought I was simply a misguided tourist, meeting a friend for some sightseeing before heading off to Bali. I didn't ask him to elaborate on the 'hell on earth' thing. It couldn't be that bad here, surely?

I peered around the queue. I could see Dwayne heading for the exit and before he went through the doors he turned and gave me a wave. I waved back and sighed. How much nicer to be arriving in Bali instead, looking forward to my first evening sitting at a beachside bar, a creamy cocktail with fruit hanging out of it, an orange hibiscus in my hair. And sitting beside me, a hand on my knee and smiling because he was on holiday with me, looking delicious and relaxed and as sexy as all get out, was Jack. Or Dwayne.

Unfortunately, I was forced to refocus when someone gave me a poke from behind because the queue had advanced ten metres but I hadn't. I looked ahead. The customs people seemed to be searching every suitcase. Sweat poured down my face. I'd never known humidity like it.

There were men in uniforms with machine guns. The backpacker in front of me had the contents of her bag spread over the search table, and two customs ladies were inspecting every item. The way they rifled through the woman's stuff, picking out certain things, made them look more like bargain-basement shoppers than officials conducting a search. One picked up a tiny travel iron, examined it and handed it to her co-worker, who walked away with it. The backpacker said, 'Hey!', but the customs lady moved on to the next person. Me. The backpacker said, 'You can't take that!' but no one took any notice, except for the guys with guns, who were moving towards her. She looked around. Our eyes met. I shrugged and looked away. She repacked her bag angrily and moved on. The customs woman opened my backpack. She pulled my hairdryer out and examined it.

'No!' I said, too loudly.

She stared at me suspiciously as she handed the hairdryer to her colleague, who walked away with it. She returned to my bag and rifled some more. Pocketed the hair wax. Picked up a packet of tampons and rattled the box, narrowing her eyes at me. Hang on, why did the box *rattle*? Oh, shit. As she opened it I remembered where I keep the bullets for my gun. She peered inside the box, signalled one of the lurking guards, and I closed my eyes. I remembered now, scooping up that packet from my undies drawer along with a few pairs of knickers and throwing the bundle into my backpack. *Idiot.* I would be imprisoned in Saint Sebastian for at least 20 years. When I opened my eyes again, the soldier was standing next to the customs lady. She slipped him the bullets; he put them in his pocket and walked away. Without further eye contact she dismissed me, and called the next person in line. I decided there and then that this type of corruption was fine by me. But as I blew out my held breath, I thought that if Jack was still alive, he would surely kill me.

I WALKED through the automatic glass doors and searched the thin, scattered crowd for Dwayne. I thought I could ask him where he was staying and go there too, but really I just wanted to see a familiar face. I changed some money to local currency, which, surprisingly, was

American dollars. I ignored the astronomical fee they charged for the exchange because, based on my experience so far, there was probably little point arguing.

I took a seat and looked around, waiting. For what, I didn't know. There were some backpackers. And some people who looked like tourists, and other people who could have been foreign workers – Aussies maybe – who sat around looking bored, like there was nothing left in Saint Sebastian that could possibly interest them.

So, where were Jack and Joe? Were they dead? No. Time to move. I stood and hoisted my pack onto my back, attached my handbag-cum-small-backpack to my chest, and left the building. I stood at a narrow road that appeared to be the main thoroughfare in and out of the airport. To the left the road presumably led to Seni; to the right was a dead end, marked by tall cyclone-wire gates. Across the road the bitumen morphed into jungle; a jungle that was so dense, the green was almost black. The humidity was so oppressive, I could imagine anything would grow in there. All kinds of fungus and diseases.

There was a bus but it pulled out as I approached. I looked for a timetable. There was none. I looked for someone who might know something about the buses. There were no official-looking people, apart from blokes with guns. I was going to go back inside to ask, but thought about the man who was now in possession of my bullets. And the stupid woman with my hairdryer. And hair stuff. What would I do without my dryer and hair wax?

I approached the first driver in a line of taxis.

'How much to Seni?'

He shrugged.

I tried again. 'Do you speak English?'

He looked away.

I walked to the next cab. The guy held up both hands, showing me ten fingers. He did that five times. What was he trying to tell me? Fifty dollars? That seemed a lot. The airport was close to Seni, I knew that much from Google. I asked the next man, who said, 'Twen fife,' and held up ten fingers.

The next driver was a skinny man with a big smile and some teeth missing.

'Hello, lady, you need taxi?'

'Oh, thank God, you speak English. How much to Seni?'

'I make cheap trip,' he said, his smile widening even more.

'How much?'

'Cheap as chip!'

I walked to the back of his beaten-up yellow Toyota – it reminded me with some misguided sense of familiarity of my car – where I waited for him to open the boot.

'Can you take me to a nice hotel?' On the flight out of Darwin I'd decided that cheap and nasty was a thing of the past for me. No more being a cheapskate. Never again.

'Nice hotel! You come.' He loaded my pack into the boot and held the back door for me.

As I sat inside the car, I said, 'How much will it cost? The taxi ride?'

'Cheap trip. Special price for pretty lady.'

We cruised from the airport at about 15 kilometres an hour and the driver talked incessantly. His name was Bruce Willis, he said with a straight face. He told me he used to be a driver for the UN, which was why he speaks 'very good English' and I assumed also why he drove at funeral-procession speed. Actually, slower than a funeral procession. I kept looking ahead to see what the hold-up was, but the road was clear. Actually, it was more like a country lane than a road and fringed on both sides by dense rain forest, which, after a couple of kilometres, ended abruptly and was replaced by cane fields.

I tapped him on the shoulder to interrupt the verbal flow. 'Can you go faster?'

'No fast. Maybe snake on road.'

'What's the big deal about running over a snake?'

'Maybe run someone. Man or lady. Look!' he said, pointing ahead.

There were indeed people standing close to the road. Two groups of boys – maybe 14 or 15 years old – stood on opposite sides of the road, and they were chucking stuff at each other.

'What are they doing?' I said.

'Dangerous gangs,' said Bruce Willis, going even slower. 'Throw rocks. Kill each other.'

'Are you serious?'

As we approached, the rock throwers stopped what they were doing and waited while we drove past, now at walking pace. Two of the young men had monkeys sitting on their shoulders. They smiled and waved at me – the kids, not the monkeys – taking bows, calling out things. The driver interpreted. 'They want to meet pretty lady.'

'Can't you go faster?'

He resumed his breakneck speed and I watched out the back window as the gang kids started throwing rocks again.

'Why do they have monkeys?' I said.

'Big monkey, big man,' said Bruce Willis. 'Important gang leader has very big monkey.'

'Maybe the gang leader is trying to compensate for something.'

THE TOWNSHIP of Seni was close to the airport. The outskirts consisted mostly of small, crooked, grubby fibro houses. We passed an official-looking building set back from a high wall with armed guards at the gates, a couple of acres of unkempt property surrounding it. That building was pretty grubby-looking, too; crumbling stucco that presumably was once white. There were open market-style shops and some cafes. Grubby.

In stark contrast to the shanty town, behind it rose a magnificent mountain range, and to my right was a surprisingly clean, white beach and ocean the colour you see only in travel brochures. A line of date palms separated the beach from the road. We could have been in some exotic resort town, except for the fact that we weren't. Bruce parked in front of a crappy-looking place called the Koala Bear Hotel. He got out of the car and walked to the boot, pulling my bag out and dropping it on the ground.

I wound the window down and called out, 'Isn't there a better hotel?'

'No better hotel. Good hotel for Aussie,' he said. 'Cheap as chip. Good bar.'

'Thank God, a bar,' I muttered and got out of the car, my inner miser taking back control. I looked around. I wanted to go back to Yvonne's. Or El Cheapo Backpackers.

Bruce Willis carried my bag the two metres from the front door to the reception desk. The space was devoid of all character. I'd say it was clinical, but it was too dirty. There were two women sitting behind the desk, looking blankly at me. You could hardly see them over the top of the counter. One of the girls handed something to Bruce and he pocketed whatever it was, turned to me and smiled, an expectant hand held out.

I looked at his empty palm. 'How much do I owe you?'

'Special price for pretty lady. Fifty dollar.'

'You've got to be kidding! That can't have been more than five kilometres.'

'Forty dollar.'

'Twenty.'

'Thirty?'

'Oh, alright.' I gave him a 50-dollar note and followed him out to his car for the change, but he sped away with his arm waving happily back and forth out the window.

CHAPTER 17

*L*uckily for me, the Koala Bear Hotel had a room available on the top floor – three flights of stairs and no lift. My room was about as inspiring as the hotel foyer, and the cleaner's mop obviously hadn't been able to reach the corners of the white-tiled floor. There were two single beds. There was no view of the beach, however there *was* a view through a small, square window directly across a filthy courtyard into another room where a couple were having sex. And making a lot of noise about it. I tried not to look, but I couldn't help it. The guy's bare bum bounced up and down, up and down. Every now and then she'd fling one or both of her legs into the air and laugh. And I was peeved, thinking that I'd like to be in Bali right now having hot, sweaty sex with Jack. Not trying to find him in some scary jungle where he probably lay dead or mortally wounded, gasping his last, raspy breaths.

I chucked my stuff on one of the beds, huffed, said to the sex couple, 'Have an extra one for me,' and left the room. I'd decided to check out the Australian Embassy first; Lucy had insisted on it. Back out the front of the hotel, I flagged down a cab. It was Bruce Willis, the rip-off driver. He hopped out of his car and held the door for me, smiling brightly.

'I'm not going with you,' I said. 'You ripped me off!'

'Sorry, lady. Free ride now.'

I hesitated. It was stinking hot. I looked around. 'I suppose,' I grumbled, got in, and two minutes later we pulled up outside the Australian Embassy.

'Here, lady,' he said.

'Well, that wasn't very far.'

'Twenty dollar.' He held out his hand.

'Hey, this was supposed to be a free ride!'

'Fifteen dollar?'

'No money!'

'Ten dollar.' He looked miserable. 'My wife, she have cancer.'

'Oh, please.'

'And dybeety.'

'Oh, for God's sake.' I slapped a ten-dollar note in his hand and got out, and he zoomed away.

At the embassy I waited in line behind a couple of backpackers and a variety of odd-looking people, all of whom I thought should be friendly – being fellow Aussies – but they weren't. They all looked unhappy, hot and tired.

It was finally my turn. As I stepped up to the counter, the guy seemed to be already looking for the person behind me.

So, what to tell him? I couldn't say that I thought Jack had been sent to Saint Sebastian by a secret Australian organisation that was also illegal, so, thinking about the Hercules I'd seen, I said, 'My friend came over here on a mission with the Australian Air Force and now he's missing in action.'

'That sounds like a problem for the Australian military,' he said.

'Well, actually, I don't know if he was here with the military or if it was . . . a private thing, but he's missing and no one's doing anything about it.'

The man spent approximately three quarters of a second inspecting his computer screen. 'The R.A.A.F. is not currently active in Saint Sebastian.'

'Well, what about the army?'

'It's all the same.' He looked past me, ready to serve the next in line.

'Can you check somewhere else?' I said, feeling desperate. I really thought he would have some kind of answer for me. My reward for being brave and coming here would be that the Australian Embassy would know what needed to be done once I'd alerted them to the problem. That they'd send troops or embassy people or something out there to find Jack.

'There is no active military here from Australia,' he said.

'But I saw the Hercules!'

'Miss, please.' He was looking really pissed off, and I was attracting attention, which probably wasn't a good idea.

Still, I leaned close and lowered my voice. 'You're wrong. He came over here on a mission and now he's missing in action. And his friend who rang to tell me about it is missing as well.'

The man, stiff and shitty, said, 'As I said, currently, there is no active Australian military in Saint Sebastian.' He looked past me again.

I leaned to the side so that I was directly in his view. 'And, as I said, you're wrong.' I choked on that last word. Damn it, why can't I just stand in a shop or at a counter and shout at annoying, unhelpful people without getting emotional? Like Lucy.

The man watched me for a moment, glanced around, and leaned in. 'Look,' he said, quietly, 'if the Australian military sent someone over for active duty, we'd know about it. Unless,' he added, lowering his voice even more, 'the operation was secret. In which case, no one would know about it, and if the operation were to go wrong, even the government might deny any knowledge.' He stared at me for a moment longer, leaned back and said in a normal voice, 'Why don't you try the UN?' Then he called, 'Next!'

I staggered away, his words echoing in my head. Is that what had happened? Was Jack here on a secret government mission that had gone wrong, and now they were denying his very existence? I thought that kind of thing only happened in movies. But if it *is* a government thing, why is JD involved?

With directions from the embassy security guard, I found the United Nations office. When I told my story, the man sitting opposite me didn't bat an eye. He just pushed a pile of forms at me and suggested I go back to my hotel to fill them in and bring them back some other time.

'But you don't understand,' I said. 'My friend might be a prisoner and they might kill him.'

'Lady, I'm due to go on annual leave,' he checked the clock on the wall, 'in exactly two hours. I really can't get involved in some fantasy you might have —'

'Fantasy?' I almost screamed the word.

'Okay, well, what you say is probably true, but my flight's booked, and I'm outta here today.' He grinned. 'Gonna visit some of those famous fleshpots in Thailand.'

I WALKED BACK to the hotel. In my room I flopped onto the creaky single bed. So, now what? I did some deep breathing. In through the nose, out through the mouth. The sex couple were still going. Or maybe they'd had a sleep and started again? I thought about being with Jack, imagined holding him, hearing his voice. The sex couple were making so much noise I could hear them through my closed window. His grunts and her squeals. I remembered being in Sydney, in the hotel with Jack. Our first time. Not that we made noises like that, I'm sure. When we'd finally made it to the bed, we'd been a bit shy with each other, even though there'd been about six months of foreplay. That night, Jack had saved me from my kidnapper, put me in a bath, brought me Krug champagne and a snow globe, then made love to me all night long. I remembered his face as he lay on me, moving slowly, kissing me deliciously, and the way he looked into my eyes . . .

He'd told me then that he couldn't get involved. Specifically with *me*. Because he already cared about me too much, he'd said, and he couldn't imagine if something even more terrible had happened because (he didn't say this) he lost his wife and parents and (he also didn't say this) he'd never dealt with the pain of that loss. But it all sounded like excuses anyway. *It's not you, it's me.* Damn straight. He didn't say that either, but I didn't give him reason to. In fact, I'd told him that I wasn't interested in getting involved – what a nightmare being Jack Jones's girlfriend! That's kind of what I'd said, even though I didn't mean it. And now we've been together again and he's made it pretty obvious he hasn't changed his mind, but it'd be nice to think that some time in the future, maybe we could make a go of it – a relationship. If I found him alive.

And then I was crying at the ceiling. Tears filled my ears and I didn't do anything about it. My attention-seeking inner victim was shoving the miser aside. It said, 'Why me? Why do I deserve a boyfriend who goes M.I.A.?' Joining the conversation I was already having with myself, a small voice somewhere in the room reminded me that a couple of shags does not a boyfriend make, not by a long stretch, and no one said I *had* to come to Saint Sebastian. I probably needed to remember all that. But Jack's still my friend, and I do love him. You never know, I thought, I might be able to do something to help. What should I do now? I tried to meditate to see if answers would come from the universe.

Go to the bar, it said.

'But I've got a hangover.'

It's after five. Happy hour.

'But I need to find Jack.'

Go to the bar and ask around, you idiot!

'Oh, alright.' I got off the bed. I was in and out of that bathroom in a shot because there was a vague smell of sewerage in there. And the bathroom had a mirror, which I didn't want to accidentally look at. And, I really needed a drink.

At the entrance to the bar I gazed around. The receptionist had told me with a giggle that it was called the Bum Crack Bar and it wasn't hard to understand why. I considered going some place else, but it was hot and I was stuffed and I had sticky-out hair, and I quite liked the idea of not having to walk too far to get home. I made a mental note to eat something.

The Aussie scene before me reminded me very much of El Cheapo Backpackers with several men and their bum cracks lined up on the stools at the bar, drinking cans of VB. A few others were shooting pool on a small, tatty table. There were rows of Victoria Bitter flags hanging across the ceiling – decoration rather than advertising, I imagined – and a solitary, filthy fan that took about a minute to complete one rotation. My feet stuck to the floor as I made my way into the room. I wondered how they'd respond if I announced I was looking for a couple of Australian soldiers who'd possibly been captured by some enemy. Or who were lying in a hole. Or dead. As I headed for the bar, a man I knew emerged from the men's bathroom. It was Dwayne from the plane, and when he saw me, a big smile lit up his face. Not that his face needed lighting up.

'Hi, Dwayne,' I said, feeling relieved.

'Well, well, if it ain't the Tupperware gal.'

I giggled. 'I think you've mistaken me for my mother.' Horrors! 'Are you staying here?'

'Here? Hell, no. Who'd stay in this dump?' He glanced over his shoulder. 'Just doin' some business.'

I lowered my voice. 'Right. Business.' I gave him a wink. Black-market stuff. Yeah.

He said, 'We should have a drink some time. I'm here a couple days.'

'That'd be really nice.' But what was I saying? I'm not here to flirt and have drinks with strange men.

'Where's your friend?' he said, looking around.

'What friend?'

He paused, giving me a pretty intense look. 'You said you were meeting a friend here for some *sightseeing*.' He wiggled his fingers in the air, making quote marks.

'Oh. Right!' Whoops. I laughed too much. 'She's, ah, been held up. Arrives tomorrow.'

Dwayne nodded, looked over his shoulder at the people sitting at the bar. 'You sure your friend's not already here?'

'What?' I checked out the people at the bar. Unlikely looking candidates. 'No, not yet.'

I forced a smile and he grinned, said, 'Wish you'd gone straight to Bali?'

I stretched my smile wider. 'Next stop.'

'Well, see ya 'round.' He gave me a lingering look as he walked away.

I sat on a stool next to one of the bum cracks and asked for a glass of wine, which was poured from a cask and which tasted like salad dressing. I pushed it aside and ordered a VB. A glance in the fridge told me there wasn't much point asking for any other kind of beer. The barman handed me a menu. It was typed on a piece of paper that had passed through many sweaty hands. I put it on the bar to avoid touching it. I ordered the fish, which was just called 'fresh local catch'. I asked if the fish was grilled or fried but the barman walked away without answering.

The man next to me made a groaning sound. I swigged on my stubby and discreetly checked him out. He had a basketball beer belly and skinny brown arms and legs sticking out of his clothes. The kind of leathery tan that gets layered on over many years in the sun until there's no chance it could ever fade or do anything but turn to cancer. Or maybe the sun just keeps burning the cancer off. He had deep lines on his face plus a bushy grey beard; looked about 60, might have been 40, and seemed harmless enough for a chat.

'Hello,' I said, smiling but hopefully not in a flirty way.

The man's right eye moved and regarded me for a moment.

'G'day,' he mumbled.

'You're Australian? I'm Erica.'

'Phil's the name. Phil Collins.'

'Ah, like the singer,' I said, but his expression – what I could see of it – was blank. And there was no more conversation forthcoming. Phil Collins stared at the fridge, his arm lifting and lowering at a steady rate.

I said, 'Do you live here in Seni?'

'Yip.'

'And you work here?' Phil Collins was wearing navy-blue shorts and shirt with a lot of black muck on them. He didn't look like a tourist.

'Yip. On the barge.' He pointed over his shoulder, and I looked, expecting to see a barge tied up outside, but there wasn't one.

'Are you the driver?' That might be the wrong word, I thought. What's the driver of a boat called? Skipper?

'Mechanic.'

'Ah.' I checked his fingernails. 'And what do you do when you're not on the barge and when you're not here in the bar?'

He hesitated and his right eye inspected me for a long moment, like he thought I might be making a joke but he wasn't sure why it was funny. 'Gardnin',' he mumbled. 'Love me gardnin'.'

'I love the gardens here,' I said. 'I love frangipanis.'

'Yeah.'

There was a very long time where nothing was said, and I thought that was the end of the gardening conversation, but then Phil said, 'Can't get no gardnin' books 'ere.'

'Why don't you order online?'

The right eye moved.

'You know,' I said, 'on your computer?'

The eye looked away. 'Get stuff from Darwin. On the barge.'

'Maybe you could get a gardening book from Darwin?'

'Nah,' said Phil and sucked hard on his beer. And stared at the fridge. And that, it seemed, was the end of the gardening conversation. A fresh stubby appeared, money was taken from the pile of coins in front of him, and Phil swapped the used stubby for the new without so much as a pause.

My meal arrived and I stared at it. 'This is fish fingers,' I said. 'Birds Eye fish fingers.' Maybe they'd run out of the 'fresh local catch'. I picked up a soggy chip and ate it. The barman hadn't given me cutlery. I waited but he was busy drinking at the other end of the bar. I snapped a fish finger in half. It was still frozen in the centre. I finished the soggy chips but left the 'fish', pushing the plate away.

Over my shoulder I watched my neighbours, the sex couple (I

recognised her legs), walk in and look around. The guy said, 'Fuck this for a joke. Let's go to Bali.' And they left. I wanted to go to Bali, too.

I fanned my face, feeling like I was in a sauna with sweat running down from my armpits and pooling in my belly button. I had two big wet circles under my boobs. I sat straighter; the sweat trickled out of my belly button and into my undies.

I said, 'I don't think the air conditioning's working.'

'Nah,' said Phil. 'It's rooted.'

'Oh?'

'Shit itself.'

'Right.'

'Fridge works.'

Yep. The fridge works. I took a swig of my beer. Actually, I was feeling much better after a couple of mouthfuls. Good old hair of the dog.

THREE HOURS later I was in a much better state than I'd been after three hours with Yvonne. And now Phil also knew all about Jack, even though I remembered too late it was a secret mission and I probably shouldn't tell anyone else. But how was I supposed to find Jack if I didn't ask?

I hadn't told Phil about my mother. Yet. He hadn't moved at all the whole time, apart from his drinking arm and his eye that swivelled occasionally in my direction. He didn't say anything. I started to wonder if he was a puppet, propped at the bar for whatever purpose. Had he eaten? Had he been to the toilet? I didn't think so. Maybe he'd nicked to the dunny while I was in the ladies'. Maybe he just sweated it all out. He didn't seem affected by the amount of booze he'd slugged down. Men came and went. There were quiet murmurings between Phil Collins and these men. Money was exchanged. For what?

'Phil,' I said, 'I saw some kids on the way here. The taxi driver said they were gangs but they were just kids.' Kids that looked angry, but not very competent. In fact, they didn't even look that angry. More ... deliberately trying to look mean in an overacting kind of way.

'Lotsa gangs 'ere. Real mean uns with money 'n power 'n guns. Kids practisin' for when they're older.'

'Really?'

Phil's arm slowly and precisely lifted his stubby; the neck of it vanished into his beard for a second, and the arm lowered again. He glanced over his shoulder.

'Yip.'

In the morning I didn't feel too bad, but nobody had warned me about the B-52-size mozzies that snuck into my room while I slept. I looked like I was growing cherry tomatoes under my skin. I swallowed another malaria tablet and reminded myself to get Aeroguard. Imagine if I got malaria! Jack would arrive home, come to visit me and be told I'd died from malaria in Saint Sebastian. On the funeral notice Mum would have used a photo of me when I was about ten with my hair in pigtails and gappy teeth. Jack would be really confused, not understanding why Mum was asking him about Bali and his trip to Europe and wondering what the hell Erica was doing in Saint Sebastian.

Anyway, in my overnight dreams I'd been in a gorgeous five-star hotel, swanning around an elegant bar with men who looked like Jack, my hair looking fabulous. I decided this was definitely a sign. I needed to wash my hair and restyle it, clearly. So, I did, making another mental note about buying styling product to replace the one that got stolen. I really didn't know what I was doing with my hair, but I tried just mussing it up and leaving it to dry, which took all of five minutes, and *voila*! It looked like Kath's from *Kath & Kim*. A 1980s perm. The kind my mother used to have. I wet it again and used sunscreen to straighten it, tugging it around my face, dragging my fingers through it to pull the curls out. It kind of worked but I needed my hairdryer. And hair wax would be better than sunscreen, I thought, although sunscreen's probably cheaper.

I paced around the room, thinking, scratching at the mozzie bites. In my head I made a list of things I could do. First, I needed a supermarket for Aeroguard and, seeing I brought bullets instead, tampons in case I was still here in a week. And that was it. My list. I couldn't think of anything else. I felt depressed.

I checked my phone. A dozen texts from Lucy. I hadn't messaged her since before I left Darwin.

Her last one read: *WHERE THE FUCK R U????????*

SS. All good. There's a nice beach!

I emailed my boss, saying my doctor had recommended stress leave. (I wondered if Kate would write me a note.) I apologised to Rosalind and said I'd be back in touch in a couple of days and that I'd work overtime when I returned. Poor Marcus; she'd probably call him back from annual leave. At least today was Friday, which meant I didn't have to feel guilty for the next two days.

I needed to call my mother. I sat on the bed instead. Now what? My room was so stuffy. I needed fresh air. Fresh air to clear the head. I thought about the nice beach, and left the hotel wearing my baseball cap, handbag on my back, and I crossed the road to the sand, looking around for crocodiles. I had no idea where they lurked, but I reckoned any water in a tropical place was fair game. Freshwater crocs were pretty harmless, apparently, only interested in fish (not that I trusted whoever said that). It was the salties that were the really scary ones. They had monster jaws full of teeth that grew in all different directions, making it easy for them to crunch bones. I saw that on Steve Irwin's show.

The beach had palm trees growing out of the sand, leaning at impossible angles toward the sea. I imagined cyclones must come through here sometimes, try to flatten the trees. I sat under a reasonably straight one, my back against the trunk, and gazed out at the water. My headspace was divided equally between wanting to hunt for Jack and finding a pool to swim in. I closed my eyes, hoping for an epiphany, but instead my phone rang. I searched my bag in a hurry, thinking it could be Joe. But it was Mum, wanting to Facetime. I hesitated, knowing I couldn't put her off forever. I answered with a big smile, holding the phone close so she couldn't see the grotty buildings across the road. Or my hair. I stood and turned my back to the ocean, so she could see that instead.

'Erica! I thought you might have called by now. Aren't you worried about your pussy?'

'Is Axle okay?'

'Well, he had diarrhoea —'

'Is he alright?'

'Yes, he's fine now. Your father gave him some beetroot.'

'He ate beetroot?'

'Yes, dear. Don't you want to know how your mother is?'

'How are you?'

'I'm fine. We went to Chadstone today to buy some underpants for your father. Myer is having a sale. It wasn't the big stocktaking sale, you know, just a small one in the men's department, and I think the homewares department has some items reduced —'

'This is an overseas call, Mum.'

'You haven't asked about your father!'

'What's wrong with Dad?'

'Nothing. He's fine. Why are you holding the phone so close?'

'Um. There's a really strong wind. I can't hear you.'

The problem with Facetime was that I couldn't pull faces, roll my eyes or do big silent sighs. I held my stiff little smile while I waited for the obvious demand.

'Where is Jack? I want to talk to him.'

'He's, ah, not here yet. His flight was delayed.'

'Where is he flying from?'

Where did I say again? 'Um. Rome?'

'Maybe he met the Pope.'

'Maybe.'

I managed to end the call by pretending the line was breaking up. I did that by jiggling the phone up and down.

I sighed, took another look at the ocean.

'This isn't finding Jack,' I said.

I headed back across the sand. A few people dashed past me and, as I looked around, I saw that the streets had pretty much cleared. I stood in the shade of a tree by the road and waited for a handful of cars to pass. One pulled up in front of me, and a black Hummer stopped right behind that car with no room for me to walk between. I was frozen momentarily, trying to decide whether to walk around the front of the first car or behind the Hummer, when two men got out of the cars. One from each. They strode towards each other, meeting on the road right in front of me. They shouted, waving hands, and then the Hummer man took a gun from inside his jacket and aimed it at the other man's head. There was part of me that thought, hoped, the men might not notice me standing there, just a few metres away. The front man held up his hands and stammered as he spoke. Shitting himself, like me. The Hummer man said something, returned the gun to his jacket, and turned back to his car. But not before giving me a long, curious stare. And there was not a part of my body that was functioning. I felt like everything had stopped – my heart, my breathing, my blood – and as soon as both men drove away, everything started again with a rush. My breath returned in a loud gasp and my blood was a torrent in my head. Shaking, I made my way as fast as possible back to my hotel room, wondering again who the hell I thought I was coming to a place like this, a place where people threatened to blow other people's heads off in the street.

CHAPTER 19

I was resigned. I would go home. It was outrageous, thinking I could do something to help. If Jack was dead, then my visit was pointless anyway. If he was a prisoner somewhere, then I'd just have to make a fuss back home until someone did something about it. Who would do something? No one. Jack would die, I knew it now, and I'd just have to live with it. I wasn't some tough special ops person. I wasn't James Bond or Lara Croft. I hadn't even been a girl scout!

I sat on the bed and cried into my hands, then I called the airport. There was a flight leaving for Darwin that afternoon, so I booked a ticket. I went downstairs with my stuff, checked out and asked them to call me a taxi. Then I stood on the pavement with my bag, staring trance-like at nothing.

Bruce Willis pulled up in front of me.

'Hello, lady!' he shouted through the window. He jumped out and held the door open.

I climbed in, saying, 'You still owe me money, Bruce Willis.'

'Free ride today.' He got into the car and drove.

I told him to take me to the airport and he seemed disappointed that I was leaving already.

'No stay longer?' He made a sad face in the rear-view mirror.

I stared out the window, biting my nails, as the horrible world rolled slowly by. I hunted in my bag for my nail scissors, but remembered they'd been taken off me at Melbourne airport. In case I stabbed the flight attendant for being a bitch, maybe.

A piece of paper floated out of my bag and onto the seat beside me. It was the note from Yvonne with her hand-drawn map of Darwin and something else I'd forgotten about. Her Seni friend's contact details. *Kitty*, it said. What had Yvonne told me? That they'd been flatmates? And that Kitty knew everyone. *Absolutely everyone*. That's right. I stared at the note for a long time, and said to Bruce Willis, 'Change of plan.'

I gave him Kitty's address and he made a fast U-turn, zooming back to where we came from so fast I was thrown back in the seat. He stopped the car right in the heart of Seni, it seemed, about 500 metres from my hotel.

Bruce held out his hand.

'You said this was a free ride!'

'Free ride airport. Here not airport.' He looked around in amazement to make his point. How could I have not noticed?

I sat there, my mouth opening and closing like a fish. 'For God's sake,' I muttered as I handed him ten dollars.

KITTY'S FLAT was above a shop with black velvet drapes covering the windows and pink writing on the door in a language I couldn't read. There was a wooden staircase running up the side of the building and I climbed it, knocking on the door over and over until I gave up and conceded that no one was home. I went back downstairs and stood in front of the shop door. What the hell, I thought, and opened it, slowly, peering in, waiting for my eyes to adjust to the darkness before I stepped inside. The shop was lit only by a couple of very dim lamps and the green glow from various sex toys. An exotic-looking black-haired woman sat behind the counter, smiling at me.

'Hello! What can I help you with today?' She jumped up and stood before me. 'We have the most exciting new products for women who are all alone at night.'

'Um. Actually, I was just wondering —'

'What about this Jumping Jack Flash? It arrived just yesterday.' She held up a green, round thing that bounced on her hand.

'Ah …' I kept watching it. It was fascinating. I shook my head. 'Do you know Kitty?' I pointed at the ceiling, indicating the flat above.

'Oh, yes, of course! Because it is me.' Her peals of laughter sounded like bells, and that made me smile.

'Oh. Hi,' I said. 'Yvonne gave me your number and —'

'Yvonne! My dear friend. How is she? You must tell me everything. Come.' She took my backpack and left it behind the counter, and retrieved her handbag. 'Come,' she said again. 'We will go to a very nice cafe and have coffee.'

I looked at my watch, considering my flight to Darwin, thinking I probably shouldn't be too long. I sighed, sent a small prayer heavenward and let Kitty push me out into the street. She locked up the shop, linked her arm through mine and marched me forward.

'What is your name?' she said.

I told her.

She said, 'Well, Erica Jewell, you must tell me all about yourself. You are Australian, yes?'

'Yes.'

'And how is Yvonne?'

'She's, um, great.' Not that I remembered much. 'She's got a nice house.'

'I love Australia, especially the snakes.'

'Snakes?' I said.

'Yes, I love snakes.'

'Have you heard of Steve Irwin?'

'Oh, yes, I was so sad when he died. I used to watch his television program all the time. Crocodiles are very nice, too.'

'They are?'

'Oh, yes.'

We arrived at the cafe and took a table inside, where it was air-conditioned, and sat by the window overlooking the main street. Kitty sat opposite me, a bright smile on her gorgeous face. She had almond eyes and flawless skin, and her straight, glossy black hair framed a delicate, almost-pointy jaw. She told me that her mother is a Filipina who lives in Manila, and her father is French and lives in Paris, and laughingly told me that Christmas is a nightmare. That she's been living in Saint Sebastian for five years – which is where she met Yvonne – and she waved her hands theatrically, describing the habits of the typical Senian with delight and much laughter. She was the happiest person I'd ever met.

'My clients,' she said, 'they are all so different, but in a way they are all so typical.'

'Clients?' I said, sipping my coffee.

'I am – what is it you Australians say? A hooker.'

I sprayed coffee across the table. Most of it landed on Kitty.

'Omigod, I'm so sorry!' I snatched up a handful of napkins, pressing them into her chest.

But she was laughing. 'That was very funny.' She laughed some more. So, if Yvonne lived with Kitty in Seni, does that mean Yvonne was working as a hooker, too? Probably.

Kitty continued, 'I want to save as much money as possible,' she said, 'so when I meet a handsome, strong, brave man we will be able to go and live in the jungle together. Like Tarzan and Jane.'

'Really? You want to live in the jungle?'

'Oh, yes. It would be very exciting. There are many snakes there.'

I smiled at the strange, funny woman. I said, 'My . . . boyfriend's strong and brave. And handsome,' and, what the hell, 'rich, too.'

'He is? You are a very lucky girl, Erica Jewell!'

She then told me I reminded her of Yvonne. 'Actually,' she said, 'you look like that actress, what is her name?'

'Halle Berry?' I said, hopefully.

'No, no. I am thinking of the one who was in the James Bond movie with Pierce Brosnan.'

'Yes, that's Halle Berry.'

'No, the English woman . . . I remember! It is Judi Dench I am thinking of. A marvellous actress.' Kitty looked at me, her head cocked. 'It is the hair, you know? You do not look as old as Judi Dench.'

'Great. Thanks,' I mumbled. It's not that I don't admire Judi Dench. She's wonderful and I'd be thrilled to look like her in about 40 years.

Kitty wanted to know more about my 'boyfriend', and I told her. Not the romantic stuff I'd told Yvonne and Phil – I got straight to the point. I said that I thought he'd been sent to Saint Sebastian on some military thing and that maybe he'd been taken prisoner. Kitty nodded, watching me, listening intently to my story with a serious expression.

She sipped her coffee and looked past me as though pondering something. She said, 'This is the rich one?'

'Jack? Yes. Do you know something?'

She picked at some fluff on her top. 'Oh, no. But I can ask around, if you want.'

'I'd appreciate it, Kitty.'

Our breakfast arrived. Kitty got stuck into hers and I nibbled at mine.

'He's probably dead,' she said with a full mouth and I dropped my fork.

'What?'

'There are some very bad people in this place. Dangerous people.'

'Jack knows what he's doing,' I said, irritated. 'He's handled dangerous people before.' *He's not dead. He's not.*

She shrugged and gazed out the window and my attention was drawn to a dark shadow swimming across the wall behind her. I followed her gaze and watched a black Hummer cruise by, my heart racing at the sight of it. When I looked back at Kitty, she was smiling.

I said, 'I saw the man in that car before. He threatened someone with a gun.'

She grinned. 'You see how entertaining it is to live in Sebastian?' She leaned towards me, still watching out the window. 'The man in that car, his name is Samson. He is a gang leader. A very powerful one. He is wealthy, and most people in Seni listen to him, including the politicians, because if they don't, well, they must have a death wish.'

The car had moved on, but its energy lingered. I shivered and watched the street.

Kitty informed me, 'He spends a lot of time driving these streets, making sure people remember that he is around. I know him.'

'You do?' My head snapped back and I stared at her.

'Yes. I have slept with him many times. He does not pay me, not directly. He pays my rent and makes sure my friends are safe. I have not seen him for some time. I think his wife must be suspicious,' she said with a wink. 'She is the only thing he is afraid of.'

I whispered, 'He's married?'

Kitty gave me a slightly pitiful look, said, 'He is married but he has many mistresses. Like so many men in this country.' She checked her watch. 'Whoops! Must go. I have a client.'

'I need to get my backpack from your shop.'

'But now I am going to my client's house. You will call in later, yes?' she said as she walked out of the cafe.

'I've got a flight to catch!' I called after her but she was already striding down the street, waving and leaving me with the bill.

OK, so, I wouldn't be flying home today after all, and for some reason, I didn't mind too much.

CHAPTER 20

I stood on the street.

He's probably dead. Just like that. I wondered how many wives and mothers of men who went to war have been told this news. Your man is missing in action, presumed dead. Killed in action. Dead. Probably dead. Obviously. I shook my head.

No. No! He's alive. I *know* he is. I'd feel it if he wasn't. What would Kitty know, anyway? I nodded once. 'Good.' Now I had things to do. I pushed away all thoughts of dead Jack, focusing instead on his very alive, beautiful self, knowing (hoping) the Law of Attraction would hear me.

I looked up and down for the black Hummer. Instead, there was a yellow Toyota that screeched to a halt in front of me. Not wanting to be the innocent victim of a drive-by shooting and have my mother find out I wasn't really in Bali, I got in.

'Airport, lady?'

'Not yet.' I asked Bruce Willis which was the best hotel in Seni.

'The Koala Bear Hotel!' he said with a big grin in the mirror.

'No, I mean the hotel where a very important person would stay.'

He stared at me wide-eyed, worried perhaps that I'd discovered he hadn't in fact taken me to a nice hotel.

'It's okay,' I said. 'I love the Koala Bear Hotel, but I need to go to the best hotel to meet someone.'

'Hotel Sebastian, lady?'

'Then let's go.'

I'd decided to see if Jack had stayed in any of the hotels in town. And I knew that the best hotel was the right place for me to search for him. Why the best? Because he wouldn't stay anywhere else, of course. I thought if I went there, I might learn something. That is, if I didn't actually find them there, Jack and Joe, lying by the pool, reading books, drinking cocktails. I'd be happy for exactly one second before I killed them both.

The Hotel Sebastian was no Grand Hyatt, but it was certainly a step up from the Koala Bear. Several steps up. I felt the relief of its cool interior, thinking it had a lovely tropical charm and I could imagine Jack staying there. The quiet, spacious lobby had polished timber floors, high ceilings and giant fans circulating the air. I had a quick fantasy about arriving there with Jack in a chauffeured car, being fussed over as we checked into our room. I thought maybe I could stay here tonight.

I stood at the reception desk and smiled at the young man in his neat uniform.

'Good morning, madam,' he said in very clear English.

'Good morning, do you have availability tonight?' I asked, grandly. 'Oh, and what is your room rate?'

He tapped his computer. 'Yes, madam, we do. Three hundred American dollars per night.'

'Oh.' Maybe the Koala Bear wasn't so bad at 80 bucks. 'Er, I'll think about it.'

He nodded, smiled.

'I'm actually looking for someone who may have stayed here recently,' I said.

'Yes, madam?'

'His name was ... *is* Jack Jones.'

Without checking his computer, the receptionist said, very

politely, 'I am sorry, madam, but I cannot give out information about a guest.'

'Oh. Well, I don't actually know if he was a guest. I just wanted to check.'

He smiled again and looked sympathetic. 'I am sorry.'

I stared at the man, having no idea what to do now. So I cried. Tears sprouted out of my eyes and the man looked horrified, glancing around.

I took quick advantage and, while fumbling for a tissue, said, 'I'm sorry, but . . . but we were supposed to be coming on our honeymoon here and I thought . . . ' I added a sob.

The receptionist looked around again and then turned to his computer. He said in a low voice, 'Can you say the name again, madam?'

'Jack Jones.' I spelled it. 'From Australia. Thank you so much,' I whispered.

After a minute he said, 'I can see here that we have never had a Mr Jack Jones from Australia staying in this hotel.'

'Okay. Well, thank you.' He probably used a different name anyway.

Just then, two men walked out of the hotel lift. They nodded at each other and one headed for the reception desk where I was standing – it was Dwayne from the plane – and the other sauntered across the lobby toward the exit. The second man was so familiar, I gasped loud enough for him to turn his head and look at me. He looked like Hugh Grant. He gave me a sly smile and continued on his way. The porter held the door for him and said, 'Good morning, Mr Berringer.'

Dwayne approached me, his eyes narrowed. He glanced back at the other man, said to me, 'You know him?'

'That man?' I watched him walk through the door and muttered, 'Berringer . . . '

'That's right. Rupert Berringer.'

'Berringer,' I said again. Why did I think I knew him? Because he looked like a famous actor?

Dwayne said, 'How do you know him?'

'What? Him? I don't.'

He gazed at me, suspicious. 'Well, can't stop and chat,' he said. 'Let's have a drink later.'

'Oh, sure,' I said, and turned back to watch Mr Berringer, who, I could see through the window, was waiting out the front, checking his watch. Dwayne dropped his key at reception, squeezed my arm, told me he'd be in touch, and left the building.

I walked slowly to the exit as Mr Rupert Berringer got into a hotel limousine. Berringer. Berringer. Who had the name Berringer? I was suddenly and so surprisingly transported back in time that I stopped dead in my tracks. I could hear JD's voice, soft but crystal-clear, drifting through the open library doors on the night of his cocktail party: *Berringer's recruiting more men every day . . .*

I bolted for the exit, looked frantically around. I waved at the porter.

Without leaving his post, he said, 'Yes, madam?'

'I need a taxi, urgently!'

'You will ask inside.'

'Never mind.' I rushed down the palm-lined road away from the hotel and was very happy to see my new friend still there in the taxi zone, leaning on the crumpled bonnet of his car, smoking and smiling.

'Hello, pretty lady. You need taxi?'

I leapt into his car. 'Come on!'

'Yes, lady!'

He threw his cigarette on the ground and hurried into the driver's seat, zooming away before his door had closed, flinging me back into my seat.

'Where, lady?'

'I'm not sure yet.' I sat forward and scanned the road ahead, then I scowled at Bruce Willis in the mirror. 'I'm not happy with you.'

He pouted. 'Sorry, lady. Free ride today.'

'You said that before.'

'Free ride now. Koala Bear Hotel?'

'No. Not yet.'

Ahead of us, Rupert Berringer's limousine appeared.

I slapped Bruce on the shoulder and said, 'Follow that car!'

His eyes lit up. 'Yes, lady,' and he zoomed up close to the limo, sitting about a metre from its rear bumper.

'Don't go right up his bum; he'll know you're there. Don't you know anything about tailing a car?' Like I had so much experience myself.

'Sorry, lady.' He slowed, and we assumed a reasonable distance. The limousine took its time, rolling down the main street of Seni, past Kitty's place, past my hotel and away from town.

So, did I have a plan? When the limousine stopped, would I leap from the taxi, point at Mr Rupert Berringer and shout, 'You stole my man!'? And would he say, 'Oh, yes, I'm really sorry. I'll go get him.' I sighed, feeling despondent again. But at least I was doing something. Something more than just wallowing in a stinky hotel room or turning into an alcoholic at the Bum Crack Bar.

After about 15 minutes, the limo turned off the main road and headed towards the sea. A sign in English and another language said that the Port of Seni was down there, and that only authorised people were allowed. Bruce went to follow the limo and I said, 'Don't go down there, for God's sake.'

'Yes, lady.' He pulled up and waited for instructions.

The limo didn't stop at the security booth but continued on, disappearing into the parking lot. I said to Bruce, 'Okay, you can go down there.'

He peered at me in the rear-view mirror and pointed. 'Down there, lady?'

'Yes. It's okay.' Probably not okay. How would I know?

Bruce Willis drove slowly along the forbidden road and stopped at the security gate. I was trying to work out what to say to the guards. I thought I'd put on an American accent and pretend to be looking for my P&O ship. But there were no security people, and the boom gate was up.

Bruce said, 'Go, lady?'

'Yes, alright. Let's have a look. And, hey, you'd better not be charging me for this.'

Bruce drove through the parking lot. I saw the limo parked near a pile of shipping containers. And a black Hummer. While I watched, a crane lifted a container off a barge and placed it carefully with the others. Samson was standing there, next to the Hummer. Rupert Berringer was talking to someone and pointing at the containers. I knew that someone. It was Phil Collins. Why was sweet, harmless Phil Collins talking to Rupert Berringer and Samson the gang man? Maybe he was the wrong Berringer. He didn't look like a bad man, after all. He looked like a movie star.

Berringer looked around – directly at us. With a yelp I ducked and Bruce Willis panicked, planting his foot and screeching through the car park, sending gravel and stones flying. I rolled around on the back seat. Everyone in the vicinity was no doubt looking at us. As soon as we were safely through the security gate I sat up and shouted, 'Are you crazy?'

'No, lady!'

'For God's sake. How embarrassing.'

Back on the main road, Bruce stopped the taxi and turned in his seat.

'Where now, lady?'

Where, indeed. I stared out the window at the busy Port of Seni, wondering about Rupert Berringer and Phil Collins, and wondering if Jack was down there. There was no way I could go home, not now that I was on a trail of some kind. No. I wouldn't leave Saint Sebastian without Jack Jones. Alive or dead.

CHAPTER 21

I called the airport and changed my ticket to an open-dated one.

As Bruce Willis drove I braced for an argument about payment. But when he pulled up in front of Kitty's he didn't say anything, just looked at me over his shoulder with big puppy-dog eyes and a down-turned mouth. Maybe he'd watched my performance at the Hotel Sebastian.

'Let me guess,' I said. 'Your wife needs a kidney transplant.'

I could see that he was considering future possibilities armed with this new information. I handed him a 20 dollar note, but only because we'd driven much further than I'd planned.

When I walked into her shop, Kitty was in the middle of a sales pitch. She had several squirming, bouncing, vibrating things lined up on the counter and the young sex couple from the Koala Bear were inspecting them. So they hadn't left for Bali yet; that was somehow comforting.

Kitty squealed my name and gave me a hug before retrieving my backpack from behind the counter.

'Kitty.' I took her arm and pulled her away from the sex couple so we could talk privately. 'Jack's not dead. I know it.'

She looked a bit taken aback by that. 'How do you know?'

'I . . . I *feel* it.'

She waved her hand. 'I think you have had a big shock, Erica Jewell. You should just go home.'

The girl customer giggled.

Kitty called out, 'I will be just one moment more.'

I shook my head, whispered, 'Have you heard of Rupert Berringer?'

Kitty went still and stared at me. 'Why are you asking about him?'

'So you know him?'

'I . . . um . . . have heard of him.'

The backpacker guy said, 'Have you got this but bigger, like mine?' and waved a giant latex penis in his girlfriend's face. He laughed; she punched his arm.

I said, 'Kitty, you know that man, Samson. I saw him talking to Rupert Berringer today. Can you ask him about Jack? He might know something.'

She stared at me a few seconds more, stony faced. 'Of course! Especially for you, Erica Jewell. Now, back to my customers.' She rushed back to the giggling couple. As I turned to leave, Kitty called after me, 'If you want, there is a party tomorrow.'

'A party?'

'You should come along.'

Whatever. I gave her a wave and left.

I told Bruce to take me back to the Koala Bear.

The receptionists greeted me with no enthusiasm or recognition. They handed me the key to the same room and charged me ten dollars more per night.

I dumped my bag and went straight back downstairs to where Bruce Willis was waiting. I sat in his cab, scratched a mozzie bite, and asked him how much he was planning on charging me.

'No charge,' he said, looking offended.

'Is there a supermarket?'

'Yes, lady.'

· · ·

THE SUPERMARKET WAS CROWDED. I scanned the aisles. Everything was white. There were boxes and bottles and various containers of things, but it was all white with writing I couldn't read – Spanish? I spoke to a girl standing next to me.

'Could you tell me where the insect repellent is?'

She looked at me, shook her head and moved quickly away, like I had a contagious disease.

There was a staff member stacking shelves. 'Excuse me, can you tell me where the tampons are?' I said and she gave me a blank look. 'Do you speak English?' No expression. How to sign 'tampons'?

A woman's voice behind me whispered, 'The next aisle.'

I turned. She was smiling and pointing.

I said, 'Thank you.'

'You're welcome.'

The queue for the checkout was long. I'd found the tampons and insect repellents, but there was no recognisable brand. Still, anything that kept those little bastards away was fine by me.

I jiggled, impatient. Why were there so many people? The checkout girl was examining each item, looking for the barcode before aligning it precisely with the scanner. Didn't she know you just wave the thing around and the scanner finds it? Why was the queue so long, anyway? 'What's the deal with this place?' I muttered.

From behind me the helpful woman from before said, 'It's the economy, my dear. Things have picked up, so everyone can afford to shop here now.'

I was embarrassed. 'Sorry.' I glanced at my watch.

She smiled and nodded.

'You speak very good English,' I said, hoping to make up for my rudeness.

'Thank you,' she said, smiling. She was a well-fed lady, by the look of it. About 50.

'What language is spoken here?'

'Portuguese, mostly, but I like to practise my English.'

'Where did you learn it?'

'I spent quite some time in Puckapunyal, and other places.

I was surprised. 'My Puckapunyal? I mean, in Australia?'

'Yes, I was evacuated there during the invasion in the seventies. You know. I quite like Australians,' she said. 'Where are you from?'

'Melbourne,' I told her.

'Ah, Melbourne is very nice. And what are you doing in Seni?'

'Um, it's kind of a long story.' I glanced ahead to the front of the queue, which hadn't moved. I wondered how much Bruce Willis would charge me.

'You're in a hurry with your snail bait, I see,' said the woman.

I looked at the 'tampon' packet in my hand. 'Bloody hell,' I groaned.

She said in a low voice, 'The goods here are mostly from Indonesia and sometimes it's impossible to work out what is what. And,' she added in a whisper, leaning in, 'things are often mis-shelved.' She gave me a wink and pointed to aisle number three. 'On the left, just down a bit.'

When I got back to the queue, the woman was second from the front and waving to me. She beckoned and made room for me ahead of her.

'Thank you,' I said, beaming at my new friend. I held up the packet, questioning, and she nodded. As I paid the cashier I said to the woman, 'It was nice meeting you and thank you again, so much.'

'I do hope we meet again.'

I waved and left the supermarket, and as soon as I stepped outside, I drowned myself in the insect repellent. It stunk, but I didn't care.

BRUCE WILLIS DROVE me back to my hotel and I gave him money because it was too hard to argue. I took about ten minutes to climb the stairs. I had no energy. And I knew, once I was in my room, that I wouldn't know what to do next. I couldn't just spend all my time at the Bum Crack Bar, waiting for something to happen, could I?

I pushed open the door to my room and froze. Wrong room? I stepped back, checked the number on the door, checked the number on my key. This was my room, but someone else had been in there, ransacking it. All my stuff was strewn around. The pillows had been stripped of their cases, the mattress had been thrown onto the floor. My heart started thumping. What if someone was still in there? I listened, stepped hesitantly forward, my hands shaking. Pushed open the bathroom door. No one there, but stuff chucked around. I opened the wardrobes, rushing back to the door in case there was someone inside.

All clear.

Who'd been in my room? What did they want?

Trembling, I started putting everything back in order. I thought maybe I should leave it and call the police, but I knew that, if I did, I'd be facing a whole load of questions that I really didn't want to answer.

CHAPTER 22

Bruce drove slowly, around and around, as I stared out the window, not really seeing anything. I was oscillating between the need to stay and do something, and the knowledge that I was completely unqualified to do what was needed – whatever that might be. But if Jack was dead, there'd be no reason for someone to trash my room. Would there?

I felt suddenly angry. Angry with this bloody hole of a country where people can just walk around with guns and trash people's hotel rooms. And the anger was good, because it made me feel brave. I told Bruce to take me to Kitty's.

Kitty's 'back in five minutes' sign in English and presumably Portuguese was on the door of the shop, and she wasn't answering her phone or her door upstairs, so I squatted with my back to the wall and waited. I pulled my cap down low over my face.

Who had searched my room and why? Who had I met since arriving in Seni? Bruce Willis, Phil Collins, staff at the Koala Bear Hotel, Kitty, the woman at the supermarket, the reception guy at the Hotel Sebastian. And there was Dwayne from the plane. Whoever I'd told about Jack knew I knew nothing. Maybe it was just a coincidence? Maybe they had trashed the wrong room? Maybe I'd go back later and find out that someone else's room had also been trashed – the right room. Maybe I'd find out that everyone's room gets trashed sooner or later; that's just what happens in Saint Sebastian. I didn't want to go back there.

Kitty finally turned up, skipping along the street, whistling, singing, laughing. 'Hello, Erica Jewell!' She waved madly and broke into a run, giving me a hug like she was greeting a long-lost sister. 'Back again so soon?'

I told Kitty what happened at the Koala Bear Hotel. She blinked at me. 'Yes, well, these things will happen in this country. You should definitely go home.'

'Home? I can't go home. I need to find Jack.'

'Even though he is probably dead? Definitely dead.'

I burst into tears.

She put her arms around me and said, 'There, there. And now I have an idea. I think you will stay with me.'

'Really, Kitty?'

'Oh, yes.'

'That's so nice of you.'

She guided me up the stairs with her arm around my shoulder. I stopped in the doorway, letting my eyes adjust to the green light. Kitty's flat looked like a Peruvian jungle. Not that I'd been to Peru, but it's what I imagined it would look like. The fake trees and vines and subdued lighting cast scary shadows on the walls. And to complete the picture, there was a fake snake curled up on her bed. Kitty rushed to her bedside table, fiddled with something, saying, 'You will have to sleep with Cecil and me, but I'm sure we can all fit.'

'Cecil?'

'Yes, my beloved pet.' Kitty picked up the front section of the fake snake, which was about five metres long and as thick as Jack's biceps. The snake uncoiled itself and raised its head, inspecting me. For the second time today, I was stunned into immobility and silence, my mouth hanging open.

'Here is Cecil. Say hello to Aunty Erica,' she purred, giving Cecil a kiss on the top of his head. 'He is very gentle,' she said. 'He can usually contain himself.'

'Contain himself?'

'Yes. He almost never tries to strangle me. You will see how gentle he is.'

'You know what, Kitty?' I stammered. 'I think I probably need to stay at the hotel, after all.'

She gave me a surprised look. 'Really? Aren't you afraid to stay there? There might be murderers.' She stroked Cecil's head and he swung himself over her shoulder. Around her neck. She pulled him away.

'Um . . . um . . . I just think I'll have better luck finding Jack if I'm in the thick of it, you know?' I tried to smile.

'Oh, well, we are disappointed, are we not, Cecil?' She gave him a squeeze. Not something I would have done, in case he got ideas. 'You are always welcome here, Erica Jewell.'

'Thanks, Kitty. I'll keep that in mind.' Way, way at the back of it.

BACK AT THE KOALA BEAR, I jammed a chair under the doorknob, had my second shower for the day, and sprayed myself with insect repellent. I was tired and wired at the same time; not sure what to do. Too scared to stay in my room just yet. It'd been a long day, and now it was happy hour. I went to the bar. Phil Collins was there, and I remembered seeing him talking to Rupert Berringer. I wondered what Phil had to do with anything. And I wondered what Dwayne from the plane had to do with Mr Berringer and if, when I saw Dwayne in the bar last night, he'd been talking to Phil Collins.

I sat next to Phil and gave him a suspicious look. I don't think he noticed, though. Or cared, probably. He raised his beer up and down, up and down.

'Hi, Phil.'

He mumbled, 'G'day.'

I ordered the Greek salad from the menu. Nice and safe. The barman retrieved it from the beer fridge and put it in front of me. I poked at the cubes of cheese. Picked one up, sniffed and tasted it. I think it was Coon Extra Tasty. There was lettuce. And that was it, my Greek salad.

'How was work today?' I said to Phil, sucking on the limp lettuce.

He glanced at me. Did he see me in the back of the taxi? Did Rupert Berringer see me?

'So, Phil, this barge of yours . . . '

Phil sucked hard on his beer.

' . . . what do you transport on it?'

'Stuff.'

'From Australia?'

'Yip.'

I leaned in and whispered, 'Do you bring stolen stuff?'

Phil didn't change his rhythm.

'I won't tell,' I said.

He shrugged. 'Maybe.'

I lowered my voice even more. 'What kind of stuff?'

No response.

I said, 'Hey, Phil, do you know Rupert Berringer?'

He tipped his beer until no more could possibly drip out of the bottle. He got off his stool and went to the men's room. When he emerged he walked straight out of the pub without a glance in my direction. Through the window I watched him get into an old ute and drive away. I rushed out to the hotel reception and greeted the ladies with a big smile.

They looked up at me from their low chairs.

I said, 'Do you know Phil Collins?'

'Yes, ma'am.'

'Do you know where he lives?'

They glanced at each other.

I said, my voice low, 'I have to meet him to pick up some . . . stuff. You know.' I gave them a wink.

'At the airfield, ma'am.'

'He lives at the airport?'

'No, ma'am. Not airport. Air*field*. That is where he has business.'

I nodded. 'Well, thank you, ladies. Could you please call me a taxi and ask them to hurry?'

'Yes, ma'am.'

The taxi pulled up outside and Bruce Willis rushed to open the door for me. 'Are you the only taxi driver in Seni?'

'No, lady!' he said, looking shocked at the very idea.

I sat in his stinky cab.

He said, 'Where, lady?' and fiddled with the meter. This was the first time he'd used it. It already had 20 dollars on it.

'The airfield.'

'Airfield?' He was staring at me in the rear-view mirror.

'Yes. I want to buy some Tupperware.'

'Yes, lady!' And off we went.

So, I thought, what's my plan this time? Knock on Phil's door and demand answers? Answers to what? What I'd figured so far was that Phil was probably involved in criminal activities, which didn't seem like such a big deal here in Saint Sebastian, and that he knows Rupert Berringer, and Dwayne seems to know them all. The answer was gurgling around in my head, but I didn't like it.

Typical of the tropics, one minute you're admiring a sunset and next minute you're fumbling around in pitch black. Bruce hit his high beam and as we approached the airfield, driving along the narrow road next to a cyclone wire fence, I watched a small plane cruising in, guided by a few dim runway lights. They were more like garden lights, actually. And the runway was more like a paddock. I told Bruce to stop the taxi and cut his lights. There was a building by the runway – an airline hangar. By the side of the road we watched the plane land and roll to a stop. The pilot and one other man got out. Then Rupert Berringer emerged from the hangar and approached the plane, waving his arm, giving instructions as crates were unloaded.

Bruce's saucer eyes were watching me in the rear-view mirror. I realised I had partly solved the riddle of why Jack had been sent to Saint Sebastian and why he was now imprisoned or dead somewhere. He'd tried to bust open a ring of Tupperware thieves.

CHAPTER 23

$\mathcal{I}$ told Bruce to wait and hitched my bag onto my back, creeping low along the road to a gate in the cyclone wire fence. There were no padlocks or security men with guns or anything like that. I pushed open the gate and it squeaked, loudly. I hesitated, waiting for the SWAT team, but there was no sound except crickets and the distant, muted noises coming from inside the hangar. I tiptoed through long grass towards the building, and froze when I became aware of sounds around my feet. Cecil came instantly to mind. I stopped breathing and my heart stopped beating. All my blood pooled in my feet. I listened. No, not slithering; more definite movements than that. I needed to know. I fumbled for my mobile phone and turned on the torch app, pointing it at the ground. I couldn't see anything at first because the grass was so long, but then something flashed past on my right and disappeared again. I hit that spot with the light. There it was – a cane toad! Suddenly, there was hopping all around me. Hundreds of bloody cane toads bouncing all around, banging into my legs, trying to *climb* my legs to get to the light. I clamped my hand over my mouth to stop the threatening scream. My body shuddered all over, kick-starting the adrenaline again and sending me flying over the grass, barely touching it, until I reached the hangar. I thumped into the side of it and froze again, holding my breath, waiting for some reaction from within. But there was none. In the distance I could see the glow of Bruce Willis's cigarette. I wondered if the metre was running. Of course it was.

THE HANGAR DOOR WAS OPEN, way down the back. Someone came out of it and I ducked back around the corner. I waited a minute and poked my head around again. All clear. Just a couple of metres from me was a narrow wooden door into the building with a window at the top. I crept low to the door, keeping an eye out for whatever horror might be lurking, then I slowly rose until I was on tip-toes. I peeked in the window. And there, grinning at me on the other side, was Dwayne from the plane.

He snatched open the door and said, loudly, 'Hey, hey! If it ain't my Aussie friend. What are you doing, sneaking around out there?'

I gawped at him. I was too scared to look around, see what attention we'd attracted.

He was smiling – he really did have nice teeth – waiting for me to say something. There were a couple of blokes moving about and opening boxes, but they weren't taking any notice of me. I couldn't see Phil Collins or Rupert Berringer. Maybe they were having a stolen-Tupperware party?

'Well?' said Dwayne, putting his arm around my shoulders and pulling me into the room.

'I, ah …'

'Yes?'

'Came here to …

'Uh-huh?'

'… buy some Tupperware for my mother.'

'Yeah? Doesn't your mom have it all?'

'Oh, no, not everything. It's Mother's Day soon and she wants something special.'

'Alrighty, then.' Dwayne whistled to a bloke who was pulling stuff out of a box. We walked over to him, and I inspected the scattered items. The Tupperware was all second-hand. Stolen, presumably. I wondered if anything had come from Chadstone. 'A customer for you,' Dwayne said to the man.

I picked up a beetroot container. That would do nicely and then I could get the hell out of there. 'My mother always wanted one of these,' I said, even though she already had one. Well, *I* didn't. I took the lid off and peered inside. 'The thing's missing.' I looked at the man and he looked blankly back at me.

I asked Dwayne, 'Does he understand English?'

'Nah, just show him what you want and he'll write down the price.'

'Well, I want this beetroot container but the thing inside is missing.'

'What thing?' said Dwayne, inspecting it.

'There's a thing to lift the beetroot so you can get it easily, but most people think it's a handle and they end up with beetroot all over the table.'

'Well,' said Dwayne, 'sounds like you're better off without the thing.'

'How much?' I said to the man.

He held up two fingers.

'Two dollars? Sounds good.' I opened my bag to get my wallet.

Dwayne laughed. 'Honey, that's two hundred. US.'

I dropped my wallet. 'Two *hundred*!'

'This is a rare find. You should take it while you can.'

I picked up my wallet, huffing. Yeah, rare because it's an old, used piece of plastic with bits missing that no one in their right mind would pay 200 bucks for. I looked around, wondering if I could get out of buying it. Or at least get something useful instead. I scratched my head. I'd forgotten for a minute why I was really here. Why was I really here?

Just then, a door at the back of the warehouse opened and Phil Collins walked in. He looked at me with a very surprised expression – I gave him a little wave – then he took a beer from a small fridge and glanced at me again before retreating. He made a groaning sound as the door closed.

'Where's Rupert?' I found myself asking.

'Berringer?' Dwayne looked over his shoulder towards a high partition at the far end of the hangar. He shrugged. 'Dealing with his shipment, I'd say.' His eyes narrowed. 'So you *do* know him?'

'No. Um, no. He's, ah, a friend of a friend.' I stepped back. 'I really should go.'

'Alrighty. So, how you gonna pay?'

'Oh, right.' I opened my wallet. 'Will he take American Express?'

'Sure will. Ten per cent surcharge.'

'Bloody hell,' I grumbled as I handed over my card.

Dwayne gave it to the other guy, who reached behind a box and produced a wireless credit card thingy. He swiped my card, I punched in my PIN and I was the proud owner of an old, used, Tupperware beetroot container with the thing inside missing.

'And now,' Dwayne said, 'I'm buyin' you dinner.'

The restaurant at the Hotel Sebastian was quite nice – linen table cloths, candles, serene waiters in white jackets – and I was very underdressed in my creased hiking pants and black singlet top. But no one seemed to notice or care, including Dwayne.

We'd left the airfield in a white SUV, stopping to tell Bruce Willis that he could go (after I paid him). At first I was worried that Dwayne might have other plans – like, dinner in his room – but he walked me straight into the restaurant and we were seated at what appeared to be the best table. A romantic one by the window, with a view of the pool.

There weren't many people in the restaurant, and our table was far away from the few others there. I remembered what Jack had told me once about candlelit dinners. That they were foreplay, always, he'd said, and thinking about that made my stomach go all squidgy.

Dwayne picked up my hand, kissed it, kept it in his. He gazed dreamily into my eyes. Should I tell him about Jack? What about Jack? We're not in a relationship. No, I won't tell him about Jack. Should I mention the candlelight/foreplay thing? In case he had ideas? Maybe not. He might get ideas.

'You've got the most amazing green eyes,' said Dwayne.

'Apparently, I got them from my grandfather.'

'Tell me about your grandfather.'

'Well, it's kind of interesting, actually. And a bit embarrassing.' Should I tell him? Okay, I'll tell him. 'I didn't know my grandfather. He was a passing ship in my grandmother's, er, port, so to speak.'

Dwayne gazed. His eyes still sparkled, even in the darkness.

I continued, 'But only once, apparently. He was Italian, very handsome, and she was swept off her feet. Anyway, that fling produced my mother, much to her distress.'

At the mention of my mother, Dwayne's face lit up. 'Tell me all about your mom.'

Must I? I sighed. Dwayne was so handsome. What was he doing here in Saint Sebastian? He kept skirting around the subject. Was he a Tupperware thief? The one in charge of the stealing and, if so, what's Rupert Berringer's role? And Phil Collins? Well, he obviously brings it on his barge.

'Why are you in Saint Sebastian, Dwayne?'

He kissed the inside of my wrist. Softly. I felt I should take my hand back, but the attention felt kind of nice. He said, his voice all creamy, 'Why are *you* in Saint Sebastian, Erica Jewell?'

I sat back, gently removed my hand. The waiter hovered; we ordered drinks.

'So,' I said. 'My mother.'

Dwayne listened with great interest as I told him about my mother. I also told him that she's very attached to her Tupperware, just in case he was getting ideas about sending his thieves to Chadstone. There seemed to be a lot of ideas to be got by Dwayne, and I worried that I might be putting them in his head.

WE ATE our lobster and drank our pinot gris. It was delicious wine from the Mornington Peninsula, near Melbourne. I thought I should go visit there some time. Maybe Dwayne would like to go with me. I felt homesick.

'Do you have a boyfriend?' said Dwayne.

'Boyfriend? Me?' Do I? 'Yes. Sort of. No.' Maybe Dwayne would be a nice boyfriend. But he lives in America. And he's a thief. But Jack's no angel either, is he? I mean, he kills people. Yeah, they're all bad, but still. There can't be good karma in his life. Do I want to be mixed up with someone who has bad karma?

'I've got a cat,' I said.

'I love cats.'

'Yeah?' That was kind of disappointing. I think men should be dog people. Although Jack loves Axle, I know he does. He pretends to be annoyed with Axle's attention-seeking, but he does let Axle climb all over him.

Dwayne paid for dinner and that won him at least a million brownie points. We strolled out of the restaurant, holding hands, and I let him walk me to the hotel lifts. He pushed the button and, while we were waiting, I let him kiss me. It was a nice kiss. Warm and soft, not too sloppy. But it wasn't Jack.

'I'm not coming to your room, Dwayne.'

'Oh?' He kissed me again, this time with an arm tight around my waist. There was urgency to this kiss. And tongue. He moaned. 'You're sure about that?'

I stepped back. 'Yes.'

'Shame,' he said and walked into the lift. He gave me a little wave and a wink as the doors closed between us, and I realised I now had to find my own way back to the Koala Bear Hotel.

CHAPTER 25

I stood naked under a pretty waterfall, the water in the pond only waist high, my hair tumbling around my shoulders, glossy and bouncy and dry, the cascade unable to penetrate it. The surrounding jungle was glorious – hibiscus and frangipani the colour of sunset, emerald foliage, giant sapphire macaws gliding overhead. Jack was there, wading towards me, also naked. He was magnificent, as always. Smiling, he held his hand out for me to take. I moved towards him, but as I did, the water started churning wildly. There was fierce splashing all around us and then, a crocodile emerged, as big as a Hummer, leaping like a dolphin into the air, hesitating at the top of its climb and, following an elegant pike, diving back into the water, straight as an arrow, its jaws wide, swallowing Jack whole.

Not my idea of a sexy dream. Definitely not. Although the first part was alright. It took me a while to recover from it, but then I was happy I'd survived another night. And I was happy I hadn't gone to Dwayne's room. I checked myself over, making sure there were no wounds I'd acquired. No more mozzie bites. I loved my new repellent. Maybe it repelled murderers and room trashers, too.

While I was responding to Lucy's latest round of panicky messages, my phone rang. It was my mother, but this time just a call, not Facetime. I hesitated before answering, which is my standard response when Mum calls.

'Erica!' she screamed into the phone, hysterical.

'Mum? What's wrong?'

She sobbed, 'Your father —'

'What's wrong with Dad?'

And then she sounded irritated. 'Nothing's wrong with your father. Why do you think something's wrong with your father?'

'Well, you're crying and you said —'

'If you'd let me finish, dear, you'd have heard the rest of that sentence, which was … now, what was it? Oh, yes, I was about to say that your father and I have been burgled! Can you believe it? Burgled!'

'Oh my God! Are you alright? Were you home? What was taken?'

'Well, as luck would have it, I was having lunch with Janice. Mary was supposed to come too, but she didn't show up. She's become so unreliable and Judy thinks she's having early dementia —'

'Mum.'

'Anyway, your father and your pussy were sound asleep and didn't even hear them come in!'

'Dad was there? Oh my God!'

'I do wish you wouldn't blaspheme, Erica.'

'What was taken?'

'Well, I'm furious. They took my beetroot container from the fridge, and I'd just put a full tin of beetroot in it. But as luck would have it, I'd hidden my limited edition lettuce crisper and padlocked the Tupperware cupboard. No other Tupperware was in the fridge, thank goodness. They left before searching the house, which is just as well because I hadn't dusted in over a week —'

I tuned out. I no longer found the whole Tupperware theft business laughable, especially after what I'd seen last night at the airfield *and* what I'd paid for that bloody beetroot container. At least now I had a valid reason for giving it to Mum. Hmm. Did Dwayne send his thieves to my mother's house? Of course he did. Probably had my room trashed, too, looking for Mum's address.

'Are you there?' said Mum.

'Is that all they took? The beetroot container?'

'Well, yes.'

'Did you call the police?'

'Of course!'

'What did they say?'

'They weren't very helpful. Not at all. I told them there was a Tupperware thief, but they already knew that. They said they'd let me know but I can't imagine they'll find those thieves. They're so shifty and shady.'

I bet those cops were rolling around on the floor back at the station, telling their mates about the Tupperware thief. If only they knew the bigger picture. Well, on the positive side, I now had my Mother's Day gift for Mum, although I'm not sure it'd impress her after the iPad from my brother. Also, it wasn't tropical, and I'd promised a gift from Bali. I'd have to think of something else.

I showered, got dressed and made my way back to the cafe I'd gone to with Kitty. I ordered breakfast and stared out the window. Now what? If Jack was still alive, where was he and was he okay? Bloody Tupperware thieves! Tears came and I wiped them. It didn't take long before I saw the Hummer, and I felt tempted to run out and flag Samson down, ask him if he knew where Jack was. But would Samson recognise me as the person who saw him with the gun? He probably wouldn't care. The Hummer moved slowly on, and I saw it again ten minutes later. Cruising. Reminding folks who's in charge. Talk about controlling. Big car; probably had a big house and a big monkey and a big wife, too. Compensating.

So, what to do next? Maybe Kitty would find out something. I felt very alone and wished Lucy was with me. Actually, I wished Jack was with me, and the thought of him sitting opposite me right now, reading the menu, made my heart skip. He would say, 'What are you having, my darling Erica?' and I'd smile and say, 'Choose something for me.' Who am I kidding? I'm not his darling and never will be. Quite aside from the fact that Jack would never bring any darling of his to such a horrible place. He'd take her to a posh hotel in Fiji, or the Maldives or somewhere like that.

It was almost too much to bear, this not knowing, this waiting. I needed to stop thinking about Jack. Or at least start being more positive. Using 'vigilisation', like my mother. I smiled. God, I even missed my mother. Maybe.

I ordered an iced coffee. Someone tapped on the window next to me. It was the helpful lady from the supermarket. She waved at me, smiling, and I smiled back, beckoning her to join me.

She pushed open the door.

'Well, hello there,' she said.

'Please let me buy you a coffee.' I indicated the chair opposite. 'You were so nice to me yesterday.'

'That would be lovely.' She sat.

'Did you buy something special?' I said, glancing at her shopping bags.

She laughed briefly. 'No chance of that in Seni, my dear. There is no such thing as something special here.'

'Really? Why is that? Maybe someone needs to open a special things store.'

'I'm afraid it wouldn't be a very successful business. Any decent goods to reach our shores would be stolen before they made it to a shop. And then sold at enormously inflated prices to foreigners.' She reached across the table with her right hand. 'I'm Emeline. And it's very nice to meet someone new. Someone charming as well.'

'I'm Erica.' We shook hands and she ordered tea from the waitress. There was a poshness to Emeline's manner that didn't seem to fit Saint Sebastian, even though she looked the part in a muumuu of bright, tropical colours. Emeline was dark-skinned with a round face and hot-pink lipstick.

'Well, Erica, tell me what on earth you're doing in this dreadful place.'

'It's kind of a long story. I'm trying to find . . . my boyfriend.' I stopped, wondering how much more I should say. Although I'd now told so many people, it'd probably be in the local newspaper any day now: "Crazy Aussie Woman's Futile Search For Man She Thinks Is Her Boyfriend".

Emeline said, 'What do you mean? Where is he?'

'That's the problem. I don't know.'

'Ah.' She nodded, giving me a knowing, yet sympathetic look. What was she thinking? That he'd dumped me and run away?

'Men,' she said, suddenly.

'Yep.' I nodded. 'Men.'

'All I want,' she continued, with exasperation in her voice, 'is a few nice things around the house. Functioning things. Things that don't break five minutes after I buy them.'

'I know what you mean.' I didn't really, but I wanted to sound sympathetic.

'You'd think my husband could source some decent things for me.'

'Oh?'

'Yes. He travels. I show him what I want. Does he get it for me? No. He's too busy with his business.'

'What's his business?'

She waved her hand and shook her head. Tired of talking about him already.

'And,' she said, 'do you think he'll pick up his dirty clothes? His wet towel off the floor? No. That's women's work, he says.'

'Tell me about it.' I remembered being married to Danny, but didn't think I should confuse the issue by bringing up an ex-husband. But, not wanting to be left out of the complaining, I said, 'My boyfriend . . . ' What? Expects me to clean his guns? ' . . . refuses to vacuum.' Which was sort of true. Jack doesn't even know where the vacuum cleaner lives in his house. That's why he has Joe and a cleaning lady.

Emeline shook her head. Our drinks were delivered.

I asked Emeline where she lives and she told me that she and her husband have a house in town and one in the mountains.

'I prefer to stay in town,' she said.

There was a minute of comfortable silence, and I asked, 'Emeline, have you heard of Rupert Berringer?'

She appeared thoughtful. 'Does he look like Hugh Grant, the actor?'

'Yes, he does.' I sat forward in my chair.

'Then I've met him. Quite recently, actually. At a dinner party at the governor's house. My husband knows him.'

Emeline suddenly scowled at the window, and I glanced outside, saw the Hummer go by.

I said, leaning in and staring at the Hummer, wanting to impress Emeline with my local knowledge, 'The man in that car. He's a gangster.' Was that right? Gang leader maybe? I continued, 'I heard he has many mistresses, even though he's married.'

Emeline said, 'Where on earth did you hear such nonsense?'

'Oh, well, it seems everyone knows what everyone's doing in Seni.' I shouldn't gossip, I thought. Kitty probably told me that in confidence.

Emeline nodded, downed her tea. She looked at her watch and said, 'I really must keep moving.' She stood.

'Oh, right.' A quick cuppa.

She gave me a tight smile. 'Goodbye, Erica. I wish you luck.'

I stood, held out my hand to shake hers. She took it briefly and left.

'Nice to meet you, Emeline,' I called after her.

CHAPTER 26

I stood on the street. Now what? I looked up and down. The Hummer came again. And while my brain was telling me to press myself into the wall, disappear, be invisible, instead I stepped forward, staring at the great beast as it rumbled by. I tried to penetrate the black glass, see who was inside, wondering if they were looking at me, wondering if they knew where Jack was.

I'd been holding my breath. I blew it out, shakily. Walked to Kitty's. She was in her shop, arranging the stock on the shelves. All the pink toys together. All the green ones. Blue, purple, yellow. Nice.

Her face was already lit by the glowing toys but it lit up more when she saw me. 'Ah, Erica Jewell, you have changed your mind, yes? You will come and stay with me?' She hugged me.

'Thanks, Kitty, but I'm okay. I was wondering ...' Wondering what? Am I really going to say this? '... if you could tell me where Samson lives?'

She took a step back, stared at me.

'Why?' she said.

'Because I want to ask him about Jack.'

She took a moment to respond. 'No, I do not know his address in the town.'

'But I thought —'

She took a step closer, as though telling me a secret, even though there was no one around to hear.

'Listen to me. You remember I told you about a party today?'

'What about it?'

'It is at Samson's house in the mountains. You can come. He does not need to know who you are. Maybe you can ask someone if they have seen your Jack.' She stepped back. 'Even though he is dead. Probably dead.'

'I wish you'd stop saying that, Kitty.'

She shrugged.

A party at Samson's. Maybe I could go to that. Ask around or at least check things out. It couldn't hurt, could it? Better than getting food poisoning at the Bum Crack Bar. But then, what if I got to the party and there was nothing to see? No one to ask about Jack? I couldn't march up to Samson and give myself away. He'd probably recognise me, anyway. And he'd be angry with Kitty. What would he do to her if he knew she was helping me? But if I didn't go to the party, what would I do instead?

I decided. 'Okay. I'll come. Just for a look-see.' She clapped her hands, jumped up and down. 'But I don't have anything to wear,' I said.

'Never mind about that, Erica Jewell. I have something for you.' She checked her watch. 'But now, you must be off. I have a client due any minute.'

When I stepped outside Kitty's shop, a man was getting out of Bruce Willis's taxi. I waited for him to finish arguing about the cost so I could take his place. As he moved away from the car we did one of those embarrassing dances when you go to pass each other but keep stepping to the same side. He was the grimiest, sleaziest-looking man I'd ever seen. He put his hands on my arms, grinned a broken-toothed grin at me, and swung me to his left so he could pass. He walked into

Kitty's shop. Poor Kitty. How could she do this work? Close her eyes and think of England? France? Yuk.

In the taxi I said to Bruce's reflection, 'Do you know where Samson lives?'

He turned his whole body and stared at me. 'Who, lady?'

'Samson, the gang guy. Do you know where he lives?'

'Yes, lady.'

'Oh, well, can you take me there, please?'

He shook his head. 'No, lady.'

'Why not?'

Another vigorous head shake. 'No, lady.'

'Well … where does he live?'

Bruce hesitated then pointed.

'Just there?' I said, nodding at the street ahead. How could Kitty not know? It's right near her place.

'Yes, lady.'

'What number?'

'Four two.'

'Forty-two?'

'Yes, lady.'

'Thanks, Bruce.' I got out of the cab and walked. I didn't look back, but heard the screech of Bruce Willis's fast U-turn before he sped away.

SAMSON'S STREET was in what I supposed was the better part of Seni – the sizeable townhouses showing some semblance of quality, although graffiti artists didn't seem to care about that, having decorated most of the fences along that road. Number four two was as expected. A very high white wall faced onto the street – the only one ungraffitied, unsurprisingly – with intercom and cameras. An arched timber gate was built into the wall. I watched as my finger reached up and pushed the buzzer. It was an automatic action – not something I was controlling. How could *I* be responsible for doing such a thing? Visiting a gang leader at his house?

A young girl's voice came over the speaker. I had no idea what she was saying.

I looked at the camera, said, 'I was wondering … is Samson home?'

More speaking, some shuffling, silence, two people speaking.

'Erica?'

I froze. A woman.

The voice was familiar. She said, 'What are you doing here?'

I still couldn't think of anything to say. I looked at the number on the wall. Forty-two. Whose house was I at?

I heard a door being opened and the sound of quick footsteps approaching the other side of the gate. It swung open. There stood Emeline, looking as surprised to see me as I was her.

'Are you looking for me?' she said.

Why was she here? At Samson's house? Did Bruce Willis give me the wrong number? Unless …

'Oh,' was all I could manage. Our cafe conversation was replaying in my head. Her abrupt departure. I am *such* an idiot.

She stared at me. I needed to speak. Something.

'I'm sorry.'

'What for?'

'For what I said at the cafe.'

'About my husband's philandering?' She waved a hand. 'I am used to it, but it does annoy me that everyone seems to know.' She tsked, just like my mother would under the same circumstances. 'You haven't told me why you are here. Oh … no, you're not one of my husband's mistresses, surely?'

'Oh my God, *no*! No, of course not. I've never even met him!' Oh, geez. 'I'm just … you see, I thought he might know … where my boyfriend is.'

'Ah. Erica, come inside. I'll make you some tea.'

*B*ack at the Bum Crack Bar, I sat next to Phil with my head resting sideways on my folded arms. I hadn't had a drink. Yet. I wasn't sure if I wanted one. I wasn't sure if I wanted to suffer in my alertness or chicken out and go to oblivion. It wasn't quite lunchtime but I was hungry.

'I think a gang has Jack,' I told Phil.

He nodded. 'I reckon.'

'I told a gang leader's wife that her husband's cheating on her.'

Phil sucked on his beer.

'But she already knew, so it wasn't so bad.'

When I'd confessed to Emeline about Jack's real reason for being in Saint Sebastian – well, what I thought was his real reason: that he'd been sent on a mission and now he was missing in action, and I thought Samson might know where he is because he seems such an important and knowledgeable fellow – she'd nodded her head and said she understood, and that she agreed that Jack had most likely been taken by a gang, because that's the kind of thing they did, but she doubted Samson would tell me, even if he did know. 'In fact,' she'd said, 'it would not be good for you to ask him such questions. Not good at all.' She'd also said, 'Besides, he is not here for the next couple of days. He is on his way to our home in the mountains.' And that was that. We'd had tea, I'd thanked her, apologised again for my idiocy, and left.

Lifting my head, I said to Phil, 'How many gangs do you think there are in Seni?'

Phil shrugged, and I wondered out loud if the gangs all beat each other up or killed each other or whatever. And if that's what happens, surely one day there'll only be one gang left.

'Different types of gangs 'ere,' said Phil. 'Rich uns 'n poor uns. Rich un's gotcha bloke, I reckon.'

'I reckon.'

I ordered the 'soup du jour' from the menu and thought about Samson. Kitty might ask him about Jack, I thought, or I could ask him later at the party. Imagine if Emeline had come into the cafe when Kitty was there!

I peered at the sea of green VB cans and stubbies in front of me, and realised it was not yet midday, and while Jack was still M.I.A., I was sitting in a bar, considering an alcoholic drink.

I said to Phil, 'How come you're not at work?'

'Day orf.'

'Ah.'

My soup arrived and I swished it around with my spoon. Suspicious-looking things floated to the top and disappeared again. It looked like something from a David Attenborough documentary. I pushed the bowl away, and said, 'Um, Phil, you wouldn't happen to know where Jack is, would you?'

He gave me a look – one that suggested he thought I might be a lunatic. 'Nah.'

'No harm in asking.'

Phil's eyes grew very wide then, staring at the fridge door. In its reflection I watched Catwoman approach. Mask and all. She stood behind me and said, 'Hello, Erica Jewell.'

I spun around. 'Kitty?'

'Yes, it is I! And I am here to collect you for the party.'

'Now?'

'*Oui*,' she said, speaking French for some reason. *Je vais au parti maintenant.*'

'Did you just say you're going now?'

'*Oui*.' She nodded. 'Guess who is going to be there?'

'Jack?' My heart started thumping.

'No, silly, the British man, Rupert Berringer.'

'He's British?'

'*Oui*.'

'And he's going to the party?'

'Yes! Come along. You can ask him about your Jack. Even though —'

'Don't say it!'

'Sorry.'

'But, Kitty, aren't you worried about me talking to Samson about it? He might be angry with you.'

She picked at some fluff on her sleeve. 'Oh. No, it is fine. I am sure.'

So, should I go to the party and ask Rupert Berringer about Jack? I admit, I was having second thoughts about it. But if I didn't go, what would I do instead? Sit here and get pissed with Phil Collins? There might be nice food at Samson's.

Phil went to the men's.

I said to Kitty, 'Alright, I'll come.' I looked at the backpack she was carrying. 'Did you bring me something to wear?'

She patted the bag. 'I have something for you in here. Let us go to your room.'

'I'm not sure I'll fit into your clothes. You're a bit smaller than me.'

'Never fear when Kitty is near.'

'It's a fancy dress party?' I said as we climbed the stairs. Kitty jogged up them. I trudged.

'No, I am dressing like this for Samson. He likes it.'

Kitty followed me into my room.

I said, 'How do you know his wife won't be there?' Although, after our earlier conversation, I was pretty confident Emeline wouldn't be.

'She never goes to the mountains.'

'Okay. Well, what have you got for me to wear?'

'I will show you. But first, I have a gift for you!'

'Really? Thanks, Kitty.'

She drew a shiny bag out into the light. 'It is a superseded model, but still a favourite of my clients,' she said as she slid the black satin down the length of a puce and lime-coloured vibrator. She held it up, proudly. 'No more lonely nights for you, Erica Jewell!'

My mouth dropped open. 'Ah, er, Kitty, I don't think —'

'No need to thank me! And see? It is very tropical. Typical of this region.'

A gift for Mum, maybe? I gave myself a mental face-slap and leaned in to inspect it. Yes. Tropical it was. A long, pink palm tree with a green head of unopened fronds and a brown monkey attached to the side of it. The monkey presumably had its own agenda.

'I would show you how it works, but you will need batteries.'

'Of course.' Batteries. I could hardly wait.

KITTY HAD BROUGHT ME A CLINGY, revealing leopard-print dress that sat just under my bum and gave me a lot of cleavage. I tried to pull the dress further down my legs but that just revealed more cleavage. I was glad I'd waxed everything last week, including my bikini line, which was almost on show as well.

'Hmmm,' said Kitty, standing back and looking me up and down. 'You have a visible panty line.'

I looked over my shoulder at the mirror. 'Yeah, visible *below* the dress. Kitty, I think this is a bit much.'

'No, it is not. You will blend in this, Erica Jewell. Believe me. But,' she added, 'you need to wear a G-string.'

'Great,' I muttered, inspecting my reflection. 'Jack would love this outfit.' *Not.*

Kitty was handing me some strappy black heels but stopped, stepped back and looked me up and down. 'Yes, I think Jack would certainly love this outfit.'

I scoffed and she gave me the shoes. I put them on. She might have a tiny frame, but Kitty had huge hoofs. The shoes were way too big. I felt like a little kid in Mum's high heels.

'I don't think I can wear these.'

'Do not worry. When we get there, you can find somewhere to sit, or take them off. Let us go.'

I picked up my bag and we made our way downstairs, me shuffling to keep the shoes from slipping off. I eyed Kitty's snug, knee-high stiletto boots, thinking they looked much more comfortable. On the stairs, she said, 'We will have to find someone to take us to the party.'

I stopped. 'You mean, you don't have a car?'

'Oh, no. I do not drive. We will hitchhike, probably.' She continued on down the stairs but I stayed where I was.

'I don't think hitchhiking's a good idea, Kitty. Isn't it dangerous?'

She waved her hand in the air. 'No, it is not. Unfortunately.'

'Bloody hell.' I stumbled after her. 'Hold on. Let me just ask in the bar.'

In the Bum Crack Bar every head swivelled to stare at us. Phil Collins was back on his stool. I sat next to him. His right eye regarded me with fear and suspicion. Poor Phil.

'Um, Phil, do you have a car?'

He grunted. 'Got me ute.'

'Could you drive us to Samson's party? I'm going to see if I can find out anything about Jack.' Imagine if I arrived and Jack was there with Rupert Berringer and some blonde, laughing and having a good time.

Phil shook his head briefly but firmly.

'Okay. Well, see you later,' I said and stood, taking in the other staring locals. 'Anyone driving to the mountains?' I called out, and in unison they all looked away.

On the street, Kitty pulled her Catwoman mask into place and stood with one foot on the kerb, the other on the road. Just like a hooker. She smiled and waved at the passing cars. They honked their horns. I hid in the shadows. For the first time since I'd arrived, I wished Bruce Willis would show up. Eventually, a truck stopped.

There were two men inside. It was a single-cab unit, no back seat. Kitty had a conversation with them in Portuguese.

She turned to me. 'Okay, these nice boys will drive us to the party.'

I rushed forward, as fast as the stilettos would carry me. The door of the truck opened and a very stinky-looking man grinned out at me. He climbed down, indicating for us to take the middle. I was about to climb up, hanging on to the hem of my dress with one hand, when Kitty said, 'We might have to have sex with them, but I'll see if we can get around it.'

I fell back and landed on my bum on the sidewalk. 'Have *sex* with them?' I shouted up at her.

Kitty frowned. 'Please, Erica Jewell, do not make a fuss. I have condoms.'

I gawped at Kitty from my seated position, knees squeezed together so the 'nice boys' couldn't see up my dress. As we all stared at each other, three of us looking impatient and one of us looking like she was shitting herself, the sound of screeching tyres made us all turn our heads. A horn blared.

It was Phil! Phil Collins in his ute!

I stood, plucked off my shoes and ran to the passenger side of Phil's car, peering in the window. 'Phil! Can you drive us?'

He gave one short nod.

I waved to Kitty. 'Come on!'

She wandered over, seemingly disappointed. I climbed in and sat in the middle; Kitty flopped in next to me with a big sigh.

CHAPTER 28

It occurred to me that Phil was probably over the legal limit. I wondered what the legal limit was in Saint Sebastian. But, I thought, his body was probably so used to being pickled, maybe he'd be dangerous if he *hadn't* had a drink. Kitty didn't seem concerned about anything as she sat with the window open, wind blowing her hair. Phil drove steadily and not too fast. And once Kitty had told him where we were headed, he didn't say a word.

Driving away from Seni and the ocean, along the snaking road that followed the base of the mountain range, I watched the landscape grow and the vegetation become increasingly lush. Without the sea breeze, the humidity was an all-consuming weight in Phil's non-air-conditioned car. We drove for about an hour and I was feeling a little guilty about dragging Phil on such a long journey. But he didn't seem to mind; there was no grumbling or change in his expression. I had no idea how we were going to get back to Seni. I had no idea what I was going to say to Samson or Rupert Berringer. I had no idea about anything, actually.

Kitty asked Phil to take us up the steep driveway of Samson's house, but he refused. He didn't say anything, just stopped and wouldn't go further. So we climbed out of his ute, me hanging onto the hem of my dress, and I thanked him. He nodded. Kitty flung her backpack onto her back. With shoes in hand I started the long, winding climb up the driveway that was fringed by soaring palms and flourishing tropical growth. I glanced back. Phil was still sitting there, watching us, wondering perhaps if he'd ever see us again. I hoped he wasn't looking up my dress.

As we trudged along, a frog hopped across our path and onto a leaf as big as a platter. I pointed. 'Look at that beautiful frog, Kitty.' It was the most vivid colour. It was as orange as … an orange.

'Yes, but you must not go near it unless you want to die. It has enough poison to kill twenty men,' she said, conversationally. 'And there are snakes that can swallow you whole and spiders the size of your face and wild boars in the jungle and crocodiles and —'

'Okay! Okay. I get it.'

My breathing was laboured from the climb and I knew I'd arrive at the party all sweaty and smelly. Nice. Kitty was striding ahead, her breathing normal. I guess having sex for a living was a good way to stay in shape.

At the top of the hill, where the driveway grew wide and the dense jungle was replaced by landscaped gardens, I asked Kitty to wait while I got my breath back. She stood impatiently, and I gazed around in wonder. The driveway circled a fountain big and ornate enough to impress the Pope, and beyond the fountain was a whopping great white house with a portico three storeys high. It looked like Tara from *Gone With The Wind*.

'Come on, Erica. Let us have a party,' said Kitty, snatching the shoes from my hand and forcing them onto my feet. I shuffled after her to the front door. She rang the bell and it was opened by a butler. He took Kitty's bag. I wouldn't let go of mine, which I was wearing on my back. Kitty barged through the house in the direction of the chatting and laughter. I followed meekly, nervous. The house was lit brightly by chandeliers and wall lights – all of them turned on, even though it was the middle of the day, because the shutters on the windows were closed. The long passage opened onto a cavernous room that was filled with drinking, cavorting men, scampering monkeys and … prostitutes. Dozens of them, all dressed in sexy costumes or clinging, animal-print dresses, just like mine. Kitty yoo-hooed at someone and dashed across the room. I spun on my stilet-toed heel with the intention of running out of there as fast as I could, hoping Phil might still be sitting at the bottom of the driveway in his lovely ute, but I slammed straight into a tuxedoed chest.

'I was hoping we'd meet again,' he said.

I looked up, and found I was staring into the face of a bastard.

CHAPTER 29

I shook my head. This couldn't be right. I blinked, looked around. Mick Jansen?

'Wh— What are you doing here?' I stammered.

'Just enjoying myself with friends. My *real* friends.'

He looked past me then, took one step back, his expression changing.

Behind me a refined, British voice said, 'Surely you'll stay for one drink?'

I knew it was Rupert Berringer before I turned to look; he even sounded like Hugh Grant.

Mick Jansen moved away, quickly.

I said, 'Ah, er, I forgot something and I need to leave.'

'Oh, but you can't leave,' he murmured, leaning close to my ear, 'not until we get to know each other better.'

I backed away. 'Well, that sounds great, but I really do have to go.'

I tried to walk past him but he held my arm.

'I don't like your shoes,' said Rupert Berringer, checking them out.

'What?'

'They don't fit.'

'They're not —'

'I wouldn't like them even if they did.' He gripped my arm. 'Come along.'

'No. Please. I need to leave.'

He smiled. His lips were thinner than Hugh Grant's, I thought. I struggled, trying to free my arm, looking frantically around. Kitty was talking to a man across the room. It was Samson.

'Kitty!' I called out.

She gave me a little wave.

'Kitty!' I screamed it.

A few people looked at me, frowning.

Kitty put a finger to her lips. *Ssh.*

'Your friend won't help you,' said Rupert. 'She brought you here for me.'

'What? No!'

'And besides,' he said. 'You won't get far if you run.' He glanced around.

Apart from monkeys, laughing men and hookers, and me, there were men with guns. Big, muscly men dressed like old-fashioned warriors – bare-chested with tattoos and topknots in their hair. They stayed on the periphery, strolling back and forth, back and forth, looking like they wouldn't mind an excuse to shoot someone.

My body sagged. Rupert eased his grip. 'That's better,' he said and took a glass of champagne from a passing tray. 'Here, this will loosen you up a bit.' He smiled. 'You need to relax, Erica.'

'You're nothing but a dirty thief,' I spat, shrugging him off. But I took the champagne.

He seemed surprised. 'Oh, but I'm so much more than that.' He smiled again and put an arm around my shoulder, tight, and led me into the crowd.

Across the room I could see Mick Jansen, talking to people, having a great time. He'd be in his element here, I thought, in a room full of violent, abusive men, and women he could do whatever he wanted with. But . . . *what* was he doing here?

There was someone else there I knew. Dwayne from the bloody plane was staring at me. I narrowed my eyes at him and he returned the look. He made his way towards me, keeping a wary eye on Rupert Berringer.

Berringer said to him, 'This one's mine; keep that in mind.'

Dwayne gave him a nod, and Berringer turned away to fondle some woman's backside.

Dwayne said, his voice low and a bit angry, 'Well, now I know why you didn't come to my room last night. I didn't offer to pay.'

And I said, 'I'm not really surprised to see you here with all your thieving friends.'

'You should have told me you were with Berringer.' Then he looked concerned, whispering, 'He know you were with me last night?'

I rolled my eyes, hissed, 'I'm not his girlfriend. I'm his prisoner!'

'Sure, sure.'

'And, hey, you sent your stinking thieves to my mother's house!'

Dwayne held up his hands. 'Not me.'

Rupert had his back to us, engrossed in conversation. There was a lot of squealing and giggling all around us. Deep laughter from the men.

'I don't believe you. You stole my mother's beetroot container.'

'You said she didn't have one.'

Pause. 'I lied.'

'I think you tell a lot of lies, Erica Jewell. Like the real reason you're here in Saint Sebastian. Like your association with the likes of them.' He nodded around the room.

'With the likes of *your* friends, you mean.' I got teary then, looking around. Rupert Berringer wasn't watching me but the warriors were, clearly under instruction to keep an eye on the one hooker who would give just about anything to be back at the Bum Crack Bar or, better still, spending a week locked in her boss's office while Rosalind droned on about said hooker's commitment to her job.

Dwayne looked worried and, his voice gentle, said, 'You really don't want to be here?'

I shook my head, looked down, a fat tear plopped onto the floor.

Rupert's arms came around me from behind and he kissed my

neck. Dwayne backed away. I gave him a pleading look, but he was already talking to someone else.

FOR THE NEXT HOUR, Rupert Berringer made me stand next to him while he chatted to men in Portuguese. Dwayne stayed away from me, but occasionally, our eyes met briefly. Apart from the fact that I was terrified out of my brain, my feet were now starting to hurt and I really wanted to sit down.

Kitty skipped over and I hissed, 'You set me up!'

'Oh, relax, Erica.'

'I wish everyone would stop telling me to relax.'

'Remember that you are the lucky one,' she reminded me in a low voice. 'Every other girl here would love to be chosen by Rupert Berringer. And besides, the champagne is French!'

I turned my head away. I would never speak to her again, I decided, if I survived.

By the time a loud clapping hushed the room, I'd sussed out every door, shuttered window, corner and crevice. I'd strained my eyes to see through walls, under the floor, trying to work out how to escape. Still standing obediently with my new 'boyfriend', I turned to see who was making the clapping noise. It was Samson, standing on a step. He spread his arms wide. Kitty was next to him, proud as punch.

Samson spoke but I didn't understand him, and an excited murmur started up around the room. Then he said, in English, 'I have something to show my friends. A big surprise!'

I looked up at Rupert and found him watching me. He was looking smug, and I decided I would wipe that expression off his face if it was the last thing I ever did. He gripped my hand as we all moved to a wall of shutters at the back of the room.

Samson said, 'There is something outside I want you to see.'

Everyone waited. In unison, the warrior boys pulled open the shutters to expose a great glass wall. Tinny trumpet music blared. Everyone stepped up to the windows and peered out. Rupert shuffled me forward, pushing through the crowd, saying, 'Excuse us, everyone, we need front row.' We reached the glass. Samson's property was big; great expanses of lawn sloped away from the house to the gardens, which really just looked like jungle. There were some mangy looking dogs. Monkeys in the trees. Warrior blokes with weapons milling around. And above them, swinging in a cage, alive and seemingly well, was the biggest monkey of all. My boyfriend, Jack Jones.

CHAPTER 30

I lurched forward, my hands on the window. Jack stared up at the house. Next to him in a separate cage was Joe, crouched like an animal, shading his eyes against the sun.

The crowd briefly applauded Samson's conquest. Mick Jansen was standing next to me, laughing. Rupert kicked my legs apart and pressed into me from behind. He held my arms above my head; my face was squished into the glass and my dress was riding high.

'Jones's girlfriend,' he whispered into my ear. 'I can't tell you how excited I am right now.'

Well, that was pretty obvious, but I didn't care. All I cared about was that Jack was alive. Oh, God. I started crying. Crying and laughing, too, because I was so relieved. What must Jack be thinking? Staring up at the squashed hooker in the window, wondering why she looked familiar. I hoped he didn't recognise me. Maybe he wouldn't with my new hair. I didn't want him to worry. Would he recognise Mick Jansen? Kitty was mimicking me, her hands on the glass, staring out at the boys. My boys.

But the relief and happiness didn't last long because Samson announced, in very clear English, 'Now that I have finally shown off my catch, I will kill them tonight. My crocodiles are very hungry.' And he laughed.

BAREFOOTED, I paced back and forth. There was a comfortable-looking bed in the room, but fear and adrenaline kept me moving. The guest room was very nice, in fact, with pretty lampshades and ornaments – a bronze statue of three wise monkeys on the bedside table. I could have imagined I was in a nice B&B if it weren't for the bars on the windows and the armed guard outside my door. And the fact that Jack and Joe were swinging in cages, ripening in the sun for tonight's feast in the croc pen. Panic welled inside me and I pushed it down. I needed a clear head if I was going to break out of here and rescue the boys. So, what were my options? Well, I could seduce the guard, give him a quickie, then kill him. An obvious solution, if I could bring myself to do any of that.

I wondered how long Rupert would keep me waiting while he finished having fun at the party. It was probably really turning him on, the waiting. I opened a cupboard, seeking inspiration, thinking I might find weapons. But instead there was Tupperware. Lots and lots of brightly coloured containers, all different shapes and sizes, neatly stacked on shelves. Spare stock that didn't fit in the warehouse? Most of it looked new, not retro, which was what Dwayne seemed to be interested in. I shut the cupboard door and resumed my pacing. *Come on, Erica, think!* But I kept coming back to the only possible solution – having sex with and killing the guard.

The door swung open and in walked Kitty with a glass of champagne. She was speaking to the guard with a sweet smile, indicating the glass in her hand, pointing to me.

'What the hell do you think you're doing?' I said.

'We, um, need to swap clothes.' She put the drink on the bedside table.

'Why?'

'Because … Samson wants me to wear your dress.'

'Well, tell him to bugger off.' I backed away.

'But, Erica, when you escape you will find this much easier to run in, yes?' She waved her hand over Catwoman.

My heart lifted. 'You're going to help me?'

'Sure.'

'How?'

'Um … I will cause a distraction.'

'Really?'

'Of course. Are we not best friends?'

'No, you led me into this trap.'

'Oh, come along, Erica. Where is your sense of fun?'

'Fun! Now, just hang on a minute. You —'

'Here, let me help you out of that dress.' She held out her hands and I found myself stepping towards her because, when push came to shove, I'd rather be dressed like Catwoman than a hooker.

Once we'd swapped clothes – the leopard print wasn't as short on her – she dashed to the door, gave me a little wave and said, 'Bye!' before rushing away.

Confused, I said nothing for a full 30 seconds until it dawned on me that I'd just been conned – again.

CHAPTER 31

At least I was more comfortable. The stiletto boots were too big, but easier to walk around in than the strappy sandals. It was hot in the lycra Catwoman suit, though.

And then, there was an explosion. The house shook; there was shouting. I rushed to the door and pressed my ear to it. Maybe Kitty *had* caused a distraction? The noise was coming from the front of the house. I opened the door a crack and peered out. My guard was standing there, his back to me, staring up the passageway.

I didn't stop to think. I grabbed the three wise monkeys, snuck up behind him and whacked him over the head. He dropped with a grunt. I raced back into the room, snatched up my bag and stood in the passageway. Now where? Not to the front of the house, that's for sure. I ran in the other direction. A door opened and I dashed through another to my left, shutting it, listening as feet ran past.

I squatted behind the door, holding my breath, waiting, wondering why my stomach was growling so loudly but knowing really that was just denial working overtime because the part of my brain that was still functioning knew the growling was coming from behind me. I turned slowly, couldn't see in the dark. Couldn't even work out what room I was in. It was windowless. But then the door opened, knocking me over, trapping me against the wall. I held back a yell as light flooded the room and I saw two dogs, big ones, saliva dripping from their fangs, snarling at me. Someone shouted at the dogs and they leaped forward. I wrapped my arms around my head and squeezed my eyes shut, but then the room was quiet and still. And dark. Dogs were gone. As my eyes adjusted, I could see a thin line of light that formed a square in the opposite wall. I crawled across the floor and touched the square. It moved. It was a doggy door, and it was big enough for me to crawl through.

I CROUCHED at the corner of the house, under the balcony. I could hear muted party sounds. There was a lot of shouting, but the party carried on as though explosions were normal. Maybe they were. Above me I heard the *shoosh* of a sliding door, the party volume increased, and another *shoosh* as the door closed again. I pressed against the house and peered up through a crack in the decking. It was Mick Jansen and a giggling woman. He lit a cigarette. They stood at the edge of the deck and he unzipped his fly. Oh, God, were they going to have sex up there? But a thin stream of yellow pee appeared in front of me. Jansen finished peeing, and *then* they started to fool around.

Down the sloping ground, not far away, I could see a cyclone wire fence. Jack was on the other side and I knew I could climb it – that wasn't the problem – but there was the small issue of men with guns and vicious dogs. Not to mention Mick Jansen above and, oh goody, something I'd heard only once before, when I visited Steve Irwin's zoo. I shivered as the deep, guttural growl reverberated through the ground and up my legs. The crocodile sound came from another fenced area and I made a mental note not to go that way.

Jansen and the woman stumbled around on the deck. In the distance, black smoke billowed in great puffs with the light wind. I could smell burning rubber. Men were still shouting and running, dogs barked hysterically, and the crocodile – I could see it now – moved its head slightly to the side. Maybe the crocodile was the best option? It looked so lazy and cumbersome. But then its whole body lifted and it ran like a speeding lizard into the water.

And so did I. Run. I bolted for the fence and clambered up it, hoping Jansen would be too preoccupied to notice me. I fell over the top, but then I was hanging. Hanging by my bag hooked on the fence. I kicked my legs. I could hear shouting from the front of the house. I straightened my arms over my head and they slipped through the straps as I fell. I hit the ground in a crouch, climbed back up for my bag.

There was a terrible growling behind me and I spun around. A dog was sprinting straight for me, teeth bared, its snarls wet and gasping. I scrambled back up the fence. The dog flew at me, snapping, barking, foamy saliva flying. I hoisted myself higher and hung one arm over the top, vaguely aware of the pain of it, kicking out at the dog, wondering if rabies was a horrible way to die. It had the heel of my boot and it shook its head wildly.

'Sit!' I shouted and the dog stopped its attack. It sat. We stared at each other. 'Um, you want walkies?' It cocked its head – the picture of innocence – smiled at me with its tongue flopping out the side of its mouth.

I couldn't keep holding on, and I couldn't go back over the fence. I let myself down, slowly, and the dog leaped at me. I held out my hands to protect myself, but it wasn't biting. It jumped on me, tail wagging.

'Sit!'

The dog sat and I wondered how many languages it knew. I looked around.

'Okay, then. Walkies.' I jogged down the hill, keeping to the side, to where I could see the boys' bamboo cages in the distance. Fido bounced along beside me. As I approached, I saw three guards unconscious on the ground in pools of blood (maybe more than unconscious), one empty cage and Joe in the other, trying to kick the side in.

'Joe!' I said as I ran up to him.

His eyes popped. '*Erica!* What the hell?' He looked around, up towards the front of the house where most of the people seemed to be gathering.

Fido barked.

'Shoosh!' I told the dog, and to Joe, 'Where's Jack?'

'Gone.' Joe kicked the cage again. It was cracking, starting to give way, and he said, 'Stand back!' as a corner of the cage floor dropped away, making a gap big enough for Joe to slide through and onto the ground, a couple of metres below.

'Where is he?' I demanded. 'How did he get away?'

Fido snarled at Joe.

'Sit!' I said to the dog. But then all the shouting and noise was heading our way. Men were running from the house towards us.

'Let's go!' said Joe, taking me by the wrist and hauling me into the trees. The dog ran with us. Machine guns fired and bullets whistled past us, exploding into tree branches. Fido yelped – I didn't look. Joe dragged me behind him. I kept my head down and arm up to take the hits and slashes from the whipping branches. We reached a high wall. Joe scooped me up and pushed me over the top, arms and legs flailing. I landed on my feet with bent knees and fell onto my side, stood quickly, and Joe was next to me in a flash, pushing me along. I could hear bullets thumping into the wall, and I stumbled along, my feet skating back and forth in my big, Catwoman boots. I'd definitely have blisters. The least of my problems.

CHAPTER 32

We ran away from the property and roads and all forms of civilisation, up a steep incline and deep into the jungle, crashing through foliage and tripping over tree roots. I wasn't capable of considering or caring about orange frogs or the variety of other things that could drop 20 men just by looking at them. I ran until my lungs burned and, finally, fell on my face onto the soft, wet ground, heaving and sucking in air. Joe tried to hoist me up but I smacked him away. 'Go,' I gasped. 'Leave me.'

And then, the sobs came, my whole body shaking. I curled into a ball on my side, wrapped my arms around my head and cried. After a while Joe's hand was on my shoulder, squeezing it. He lay next to me on his back, breathing hard. I finally sat up, wiping my face, and pulled the bag off my back, finding my bottle of water and holding it out to Joe.

'You first,' he said. 'Water won't be a problem.'

I took a drink and gave him the bottle. 'They're not coming after us,' I said. The pursuit had ended at the wall of the property.

'Too late in the day. They're afraid.'

'What are they afraid of?' Apart from the obvious horrors. I looked around.

'Christ, Erica.' He stared at me. 'What the *fuck* are you doing here?'

'I came to rescue you.'

He let out a laugh and then shook his head. 'I shouldn't laugh.'

'No, I don't think you should.'

'How did you get to Samson's? *Why* were you there, by the way?'

'Long story, Joe.' Where to start? 'How did Jack escape? I saw him from the house in the cage.'

'A woman. She shot the guards and took Jack.'

'What woman?' I said, but I already knew. 'Kitty!'

'Yeah. We met her in Seni.'

'You *met* her?'

Joe nodded, took another mouthful of water and handed it back.

'Jack tried to get information from her about Berringer,' he said.

'She didn't tell me. Why didn't she tell me?'

He shrugged.

'Did she give it to you?' I said. 'The information?'

'No, but she offered … something else.'

I knew exactly what Kitty would have offered Jack. 'Did he —'

'No.' Joe frowned at me. 'Of course not.'

The thought of him with Kitty!

'Why didn't she rescue you, too?' I said. 'Why did they leave you?'

'She had a gun. Jack tried to convince her to release me but she threatened us, saying she just wanted him.'

'That'd be bloody right,' I mumbled, remembering her plans for a life in the jungle with someone handsome and strong. 'Still, I'm surprised Jack left you.'

'He had no choice. Another guard came and she shot him. They had to take off. Jack would've come back.'

'And then there was the explosion.'

He looked at me, sceptical. 'Did you do that?'

'Me? No, I thought it was Kitty.'

Joe shook his head. 'We need to get going. Here,' he said, holding out a hand. 'Give me your boots.'

I unzipped them and when I pulled them off, the relief was instant.

Joe snapped off the heels and handed them back.

'I don't think I can wear these,' I said. 'They're way too big and they're killing me.' I inspected the puffy red circles on my heels.

'You'll have to.' He ripped the sleeves off his camouflage shirt. 'It's just pain, Erica. Put it out of your mind.' He handed me his shirt-sleeves. 'Here, wrap these around your feet.'

As I pulled the sleeves over my feet, tucking the ends under my toes, I thought about Kitty and how she'd made me change clothes with her. 'Bloody Kitty,' I muttered. Why did she do that? Of course. She wanted to wear the skimpy dress for Jack!

THE JUNGLE CHIRPED, squawked and sang around us. Buzzed, slithered and rustled. I kept looking around and behind me, but not for humans. Joe walked ahead slowly and I followed. I told him what had happened with Phil Collins and Dwayne from the plane and Rupert Berringer and Samson and Kitty. He kept looking at me over his shoulder with raised eyebrows, as though he might see something in my face that suggested I was making it all up.

I said, 'And guess who was at Samson's cocktail party?'

'Mick Jansen.'

'How did you know?'

'He's the reason Jack was captured in the first place. He teamed up with Berringer.'

'What, he just flew to Saint Sebastian and introduced himself?'

'In a way, yes. He'd done some time here with the air force; he knew people. It was the best way he could pay Jack back.'

Guilt engulfed me. If I'd never pointed the finger at Mick Jansen, this wouldn't have happened. 'How did you get caught, Joe?' I said.

'Trying to rescue Jack.' He shook his head, said, 'Idiot.'

As we walked, I kept running into the back of Joe and stepping on his shoes because I was so busy looking around for crawling things.

'Are you alright?' he said.

'No.'

'Can I do something?'

'Call for a helicopter? An Australian one, preferably.'

The Catwoman suit was like wearing a sauna. Lycra in the jungle. Good name for a song. But not good for my situation. I was really happy with my haircut right now.

Apart from the buzzing, chirping, squawking, etc there were cracking and crashing sounds way, way above us and I kept peering up, trying to see what it was.

Joe said it was falling branches. 'You need to keep an eye out,' he said.

'What's causing them to fall?'

'Something sitting on them.' He shrugged. 'Just nature doing its thing.'

'What would be sitting on the branches? What's up there?' I couldn't see anything. It was too dark and too far away.

'Monkeys, snakes —'

'Snakes in the trees?'

Joe stopped suddenly and I bounced off his back.

'Ow.'

He held up a hand. 'Ssh.'

And then I could hear what he was hearing. Another woman's chatter. A voice I'd come to know very well. I lunged forward, but Joe held me back.

'Wait!' he hissed and we listened. Joe whispered, 'Wait and see. Might not be them.' He pulled me into the shrubbery and we hid as Kitty's voice got closer.

I could hear her clearly.

'I think you will enjoy living in the jungle with me . . .'

Then I could see Jack and my heart flipped with happiness. But he stopped walking, turned and gripped Kitty's shoulders; she put her arms around his waist. Was he going to kiss her? I shot out of the trees and slammed into her. She hit the ground and I straddled her, slapping her face.

'You *bitch*!' I swung my arms, shouting, 'You. Knew. All. Along. He. Was. Alive!' After a while I stopped hitting Kitty and sat there on her, panting. Her arms covered her face. There was a gun on the ground nearby.

Behind me I heard Jack say, 'Were you followed?'

'No,' said Joe.

Jack said, 'Who's that?' and a pair of hands gripped my waist, lifted me in the air and stood me in front of him.

I flung myself at Jack, arms around his neck, sobbing into it. He was stiff. Didn't he know me? Finally, he pushed me away, held me at arm's length and looked into my face as I laughed and wiped the tears.

'Hi,' I said between hiccups.

'Oh, no.' He reeled back, releasing me like he'd been burnt. 'No, no, no, NO!'

I stepped forward, reaching a hand towards him. 'It's okay —'

But he covered his face with his hands, turned and walked away.

CHAPTER 33

Kitty tried to pick herself up off the ground, having been pummelled into it by me, and I gave her a warning glare. She crawled over to Joe and stood behind him. Joe picked up the gun and flung it deep into the jungle.

'Hey! That is Samson's,' she said.

Joe said, 'It's empty.'

'You Australian people are not fun,' said Kitty and stamped her foot. 'Not fun at all.'

But I wasn't listening because Jack was walking towards me again, eyes fixed on my face, looking angry, dismayed, horrified, lots of different things. But not happy.

He stood before me, fists on hips, breathing hard, staring at me with disbelief in those tell-tale eyes. I stayed silent, waiting to see what he'd do next. His gaze travelled up and down my body and he said to me, his voice hoarse and soft, barely a whisper, 'How am I going to get you out of here alive?'

'I —'

'How?'

I shook my head. 'It'll be okay —'

But he was walking away again.

I asked Joe if we should go after Jack, but he said no, that we should just wait. He said that Jack had had a big shock and needed to get his head around what had happened. I wasn't sure what big shock Joe was referring to. Getting captured? Kitty trying to bonk him? My hair? By the time Jack turned up again, Joe was sitting against a tree and Kitty was looking impatient, staying very close to Joe and saying again that she no longer liked Australian people because we are all so boring. I stood in a clearing because I figured that was the least likely place to find something crawly.

Ignoring me, Jack took Kitty by the arm and pulled her away from Joe. I made a move towards them — I hated seeing Jack touch her — but Joe stood, a hand out to stop me.

Jack said to Kitty, 'You know how to find Berringer's camp from here?'

She pouted. 'Perhaps.'

'You'll take me there.' He turned to Joe. 'Take Erica to the coast.'

Kitty clapped her hands.

I said, 'No!' and Joe moved in.

'What's the deal?' said Joe, quietly.

Jack said, 'I came here to do a job. I'm not leaving without finishing it.'

I said, 'You mean Rupert Berringer?'

Joe said, 'We'll find the camp. We don't need her.' He glanced at Kitty.

'No, we don't need her,' I threw into the ring.

Joe added, 'You've got no weapons.'

'He stole my knife,' Kitty complained.

There it was, strapped to Jack's arm.

Jack said, 'I'll have weapons when I get there.'

'No way, man,' said Joe.

The tension around us spiked. Jack and Joe faced off. I shuffled back. Kitty leaned in, thrilled, wallowing in the testosterone.

Jack said to Joe, his voice icy, 'You got a problem, soldier?'

'Yeah, I've got a problem.'

'Boys,' I said, but Jack held up a hand and my mouth snapped shut.

To Joe he said, 'That's a direct order.'

'This is bullshit,' said Joe. 'We need to discuss this.'

'Nothing to discuss.'

Joe stepped up to Jack and they were almost nose-to-nose. I squeezed between them, facing Jack, my hands on his chest. It was like standing between two brick walls. Two stubborn brick walls.

I said, 'I think I have a right to be part of this decision making.'

Jack glanced down at me, barely tilting his head. His glare changed to a small frown and it was enough to break the tension. Gripping my upper arms, he lifted me and placed me behind him, next to Kitty. That action put a slightly larger space between the boys, and probably bruises on my arms. Kitty scooted around to the other side of the boys.

Joe said, 'Erica's right. We should all discuss this.'

Jack turned away. 'No discussion, lieutenant. That's an order.'

Joe stormed off into the jungle.

I said to Jack, 'You're being a bully,' but he ignored me. Again.

THE FOUR OF us stood in a clearing. Joe with fingers splayed on his hips, looking at the ground; me with arms crossed, tapping my toe, mouth pursed like a cat's bum; Kitty looking as smug as the proverbial cream-eating puss.

'You know what to do,' said Jack. 'Joe, you hearing me?'

Joe nodded once. Poor guy.

Jack said to me, 'You'll do *exactly* what Joe tells you.'

I turned my head, looked away. He gently held my chin, forced me to look at him. And that's what we did for about ten seconds – just looked at each other. Even grim and grubby he was beautiful and my resolve to hate him forever melted a little. His lips parted and I wondered if he was going to say something. But instead he ran his thumb down my cheek; it was so swift and light it might have been an accident. He walked away, with Kitty trotting after him. She gave me a wave and I gave her the finger.

I called out, 'So, we'll see you at home?'

Jack lifted his hand, but didn't look back.

started crying again, more from anger than distress. And then I was angry with myself for being such a baby and I stamped my foot, picked up a rock and threw it. Joe stepped away. I huffed, turned my back on him and glared at a tree. Joe patted my shoulder, tentatively, said, 'I know how you feel.'

'Sorry, Joe.' I looked at him.

'It'll be alright,' he said. 'Jack knows what he's doing.' But he didn't sound very convinced.

I nodded. Let's pretend, I thought.

'What went wrong with the mission?' I said. 'What happened?'

'I'll tell you. Let's walk.'

And we did. Walked and talked. I told Joe I'd figured out that Rupert Berringer was their target and he told me more about our friend-turned-bad-guy Mick Jansen and his military history with Saint Sebastian – the reason he was recruited to Jack's team in the first place. Joe told me how Jansen managed to sabotage Jack's plans to find and kill Rupert Berringer, and led him into a trap. I didn't think Tupperware thievery necessarily deserved a death sentence, but maybe it had political ramifications that needed to be addressed. Like the JFK/Marilyn Monroe situation. But different. It occurred to me again that if I'd never pointed the finger at Mick Jansen, none of this would have happened.

'What about Samson?' I said. 'How did you end up prisoners at his place?'

'Samson and Berringer are friends.' Joe shrugged. 'Berringer didn't care if we lived or died. He just wanted us out of his way. So he gave us to Samson to show off to his mates.'

I remembered what Samson said, something like, *now that I've shown off my catch* . . . Jack and Joe had been on death row. I wondered if they knew.

Joe said, reading my thoughts, 'Don't know how long he would've kept us. I reckon we were croc food.' And while on that subject, 'We should eat.'

I looked around. 'What do we eat? Or will I be sorry I asked?'

'I'll fix something.'

Joe the fixer. He's the fixer back in Melbourne, too, doing what-ever needs to be done: bake a cake, mow the lawn, blow up a car, kill someone. But whatever Joe does, he's always got Jack's back. That's what he cares about most. And now he's been ordered to watch his friend walk away to certain death, probably, and he's supposed to be okay with that. Jack was being a bit of a bum-hole, and I realised suddenly that I had no intention of going back to Melbourne without him. God, I'd come this far. As if! And as if I was going to let Kitty get her grubby mitts on him. Now, I just needed to work out how to wangle that – escaping Joe and finding Jack again.

Joe appeared with two bananas. They weren't all nice and yellow and smooth like the ones at the IGA. Something had already nibbled on one of them.

'I saw some coconuts,' he said, handing me the un-nibbled banana. 'I'll get them.' And off he went again.

Off I went, too, banana in hand, retracing my steps, trying to remember which path Jack had taken, wondering how the hell I was going to find him and hoping like hell Joe would find me if I didn't.

.   .   .

BY THE TIME Joe did find me I was hysterical, awed by my own stupidity and gall. Imagine if I'd gotten completely lost in the jungle, never to be found again. Jack would carry on with his mission, perhaps succeeding, and then he'd fly home to Melbourne – falling asleep on the plane with a smile and visions of beer and fat steaks on the barbie, with his buddy, and me there ready to take him to bed and do pretty much anything he wanted – not realising in fact that his charges were still roaming the wilderness, one in a Catwoman suit with little but tampons in her survival kit, the other trying to find the stupid girl, knowing his buddy would kill him if he didn't.

The reason Joe found me was because I was making so much noise, what with an 80-denier cobweb wrapped around my head, its bulbous resident trapped against my temple, both of us scrabbling to be free of the other. It had dropped at my feet and fled into the jungle, and I'd stood there in shock for a full minute before the horror swarmed through me, causing my body to spasm as I swiped and slapped myself all over to be rid of any trace of the creature from the very deepest, darkest part of hell. I'd definitely need counselling for this.

When I saw Joe I threw myself at him, sobbing on his chest. He took me by the shoulders and shook me. 'What were you thinking?'

'I'm sorry. I'm sorry!'

But I think Joe wanted to cry, too. Cry with relief that he'd found me, because the consequences of him *not* finding me were not worth considering. He was worried, of course, that the spider had bitten me and whether or not it was deadly. But I didn't care because I thought death would be better than living with the memory of it, anyway, that it had been *on* me was a knowledge I'd have to bear for the rest of my life, its deadliness just an aside. It didn't bite me, though. I think it was too terrified. Maybe it had a heart attack. Maybe *it* would need counselling. Maybe I'd meet it in the shrink's waiting room. Maybe I needed to stop thinking about it.

Once I was able to make any kind of sense, Joe tried to turn me around, head back to where we'd been. Automatically, I tried to obey him, walk with him, but every part of my being was pulling me towards Jack. I felt sick. I stopped.

'Joe, I want to be with Jack. I've come too far, been through too much. I can't go home without him.'

'We can't,' he said, unconvincingly. 'Jack will kill me.' Joe probably would have liked me to have some kind of rank so he could say, 'That's an order, soldier.'

'We can. And of course he won't kill you. You're his best friend. Besides, I'll take the blame.'

I think he said a small prayer then, looking skyward, before shutting his eyes briefly and taking a big breath. Joe wanted to be with Jack, anyway, I knew that. He just needed a good enough excuse to disobey those direct orders, and I was giving him one. Erica kept running away, he could say.

'Alright,' he said. 'Let's go find Jack.'

I stepped aside. 'You first.'

WHEN THE RAIN falls in this region it comes like it's avenging something. Angry and hard, it threw itself at the forest canopy above, pounding through it, descending on us like a heavy, wet blanket. But at least we had water and Joe used a furled palm leaf to fill my bottle in about three seconds flat. I drank from that leaf until I couldn't drink any more.

'Watch for leeches,' Joe said as he led me through the waterfall that used to be a jungle.

'Leeches? Great. Let me see now. I need to watch out for snakes, crocs, wild boar, Jurassic-sized spiders and, of course, there's those cute orange frogs —'

'Erica.'

'Well, I'm sorry, but it'd be good if you didn't actually mention these things.' At least with the rain I could no longer hear the jungle moving around us. I couldn't hear anything, in fact, so imagine my surprise when I was grabbed from behind, hand over my mouth and knife at my throat.

'Jesus Christ!' said my captor, releasing me, pushing me away.

Joe spun, alert, horror on his face when he saw what had happened. That Jack had very nearly sliced my throat, which of course would have defeated the purpose of Joe being charged, by Jack, with my protection. Kitty was peering at us from behind a palm frond.

There was the expected argument between Jack and Joe that threatened to turn violent, but I ended that by stepping between them and announcing that it didn't matter what Jack said, I wasn't leaving him and he couldn't make me. Well, he probably could, but not without a big fuss from me, which could include some life-risking stupidity.

Kitty called out, 'I think you should go home, Erica Jewell!' and quickly hid again.

Joe said, 'Look, you take Erica and I'll find Berringer.'

Kitty said, 'No!'

Jack's anger was softened by that very generous offer. He said, 'You know I won't allow that.'

'And yet you expect me to,' said Joe.

They stared at each other for a few seconds more, and Jack hung his head.

I said again, 'I'm not leaving you, Jack. You don't know what I've been through to get here.'

He walked slowly away from us, eyes on the ground. Finally, he returned, and looked at me. 'If you're killed or hurt because of me —'

Kitty said, 'What if *I'm* killed or hurt? You would be unhappy, yes?'

'I'm the one likely to hurt you, Kitty,' he said without taking his eyes off me. 'Be quiet.'

I nearly poked my tongue at her. Instead I said to Jack, 'You were saying?'

He regarded the three of us in turn, taking his time. He looked at me for the longest time. 'Alright,' he said. 'Let's go home.' Kitty pouted and stamped her foot. I felt like clapping my hands. But I didn't because it was all such serious business, and there was of course the fact that we might not survive anyway.

CHAPTER 35

For the next little while, we seemed to head north. I mean vertically. We were going up, up, up a mountain and I thought we'd never finish climbing. Up and over the mountain to the coast, apparently, where we would dump Kitty, bribe our way onto a boat headed for Indonesia, and hopefully squeeze in a romantic holiday in Bali before flying home to safety.

We walked in single file: Jack first, Kitty, me, then Joe. These were Jack's orders. Kitty walked easily in her stilettos, sometimes trotting to keep up with Jack. She'd asked for her Catwoman suit back and I'd said, 'Over my dead body.'

And she'd replied, 'I think death would suit you, Erica Jewell.'

I hoped the mozzies were munching on her bare legs. They were leaving me well and truly alone. My feet were much better, wrapped in Joe's sleeves, and I was happy to not be wearing those stilettos. I wondered if Jack had offered to snap off Kitty's heels, like Joe did for me.

The rain had stopped and we pushed our way through the jungle just as the sunlight tried to infiltrate the canopy. It succeeded in spots here and there, the light catching droplets of water hanging off the foliage so they looked like tiny light globes.

Jack wasn't being nice to me; I think he was angry that his mission had been ruined. I felt pretty shitty about that. He probably wouldn't be alive if I hadn't come. Kitty wouldn't have thought to rescue Jack if it weren't for me. When I tried to talk to him he just told me to be quiet. We were all silent for a long time. I kept my eyes on Kitty's back, imagining taking the knife off Jack's arm and stabbing her, but then retracting that thought because, well, yuk.

After a while I asked if I was allowed to talk yet, and Jack said, 'No.'

So I said to Joe, 'Don't you want to know how I found you guys?'

'You already told me,' said Joe, quietly.

'But I haven't told Jack.'

I peered over my shoulder at Joe and he gave me a look, and I thought I should probably stop being deliberately annoying. With that in mind, I said to Jack's back, 'I want you to know, I nearly had to have sex with a truck driver for you.' But there was no comment or change in his pace.

Kitty piped up. 'What about Rupert Berringer? Did you like having sex with him, Erica Jewell?'

Jack stopped walking and the rest of us had no choice but to stop as well. He stood there, stiff as a rod.

Joe said, 'Shut up, Kitty.'

Jack turned. We were all still and silent, watching him. He said to Kitty but pointed at me, '*This* is the Australian girl you said he was with?'

Kitty nodded, enthusiastically.

I was so horrified by the suggestion of it my voice was barely a whisper when I said, 'I didn't.'

I wasn't sure what I was seeing in those eyes of his – certainly murderous intentions, but for whom? Joe pushed past us and, with an arm around Jack's shoulders, kept him walking ahead. It was a good ten minutes before Joe removed himself as buffer boy and resumed his place behind me, but not before giving Kitty and me another disapproving look, just like the look I get from my mother. At least Joe didn't tsk.

At our next resting place, Jack took my compass and disappeared into the trees. I grabbed that opportunity to ask Joe, 'Why is he so angry?'

Joe sighed, said, 'So many terrible things have happened and he feels responsible for all of it. The mission failed, he got captured, then I got captured, and now you're here with your life in danger, and that's his fault. He can't deal with it.'

'But it's *not* his fault. He didn't ask me to come.'

'You don't understand. Where would you be if you'd never met Jack? You'd be safe, Erica.' He sighed and I sat there, considering all that.

I STUMBLED ALONG, struggling, but didn't dare fall behind. My legs ached, my feet burned, and I wanted to curl up on the ground, anywhere, and sleep. Joe would occasionally support my elbow, helping me when I tripped, which was often, but Jack behaved pretty much as though I wasn't there. He wore my bag on his back; it was really a handbag but I didn't tell him that. Maybe I should.

Kitty seemed to have no problem in her stilettos, but I noticed she was starting to slow. At one stage I'd elbowed my way past her, shoving her into the bushes, and pushed my hand into Jack's, forcing him to acknowledge me and help me along. Which he did, in a way, by letting me hold his hand. He even squeezed it. A bit. And let go after a minute, making me go back to my place in the line.

Along the way Jack and Joe had collected stuff we could eat – some scrawny bananas and a coconut. They'd also filled their pockets with red berries that we weren't allowed to eat yet. Jack had squeezed berry juice onto the inside of his elbow; Joe explained that if it didn't cause burning or itching, he'd put some juice on his lip and see what happened. I thought we should just feed the berries to Kitty and see if she carked it. The boys also found some protein. Jack peeled back the bark of a tree and there it was, in the form of squirming grubs. Big, fat, juicy ones. Watching that thing explode in Jack's mouth when he bit down on it, I knew I'd never kiss him again. Kitty ate the grubs, too, probably just for the fun of it or to impress the boys. I stood there gagging, quite comfortable with the idea of death by starvation.

'Didn't Samson feed you guys?'

Jack snapped, 'We weren't in a hotel, Erica.'

The light faded. There was a sudden and terrible screaming, screeching noise, like ten million birds, insects, all kinds of creatures in pain. The noise grew and grew until it was terrifying and deafening. Kitty explained, loudly, about the locals and their belief that the animal spirits wake at dusk and hunt, which is why we weren't pursued back at Samson's. 'They're more afraid of the animal spirits than anything,' she said.

'When will it stop?' I said.

'Soon.'

We arrived at a small clearing flanked by two trees, each with a girth the size of a small house. Jack indicated we should sit and ride out the noise, which we did, in a circle with our backs to each other, and I put my hands over my ears. The cacophony lasted about 20 minutes, and died as quickly as it started. It was getting dark. Jack said we'd make camp there, although we had nothing but the wet clothes on our backs, my bag with its meagre contents – contents suitable for a party, not the jungle – and a knife, so I didn't know what he intended us to make camp with. A tent would be nice, I thought. And one of those showers you hang off a tree. And a port-a-loo.

Jack said to Joe, 'I'll take first watch. Get Erica sorted.'

I said, 'What about her?' pointing at Kitty.

'She's with me,' said Jack. Kitty squealed and blew me a kiss and I gave her daggers. She skipped over to Jack and took his arm as though they were off somewhere together. He shook her off and pointed to a fat old tree root. 'Sit there,' he said and she sat, pouting.

I said to Joe, 'What am I supposed to do?'

'Sleep,' he said, peering up the trunk of the ancient tree with branches as round and thick as my father's stomach. 'With me.'

'Oh.' I looked around. 'On the ground?'

'No. There's snakes, bugs, wild boar —'

'Oh.' I let out a whimper. 'Aren't there snakes in the trees, too?'

'Yeah.'

I waited for the 'but', but it wasn't forthcoming.

Joe climbed to a low branch of the tree and held his hand down to me. I gripped his rock-hard forearm with both hands and he hoisted me up. I straddled the gnarly old branch. 'Now what?'

Joe squatted with his back against the main trunk, knees spread. There was another, slightly higher branch next to him, and he leaned against it. He beckoned, inviting me in. 'Here.'

I shuffled closer.

He said, 'Lean on me.'

I moved in, crouching between his legs, and curled up against him, my head on his chest. He put his arms and legs around me and rested his chin on my head. I peeked down at Jack and caught him watching us. He looked away.

Darkness fell on the jungle in an instant.

I closed my eyes, imagining that Joe's body was a bubble of armour all around me, keeping out the scaries. But then I felt claustrophobic at the thought of being trapped in a bubble of armour and I opened my eyes, sucking in air. I tried again. I was in a bubble of flywire, the tough stuff that burglars can't get through. That was better. I could breathe, although the hard flywire wasn't very comfortable.

I whispered, 'What if something comes to check us out? Something like a snake, for example?'

'We're not being threatening,' he said. 'No reason for anything to attack us if we're still.'

An image of a snake slithering over me in my sleep flashed through my mind, but I let it go with a shudder, conjuring up the more pleasant thoughts I have when I don't like what's happening in my world. Usually when my boss wants time with me. Or when I'm at my mother's. And the thoughts I turn to are about Jack being naked. I didn't like him any more, but he still looked good. I wondered if he still looked good naked. I couldn't see why not. He seemed to have lost weight. Maybe I should give that a go — getting locked in a cage for a few days. I could sell the idea to Hollywood and make a fortune.

Thinking about Jack naked made snake thoughts come back and I pressed into Joe. I tried meditation. Being in the moment, *aware* of the moment, and after a few minutes I couldn't help being aware of the intimacy of this moment, and I was embarrassed, trying not to think about being intimate with Joe. If I'd felt in any real danger it would have been different. But I didn't feel in danger because Jack was down there and Joe was my armour. I felt safe, in fact. And intimate with Joe.

'This is really weird,' I said, tensing up.

He huffed a laugh. 'It's survival. Don't think about it.'

Survival. I can do that. I can survive. But that small issue aside, I did wish it were Jack sitting here with his arms folded around me, hard and strong, warm and sensual. Joe's arms were . . . dutiful. They weren't holding me, exactly; they were just there. And effective enough, I supposed. I felt warm. And I did feel safe.

'You haven't said anything about my hair,' I said.

There was a long silence, then, 'There's been other stuff to think about.'

'So? What do you think?'

Pause. 'It's nice.'

'Don't lie.'

'No, really, I like it.'

'Goodnight, Joe.'

'Night, Erica.' He gave me a little squeeze.

It was agonising, of course, spending hours like that with the jungle seething around us. I couldn't possibly have gotten closer to Joe. He slept for a while and I felt his arms relax. I pulled them tighter and held them in place. I tried every trick to avoid thinking about it — the horror of our situation — and finally gave up, deciding that what would be would be, and this seemed to work. I nodded off for a while, curled up against Joe's great expanse of a chest.

I was woken by Joe gently pushing me away.

'What's happening?' I said, sleepy.

'Changing guard,' he said. 'Hold on.'

I shuffled along the branch to give Joe room to move. He dropped to the ground. I heard rather than saw him and Jack whispering to each other, and then Jack was with me in Joe's spot. Well, I assumed it was him. Couldn't see a thing.

Jack said, 'Come here,' and I flopped against him, squirming to get as close as I could. He kissed the top of my head, squeezed me tight, and I snuggled closer, pressing my face into his neck. But it wasn't the pleasant experience I was hoping for.

'Pee-ew,' I said. 'You smell.'

'You don't smell so great either,' he murmured. He sounded a bit friendlier. At least he was talking to me.

'That's my insect repellent.'

'It's not insect repellent.'

'Yes, it is.'

'No, it's not. I saw it in your bag. It's Indonesian perfume and it's disgusting.'

Well, at least it kept the mozzies away, and that's all I cared about here in the jungle, in survival mode. Although, this survival business didn't seem too difficult with Jack and Joe around. He tightened his arms around me, and I didn't mind the smell of him so much. I wriggled closer still and felt his chest expand and relax as he sighed, very deeply.

My idea of a perfect world is one where Jack and I are permanently entwined, disentangling ourselves only to perform necessary human functions. But I was so uncomfortable in that tree that I was happy when the first glow of sunrise lightened the canopy above. At least I was, until I saw what was sitting there on the branch, looking at us.

I threw myself forward, screaming so loudly the monkey shot up the tree and Jack and I fell out of it. Poor Jack thumped onto the ground and I landed on him. I stood quickly, staring into the treetops as Jack staggered to his feet, saying, 'Jesus Christ, Erica —'

'There was a monkey!'

He sighed, looking up, and stretched his back.

CHAPTER 36

Daylight didn't come easily to this place. I squinted into the treetops to see what else was up there, hearing the movement but not seeing anything. I walked away from the tree in case the monkey jumped on me. Or did something else on me.

Kitty was propped on the same root, leaning against a tree. Asleep by the look of it, though I don't know how she could have slept through my noisy performance. I felt a twang of sympathy. She looked so tiny there. And vulnerable. I wondered if things had crawled on her in the night. She probably would have liked it.

Jack and Joe were talking quietly.

I patted down my sticky-out hair. Kitty woke and yawned. She stretched out her limbs and smiled at me. I tried to feel angry with her, but the anger was gone. I found myself smiling back.

Joe disappeared and Jack emptied the contents of my bag onto the ground. He tossed the water bottle to Kitty and she drank from it.

'What are you doing?' I said to him.

'Seeing what we've got that we can use.'

There was a small box of tampons. He opened the box and seemed to be counting. I wasn't sure how etiquette and good manners were supposed to work in survival situations. Maybe I shouldn't be getting snippy about privacy and women's handbags here, now?

Joe appeared with two long pieces of bamboo. Jack put my bag aside and started whittling the bamboo with the knife to make spears. This made me think of food. I wondered if there were any berries left. Or coconuts. My stomach rumbled and I looked up in the trees. I hadn't been able to even consider food since watching the grub eating.

Joe had disappeared again and Kitty went with him. Jack sat with his knife and the bamboo.

'Are you going to talk to me?' I said, and he looked at me. There was a tiny glimmer of warmth in his eyes. Really tiny.

'What about?' he said and our eyes held for a few seconds. He resumed his whittling and silence.

I needed the toilet, preferably one that was a long way from everyone else. I walked to the edge of the clearing.

'Where are you going?' he said, without looking up.

'The toilet, obviously. We can't all just pee on a tree, you know.'

'Don't go too far.'

But I *did* go too far because I didn't want any noises or smells wafting back to our camp, and I realised my mistake when I was zipping up Catwoman and glanced up to see what was making the grunting noise nearby. A boar stood only a few metres away. It had tusks. Nasty, pointy ones. And I thought it could probably outrun me. I could feel a wail building in my throat. The boar pawed the ground, lowered its head, snorting.

I backed away.

The boar charged.

Something whizzed past my head as I turned to run and saw Jack standing there, legs astride. I clawed at him, trying to climb his body, and he clamped his hand over my mouth, said, 'Ssh!'

He set me aside, pulling the knife out of its sheath. The boar was making a hell of a racket with Jack's spear in it. I turned away, hands over my ears and eyes squeezed shut. Poor thing.

A minute later Jack strode past me, carrying his spear and the dead creature slung over his shoulder. I followed him back to our campsite, checking behind me every two seconds. He let the boar drop.

I noticed a solitary tampon on the ground. I picked it up, said, 'What did you do with the box?'

'Didn't touch it.' He looked around, and up in the trees. 'The monkeys are thieving bastards.'

I peered up, searching. The light created pale shapes in the canopy, but it was still dark up there. I could hear rather than see movement in the trees.

'Are they vicious? The monkeys?' I shivered, no longer liking this survival business. Like I'd ever liked it anyway.

'No. Just annoying.' He looked at me then as though I reminded him of the monkeys. He said, 'Did you need them?'

'The tampons? No. Well, not unless we're still here in a few days.'

He nodded and I suddenly had high hopes about his reason for asking. In fact, my curiosity burned and I couldn't help saying, with fluttering eyelashes, 'Why did you want to know?'

'Know what?'

'If I need the tampons.'

'Because I'm concerned about your personal needs, Erica. Don't get excited.'

'Excited?' I squeaked. 'God, you . . . bloody . . . arrogant . . .'

But he moved into the trees, ignoring me, and I hated him again.

I stomped around in circles for a minute, but all the rustling sounds made me feel nervous and that killed my anger. So instead of stomping, I moved cautiously, peering into the jungle. Jack reappeared with a coconut. He drilled a hole in it with his knife and handed it to me. At last, something that resembled real food. Food you could get in the supermarket. I drank.

'Where's Joe?' I said.

'Hunting for breakfast.'

'Oh. Can I do something?'

'Not unless you know how to skin a boar.'

He pulled off his camouflage shirt and T-shirt. 'I'm going for a wash,' he said.

'A wash? Where?'

But he was already striding off into the jungle again.

I sat and looked around. Piggy was watching me. I covered its face with a palm frond. I wondered where Joe was and was amused when I thought about the fact that he has to organise breakfast for Jack in Melbourne as well. I heard more rustling in the trees and I jumped up, squinting into the darkness. Maybe the monkeys could be vicious if they wanted something enough. And there might be other boars and various critters around. And maybe even human critters, who were scarier than any other life forms in Saint Sebastian. I took the empty water bottle and went looking for Jack.

CHAPTER 37

I found Kitty first. She was watching Jack, who seemed to be naked, standing with his back to us in the middle of the gently bubbling brook, just like the one in *Bambi*, scrubbing his body with his fingers.

Jack's boots were there and his other clothes that were folded neatly on the ground next to the spear, which had a small crayfish stuck on the end of it. The water was quite a bit deeper than a brook, actually; deep enough to cover his lower region. I stood at the water's edge, admiring him, remembering my jungle dream and the naked water scene – before the crocodile part – which looked remarkably like this one. Except in my dream, and all related fantasies, Jack is very, very nice to me.

Kitty started wriggling out of her dress. I put a hand on her arm, said, 'Unless you want that spear through your heart, you'll leave right now.'

She stared at me, trying to determine if I meant it. Sure I meant it. I was in survival mode.

Jack was now watching us. Kitty gave him a long look, sighed a huge sigh, turned and left.

Jack gazed at me and I returned it. Except for the moment or two when my eyes wandered low to where the waterline sat just below his navel. I watched him, wondering what he was thinking. He stood there motionless, watching me.

He crooked his finger. 'Come here.'

I looked up and down the creek, along the banks, and at the cray on Jack's spear. I shook my head. 'I don't think so.' He looked very tempting, though, with his gleaming torso, now much cleaner. Yes, he was beautiful in all his naked glory. And yes, he was thinner, but it suited him. His muscles were even more pronounced.

'I want to wash that stinking perfume off you,' he said.

I crossed my arms, lifted my chin. 'You're not being nice and I don't like you.'

'I know.' He beckoned again. 'But come here, anyway.'

I hesitated, looking for excuses, when all I really wanted to do was dive on him. 'There might be piranha,' I said.

He shook his head, slowly.

'Crocodiles?'

'Then you shouldn't be standing there.'

I looked around in case there was a crocodile, and when I turned back, Jack was wading slowly towards me. The water grew shallower, revealing more of him with every step.

'What the hell,' I muttered and stripped off all my clothes in two seconds flat. I splashed into the water, not caring about the sub-zero temperature. When I was close, Jack reached for my hand and pulled me gently into deeper water. We stood gazing at each other as he washed my shoulders, lightly running his hands down my back and my arms. I shivered, but not from the cold.

'Whatever possessed you to come here?' he said, softly. 'I can only assume it was some kind of temporary insanity.'

'You left without saying goodbye.'

He was still for a moment, staring into my face, his hands on my arms.

'Look,' I said, 'I came to rescue you because no one else would.'

'It's not your place to make that call.'

'And it's not your place to tell me I can't. It's my life, Jack. I'll do what I like with it, and I chose to come here, so suck it up.'

He stood a bit taller, stiffer, wanting to remind me who's in charge. Captain or Major or Colonel Jones, whatever he was. But his shoulders drooped as he shook his head. 'I just can't get past the danger you've put yourself in.'

'Danger schmanger.'

He pursed his lips, exasperated.

Looking into his face, a face I'd thought I might never see again, I felt suddenly shy. My heart was filling with a sentiment I didn't really understand. Love, I suppose; a kind of love I'd never known before, and then I remembered telling Jack that I loved him. I dropped my gaze and pretended to look for things in his chest hair, like monkeys do, but he put a finger under my chin, tilting my face up, forcing me to look at him.

'I didn't mean what I said,' I lied, blushing and hot despite the icy water. 'The night before you left. I didn't mean it, not like that. I was drunk.'

He smiled. 'You were shitfaced.'

'Is that why . . . is that why you didn't say goodbye? Because of what I said?'

'I told you I was leaving the next day.'

'You didn't!'

'I did. When I was tucking you into bed.'

'Oh.' I let that knowledge sink in. So he hadn't just run away without a word. 'You could've sent me a text.'

'No phones on this mission.'

'But Joe called me.'

He shrugged. 'Used someone else's, I suppose.'

I wanted to suggest that Jack could have called me from someone else's phone, too, but I let it go. Standing there naked in a creek, living out one of my fantasies, I decided there could be a better time to bring it up.

I went to say something else but he shushed me with a finger to my lips, said, 'If we make it out of here alive —'

'Yes?'

He blew out his breath, mouth still tight.

I said, 'Do you like my hair?'

'No.' He pulled me close, arm around my waist. He bent his head and breathed deeply.

'Better,' he whispered, and softly kissed my neck, my face.

'I'm not kissing you,' I said. 'You ate those disgusting grubs.'

He took my face in his hands and kissed me anyway, said, 'Are you taking malaria tablets?'

'Kate gave me some.'

'Kate knows?'

'Yes.'

'Don't tell Joe.'

He kissed me deeply then and I felt the overwhelming rightness of it, being naked with Jack Jones. Even though his face was prickly and he didn't taste very nice. But I probably didn't taste very nice either.

I felt a sting on my thigh then, like a mosquito bite, and I stepped back, feeling down my leg. 'What was that?'

'Water snake?' he said, with a very small smile.

'No, it's … OMIGOD I'VE GOT A LEECH ON MY LEG!' I thrashed my way back to shore, shot out of the creek and hopped around, flapping my arms as Jack emerged from the water and inspected the tiny black sucker.

I bounced up and down. 'Yuk, yuk, *yukky!*'

Joe and Kitty appeared from the bushes. Joe said, 'What happ— Oh.' He turned his back, but Kitty watched on.

'I've got a leech!'

Jack hissed, 'Hold still and be quiet.'

'Get it off. Get it off. GET IT OFF!'

'Can I do something?' Joe called over his shoulder.

Kitty was staring at Jack, magnificent in his nakedness, and I shouted at her, 'Stop looking!'

Jack said to Joe, 'Can you get Erica's bag?'

Joe left. Kitty stayed.

'Get it off, Jack, *please* get it off.'

'Be *quiet*, Erica.' He was getting dressed. 'You'll have to wait. It's hooked on.'

I bounced around with my hands over my eyes so I couldn't see it.

Kitty said, 'It's alright, Erica. Leeches are very useful.'

I heard Joe say, 'Here.'

I moved modestly behind Jack, peering at Joe, but he was covering his eyes with one hand and tossing the bag with the other. He left. But Kitty was still standing there, smiling.

Jack found my insect repellent and gave the leech a quick, short squirt. It dropped off straight away.

'See,' I said. 'I told you it's insect repellent.'

'That stuff would repel anything.' He wrinkled his nose. 'But don't use it again.'

'Why not?'

'Your scent, Erica. We don't want to be found by the guys with guns, remember?' He scooped up some water and rubbed where he'd sprayed the perfume, muttering, 'Although you're making enough noise for the entire population of Sebastian to hear us anyway.'

My leg bled where the leech had attached. Blood poured out in a thin, steady stream.

'I'm bleeding!'

'Don't worry, it's normal. It'll stop soon.'

I pressed a tissue onto the wound and got dressed, thinking with regret about what I'd just missed out on because of that stupid leech.

CHAPTER 38

When Jack and I got back to our campsite, Joe and Kitty were munching on thin slices of raw snake. The part they weren't eating was on the ground, guts spilling out of it. Joe tossed a big egg to Jack. He punctured the end of it with the spear and sucked the contents out. Then pulled apart the raw crayfish and handed bits around. The poor dead boar was gone. Ran away in case someone decided to munch on its hindquarters?

'Where's the boar?' I said.

'Fish food,' said Joe, who'd been cleaning up Jack's mess, as usual.

On the verge of not coping, I decided to meditate, aiming for an out-of-body experience, which usually never works, but this time it did. Even though I was still there in body, my spirit seemed to have removed itself from the scene and was watching from afar. So calm.

I sat on a rock. Joe tossed me a coconut.

'What kind of egg was that?' I said, knocking the coconut on the rock between my legs.

Jack gave Joe a quizzical look. 'Anaconda?' He took my coconut and smashed it apart.

'There are anacondas here?' my floating spirit asked, interested.

'It's a croc egg,' said Joe. 'You want one?'

189

My out-of-body experience was coming to a close, I could tell. So I thought I should focus on pleasant things as I scraped the coconut flesh with my teeth. Pleasant thoughts. Jack naked. Looking good. And he was being much friendlier now, and that was nice. I thought that if we'd finished what we started in the water, he'd be even friendlier. But those lustful thoughts ended too soon because something hit my shoulder with a fair force. I let out a yelp, jumped up, dropped the coconut. Was it some creature? Jack, Joe and Kitty were searching the treetops.

'What was that?' I said, looking around.

'Berries,' said Jack. 'Monkeys threw them.'

I scanned the trees above before I sat again and picked up the coconut. I hadn't taken another bite when a huge pile of berries rained down on my head. I jumped up again and glared skywards. I could hear screeching now, which sounded like hysterical laughter. And the monkeys weren't the only ones laughing.

I glowered at the boys. 'Did they throw berries at you?'

Kitty tittered behind her hand.

Joe shook his head, trying hard not to laugh. 'Sorry, Erica.'

I stood in front of Jack. 'Swap places?'

'No way.'

I kicked his shin.

He stood, laughing still, and I sat in his spot. He moved to where I'd been and it was my turn to smirk. We waited, gazing into the treetops. Nothing happened. I focused on the coconut. And then, something dropped right on my head, bounced and landed in my lap. It was one of my tampons. I could feel the anger brewing, and then the rest of the tampons fell like hail around me.

I jumped up, scooped up the tampons and berries and hurled them back into the trees. 'You stupid, bloody, shitty MONKEYS!'

Jack was trying to tell me to be quiet, but it's hard to do that and wet your pants laughing at the same time. I screeched and chucked stuff that sailed only a few metres into the air before dropping all around us again. So I started throwing the stuff at the boys and Kitty, yelling at them to stop laughing, and they held up their hands, ducking their heads. Finally, Jack stood and held me in a bear hug to stop the onslaught. And the noise.

I blubbered into his chest, 'Stupid monkeys, stupid jungle, stupid everything! *I hate my hair!*' I cried and cried and Jack's arms were tight around me, but he was shaking with silent laughter. I shoved him and punched his chest. 'And I hate you!'

He looked a bit surprised at that but pulled me close again and this time murmured in my ear, 'Sorry.' He stroked my hair and told me it would all be alright and finally, with great shuddering breaths, I calmed down and pushed away, wiping my face and looking around. While I was having my tantrum, Joe had erased our campsite and collected our stuff, including the scattered tampons. We were ready to go.

As we walked – same line-up as before: Jack, Kitty, Me, Joe; boys with their spears – a familiar but weirdly out-of-place noise came from my bag. I pulled it off Jack's back, finding my phone at the bottom. And so it seemed that the Universe, which had a fabulous sense of humour, and which had worked so hard to get me to Saint Sebastian, had now aligned all its planets in such a way as to ensure I had a mobile phone signal in the jungle when my mother wanted to chat. She wanted to Facetime, and in my speedy move to hang up on her, I accidentally answered, and her face loomed large in the screen.

'Erica! Do I have to be the one who always calls you?'

I glanced at the others, who were gaping at me.

'Hi, Mum.' I smiled, holding the phone close so she wouldn't see my hair or anything else, like Jack and Joe looking like soldiers. 'Sorry, I've been so busy.'

Jack picked up my bag, shaking his head, and we all kept walking, me at the back now.

'What *are* you wearing?' she said. 'It doesn't look very colourful.'

I fixed a smile on my face and gave her a brief glimpse of Catwoman. 'It's, um, a new style of bathers.'

'But you're completely covered.'

'Yes, so I don't get skin cancer.'

Kitty called out, 'Hello, Mrs Erica Jewell!'

'Who's that?' said Mum.

'Oh, just …' some hooker 'a girl we met.'

'And what have you done to your hair? It looks like you've chopped it all off! I don't expect Jack likes it.'

'Jack thinks it's nice, Mum.'

'Where are you now?' she said. 'Is Jack with you? Are you walking?'

'Ah, yes, he's here and we've just finished breakfast.' I looked around. 'We're walking to … our bungalow. I mean, Jack's bungalow. And then I'll go to my bungalow. It's very lush here, like a jungle.' I flashed the phone around so she could get a glimpse of the lushness.

'What part of Bali are you in?'

'Um, Singapore.'

'Let me talk to Jack.'

Jack stopped walking, stiff as a rod. He turned, glared at me, disbelieving. But Mum wanted to talk to him and I couldn't think of a single reason why she shouldn't. So I held the phone out, pointing it at the ground. The disbelief deepened – his jaw grew even slacker. He slowly reached out for the phone.

I said, 'It's Facetime. So you can *see* each other.' Hint, hint, stop scowling, Jack!

He rearranged his expression, took the phone, holding it close, and continued to walk ahead at a much faster pace. I heard him say, 'Mrs Jewell, you're looking well,' and then just murmuring.

I looked at Joe and shrugged, and again he was trying not to laugh. Joe was having a ball here, surviving in the jungle. When Jack handed back the phone, I was delighted to see that they'd hung up. I was busting to ask what they'd talked about, but I didn't dare.

'Maybe we could call for help,' I said, checking out my phone. 'I'm surprised we've got a signal here.'

'We don't need to make calls, Erica,' said Jack. 'You've made enough noise for the entire north coast of Australia to hear us.'

I lowered my voice. 'Well, we could call the local police.'

'You mean the Chief of Police? Best mate of the bloke who had me strung up in a tree for almost a week?'

'Are you serious?'

Kitty said, 'I know him. He is my client.'

Jack said, 'Turn off the phone.'

CHAPTER 39

Jack stopped abruptly and held up his hand.

I said, 'What —'

He clamped his hand over my mouth and pulled me roughly into the bushes, dragging me deep into the thick foliage. Joe did the same with Kitty. I struggled to prise his fingers off my nose so I could draw breath. We crouched there, and while my body shook, his was still and silent. I could hear footsteps. Lots of them. From within the jungle we watched a line of men walk past, Rupert Berringer in the lead. I stopped breathing. The blood crashed through my head. Jack was so still it was like being held by a rock. I could feel his heartbeat against my back. Slow and steady, unlike mine.

After Berringer, there was a bunch of those warrior guys, maybe ten of them, and Mick Jansen brought up the rear. I glanced sideways at Kitty, being held by Joe in the same way as Jack held me. I wondered if she wanted to call out to her buddies. She wasn't struggling, but I saw her eyes widen as she watched the procession. Jansen was maybe 20 metres away from us, but the boys hung on, not moving for another few minutes.

Jack turned my head so I could see his face. He released his hand, his expression warning, finger to his lips. He slid the knife slowly from the holster on his arm and held the point at Kitty's throat. She blinked at Jack, nodded.

Joe moved his hand. Kitty was quiet. Jack jerked his head, indicating for us to follow as he led the way slowly, silently out of the bushes and back onto the narrow track. We were so quiet that the jungle noises seemed even more pronounced. I could hear the birds and insects, the monkeys hooting, branches crashing above us. I glanced up, and stopped walking as I took in the strange sight, not understanding for a moment what it was. By the time I registered the writhing, plummeting snake, seeking in vain something to grab, it was too late. The snake landed on my shoulders, flung itself around my neck, and as Joe was trying to wrestle it off me I screamed loud enough to wake the dead in Melbourne Cemetery.

Next thing that happened was the distant shouting. Joe threw the snake. Jack said, 'Move!' and lunged at me, grabbing my wrist. 'Split up,' he said, and Joe turned off the track, taking Kitty with him. Jack pushed me along.

I gasped, 'I'm sorry.'

'Run!'

We charged through a clearing, and then I was falling. Not falling, flying! Flying through the air, straight up like a reverse bungy, screaming my lungs out.

I SWUNG IN THE NET, around and around, back and forth, a tangle of limbs. I could see Jack by a tree with his knife, trying to release the rope. But running feet were coming, lots of them.

Men charged into the clearing and surrounded Jack. He spun where he stood, knife and spear up, but dropped the weapons in an instant and put his hands on his head. The reason for his sudden surrender walked casually into the clearing, gun aimed at me.

Rupert Berringer said, 'Ah, there you are, my love. Funny little minx, running off like that. Fancy a game of chasey, eh?'

My mouth started to water. Motion sickness and fear. I fought it down.

As I swung I had snapshots of the scene beneath me. More men emerged from the jungle carrying bows and arrows and with machine guns slung over their shoulders. Berringer was smiling. 'Jones, old chap, we meet again. How nice.'

Mick Jansen walked up to Jack and punched him in the stomach.

Jack doubled over and two guys jerked him upright. Jansen punched him in the face and Jack's head snapped back.

I screamed, 'No!'

Then something was poking me. Something sharp. I squealed. Whoever was doing it was laughing. I squirmed, twisted in the net. It was one of Berringer's men, jabbing me with Jack's spear.

I cried, 'Make him stop.'

Jack yelled, 'Back off.'

Without taking his smiling eyes off me, Berringer lowered his gun slightly and fired. It was a muffled pop, not loud at all, almost harmless sounding. I heard a thud. Jack said, 'Jesus Christ', and I twisted to try to see what had happened. The other men were backing away. And then I could see. Under me was the poking man, dead on the ground in a growing pool of red. I whimpered and swung in the net.

Berringer said something in Portuguese, raising his voice. He addressed Jack. 'I've told them to treat my girlfriend with respect. You don't mind sharing, do you, old chap? We've been through so much together already.'

Jack said, 'Sharing what, Berringer?'

Berringer looked up at me, smiling, enjoying himself.

'Help yourself,' said Jack.

What?

'Not very loyal of you, Jones. If she were mine,' he laughed, 'which she now is, I wouldn't let another man near her.'

Jack shrugged. 'She's nothing to me.'

'Really,' said Berringer. 'We'll see.'

Jansen said, 'He's lying,' and punched Jack again.

Berringer said to Jansen, 'Leave it, man. Don't want to have to drag him.' He spoke again to the men and they lowered my net. I hit the ground harder than I would have liked, the net fell open around me and I stood, staggered.

Berringer holstered his gun and stepped over the net, pulling me into a tight hug. 'Ah, I've missed you, poppet.' He kissed me on the mouth. I clenched my lips together, pushed him away and slapped his face.

He slapped me back, limp-wristed, mimicking me.

I raised my hand again, this time with a fist.

Berringer laughed.

Jack said, 'Erica, don't.'

I lowered my arm and took a couple of steps towards Jack, but he shook his head, his expression grim.

'Where's your friend?' Berringer asked Jack.

'Which one?'

Berringer smiled.

Jack said, 'He's dead.'

'Really? How?'

'Took a bullet last night.'

'Don't believe him,' said Jansen.

One of the men tied Jack's hands while Berringer stood with his arm around me, giving me the occasional, comforting squeeze. His gun was drawn again, jammed against my temple. A lesson for anyone wanting to know how to be sweet and vile at the same time.

We all walked in single file through the jungle, one man ahead of Berringer and me, the rest following. I kept checking over my shoulder for Jack, but couldn't see past the guy behind. When there was room for us to walk side-by-side, Rupert held my hand as though we were on a romantic stroll through the Botanic Gardens. I kept squirming, trying to free my hand, but there was little point. I wondered where Joe was.

Berringer called out, 'Tell her what a failure you are, Jones. Tell her how much smarter I am. She'll enjoy spending time with a real man, I think.'

Jack called back, 'You're a cheat, a murderer and a traitor, Berringer.'

'Cheat,' echoed Berringer and laughed. 'How do you come to that conclusion, Jones?'

'You're no better than your lacky Jansen.'

'Oh, but I am. Much, much better in every way.'

WE WALKED FOR A LONG TIME, a couple of hours, I reckoned, mostly downhill. Rupert helped me along, gentleman that he was. I felt frightened and I was so tired and hungry, but more than that, 'I'm thirsty,' I said.

'I've got a nice Australian shiraz back at the camp.'

FINALLY, we arrived. Rupert's camp. There were some tents. Rupert got Jack sorted first. Had him tied to a tree. The men scattered. Some lay on the ground to rest. Jansen hovered around Jack. He looked like he wanted an excuse to keep beating him. Jack gave him one.

'You know what we do to scum like you, Jansen?' said Jack.

He punched Jack in the stomach.

Rupert called out, 'For Christ's sake, man. Leave him.'

Jansen stalked off and into a small tent.

I asked for water and Rupert sent one of the men to fetch it for me. Then, in the middle of the camp, with everyone watching, Rupert pushed his hand through my hair. 'I like your hair,' he said.

At last.

Jack called out, 'Let her go, Berringer. She's done nothing to you.'

Even if Berringer did release me, where did Jack think I'd go? Into the jungle to get taken by all those creatures of the darkness? Or stumble around forever, avoiding orange frogs, thinking how nice it'd be to be Rupie's girlfriend instead?

'Really, Jones,' said Rupert. 'You have no idea. This little minx has been following me all around Sebastian. I think she's in love with me.' He turned me to face Jack and stood behind me, his arms around my waist, kissing my neck. He fondled my breasts and I pushed his hands away. He laughed, and ushered me to his tent.

Jack roared, screaming abuse at Rupert Berringer. I watched over my shoulder as men rushed at Jack to subdue him; I think he'd nearly broken out of his ropes.

Rupert's was a big tent with a table, two chairs, a double bed, a leather armchair and a heavy-looking chest in a corner with a monkey sitting on it, scratching its testicles. I stood in the middle of the tent, looking for a way out, but pretty much resigned myself to the fact that I was going to have sex with my captor. This theme was getting a bit too familiar – Jack's enemies forcing themselves on me. Why didn't they just torture Jack if they wanted to piss him off? Why couldn't they have sex with *him* instead? Rupert shooed Cheeta off the chest and opened it, taking out a long, blue, sequined dress.

'You're a cross-dresser?' I said before I could stop myself.

He thought that was hilarious. 'Oh, no, sweet one. This is for you to wear.'

'It's not really my colour.'

'We're having a romantic lunch – just you and me.'

Lovely. Just lovely.

CHAPTER 40

The table and chairs from Rupert's tent were carried outside and Rupert left me in privacy while I changed into the sequined dress. More strangely gentlemanly behaviour, considering his obvious plans for me. The dress was not my usual get-up for a casual lunch in the jungle, but who was I to argue? As I emerged from the tent, Rupert gasped and rushed to hold a chair out for me.

'God, but you're beautiful,' he said.

What drugs was he taking? I took the offered seat and he kissed my shoulder, and sat opposite me. On the table was some bottled water and that Australian Shiraz I'd been promised (a nice one from Coonawarra). Jack was still tied to the tree, across the clearing, watching us.

I indicated the wine. 'Did you steal that?'

'Of course. I refuse to pay fifty dollars for one bottle of wine.'

'So you just took it.'

'That winery should be pleased I've chosen theirs. There are plenty of good Australian reds to steal.' He laughed.

There was a lot of smiling and laughing. I guess when everybody and everything was at your disposal, there was plenty to smile about. And sometimes things to laugh about. Rupert checked under the table.

'Let me see your feet,' he said.

'Okaaay.' I held them out. As well as the dress, Rupert had made me wear a pair of second-hand, glittery shoes. Unlike Kitty's boots, they were a perfect fit and divinely comfortable, even though they had quite high heels.

Rupert admired them, made me get up and walk around. He sighed.

Jack called out across the clearing, 'You *will* die today, Berringer.'

'At your hand, Jones? You and whose army?' He roared laughing.

A warrior guy with topknot hair brought some coconuts and put them in front of us. My stomach rumbled and I was reminded vaguely of *Gilligan's Island*, with MaryAnn making coconut cream pies. I loved that funny old show. The guy lifted the lid on the coconuts with a flourish. And inside … not coconut cream or anything that resembled something edible. I stared at the steaming lump. I knew what it was, even though I'd never seen one before – well, not like this, in front of me.

'Monkey brain,' said Rupert. 'Served slightly rare. Delicious and fresh as a daisy.'

Daisy? I wondered about Cheeta.

He informed me, 'Usually the brain is served in the monkey itself, but I'm an animal lover, obviously, and I don't like to see them hurt.'

Obviously. 'Why don't you become a vegetarian?' I thought about the poking guy's brains that were now splattered around the jungle. Not a lover of *all* animals.

'We humans are carnivores. We can't help it.' He pointed at my meal. 'Eat.'

'Um. I'm not hungry. I had snake for breakfast.'

'You need your strength. Eat up.'

'No, really, you can have it.' I pushed the coconut away.

He pushed it back. 'Eat.'

Should I pretend to faint?

Rupert leaned across the table with his knife and fork, ready to feed me like a little kid.

'I *will* vomit if you make me eat that,' I said.

He seemed to consider that for a moment, nodded once, and tucked in while I watched, fighting down bile. I sipped my wine.

'What's your background?' I asked him. 'What did you do before turning to a life of crime?'

He dabbed at the corner of his mouth with a napkin. 'I don't like conversations with women.' He considered me. 'But I'm prepared to try it. For you.' He sat back, folded his napkin on his lap. 'I'm both business and military trained.'

'Well, why steal all that stuff?' I said. 'What are you trying to prove? Who do you want to hurt?'

'I'm not *trying* to hurt anyone, my love. I'm simply building an empire.'

'So, it's just about money?'

'Power. One day I'll rule the world.'

'The whole world?'

'Uh-huh.'

'Can't you be happy with just one country?' I said. 'But not mine,' I added, quickly.

'I'll start with this one. And then yours, probably.'

I looked at the warriors, mostly loafing around. They were tough-looking but didn't seem very competent.

Rupert clapped his hands, pushed his empty coconut shell aside and turned his chair to face the clearing. 'Let the games begin!' he called out.

Games?

Four men with guns surrounded Jack while two others untied him. He walked slowly, suspiciously, to the middle of the clearing. I tried to stand, but a warrior guy pushed me back onto my chair. The guys with guns kept close to Jack.

A small line of dried blood ran from the corner of his mouth, the result of Jansen's earlier punch.

'Who's first?' said Rupert.

Warrior guys rushed in.

Rupert yelled something, then muttered, 'Idiots.'

The men all backed away except one. He waved a machete around.

I clamped my hands over my eyes. After a minute I looked. Jack had claimed the machete and the guy was on his back on the ground, the blade at his throat, Jack's foot on his chest. I clapped my hands.

Rupert called out, 'This is boring, people. Next!'

The men lined up like they were in a queue at McDonalds. Jack beat them all, but he was getting tired. Each fight took longer to win. Eventually, Jansen stepped into the ring, saying, 'I want him while he can still stand.'

'You should be ashamed of yourself!' I called out.

Jack stripped off his camouflage shirt. He and Jansen were now dressed the same. Camouflage pants and black T-shirts. Jack held up his hands, beckoning. 'Come on.' His fists clenched and his biceps bulged. Awesome. But, shit, Jansen was so much younger.

Jansen moved towards Jack. Through the blood on his face I could see Jack smile. They started fighting. I put my face back in my hands; couldn't watch. I could hear the punches and the grunts. Men cheered. Rupert yelled, 'Woo!' and clapped his hands. It went on for so long. Minutes passed. I put my hands over my ears. Squeezed my eyes shut.

And then, the cheers changed to jeers. I had to look. Jack was on one knee behind Jansen, his arm around Jansen's throat. Jansen was half-lying on the ground, kicking out, struggling, clawing at Jack's arm, but then he was still. Jack kept up the hold, his face contorted.

Rupert shouted, 'Let him go!'

Jack held on.

Rupert stood. The men moved in, looking to Rupert for instructions.

Rupert strode across the clearing as Jack released Jansen, stood and wiped his arm across his bleeding face. His chest heaved.

Rupert said, 'Good God, Jones, I think you've killed him.'

Killed him? I sat, relieved and horrified.

Berringer put a finger to Jansen's neck. 'He'll live,' he announced, and two guards dragged Jansen to his tent. Rupert laughed. 'Anyone else?' He looked around.

I jumped out of my seat, hitched up my dress and rushed over to Jack. He pushed me back.

Rupert took my arm and I fisted his shirt, pleading, 'Let him go now. *Please* let him go. He's proved himself. I'll do whatever you want.'

'Quiet, Erica,' Jack said and staggered. He dropped to the ground and sat there.

I said again, looking down at Jack, 'I'll do whatever you want.'

I HAD mixed feelings when I saw Cheeta alive and kicking in Rupert's tent. I was pleased that he wasn't lunch, but I wasn't very happy that the monkey was masturbating, and he seemed to like that we were watching. Outside, Jack was tied to the tree again. I'd cast a quick look over my shoulder as Rupert ushered me away. Jack was slumped forward. Rupert couldn't decide what to do with him, Jack having unexpectedly survived all the beatings so far.

'And now,' Rupert said, 'alone at last.'

'Does Cheeta have to be here?'

'The monkey? He likes to watch.'

Surprise, surprise.

Rupert sat in his armchair, waved his hand. 'Walk around for me.'

'What?'

'Walk around. Let me see how you walk in those shoes.'

I did it. Walked in small circles.

'Lift the dress a bit, so I can see. Yes, that's it.'

He knelt at my feet. 'Lift your foot,' he said.

I did it. He slid the shoe off, then very gently on again.

'Yes. Perfect,' he said. 'Absolutely perfect. I want you to wear nothing but the shoes.'

He slipped the straps off my shoulders. I pushed him away. He moved back in. I held up my hands to stop him. He swiped them away and kept doing that as my hands kept springing back. Finally, he held my wrists together in one hand.

'Be still, my sweet,' he said. He tugged the dress down until it was pooled at my feet. He looked me up and down. Under the dress I was wearing a bra and G-string – sexy, but I'd had them on a couple of days. Shame I wasn't still wearing the insect repellent.

'Now sit on the bed,' he said.

'No.'

His smile vanished.

'Ah, I need to go to the toilet. I'm busting.'

He slapped my face. It stung. And shocked me. Tears threatened.

Rupert walked me backwards to the bed. Over his shoulder I saw Cheeta playing with something – something other than his genitals. He was tossing a brown thing from one hand to the other. Rupert pushed me onto the bed and knelt at my feet again, admiring them. I kept an eye on the monkey. There was something not right about what it was doing. Cheeta threw the thing. I watched it fly in an arc, right for us, and as it got closer I could see it was taking a very specific shape. I knew that shape but my brain wouldn't form the word. The thing landed next to me. I remembered now what it was called. *Tarantula*. Easily the size of my hand. It reared up at me.

There was a moment of shocked stillness before I started screaming. I screamed and screamed, flinging my arms around, scrambling away from the spider. Somehow in all my panic I flicked it and it landed on Berringer's face. He fell sideways, grunting. The spider hung on. Rupert threw himself backwards. Knocked over the chair. Stood. Staggered. Toppled like a felled tree, crashing to the ground next to the chest. I sat there staring at Rupert as he stared back at me. What would he do now? The spider dashed across his shoulder and disappeared behind him. I waited. Did the spider bite Rupert? Would he be angry and make me pay? But he did nothing. Just kept staring.

I stood warily, watching him, and walked slowly across the tent, looking out for spidey, watching for Rupert to make a move. There was a trickle of blood from his temple. He'd hit his head on the corner of the chest? I stood close and leaned in, felt for a pulse in his neck, all the time expecting him to make a grab for me. I pressed my fingers to his throat, holding my breath, waiting.

No pulse. Rupert Berringer was dead.

I fell back, hand over my mouth. Cheeta and I locked eyes. He dashed out of the tent. Would he tell? Of course he wouldn't. Why weren't men rushing in here with all the noise we'd been making, screaming and carrying on? Okay, they're the noises they'd be expecting.

So, Rupert Berringer was dead, the monkey had run away, there was an Amazonian spider on the loose and a dozen armed warriors waiting outside. What the hell should I do now?

CHAPTER 41

I paced around the tent in my blue sequined gown and sparkly shoes. First things first. Rupert's gun was in his shoulder holster and I took it, avoiding touching him and keeping an eye out for gigantor. I checked the safety thing, like Jack had taught me. Where to hide it? If I got back into Catwoman, I couldn't. So I stayed in the long dress, but put my boots back on, and pushed the gun down one of them. The benefits of having skinny legs.

I wondered where the spider was. Rupert probably would have died from its bite, anyway. And it would be a horrible, slow death, so in a way I did him a favour. Yes, that's it. I didn't kill Rupert Berringer. I did him a favour.

Jack and I were goners, as good as dead when the others discovered what I'd done, especially Jansen. Rupert was probably the only one with a reason for keeping us alive. What to do? Charge out of the tent, shooting randomly? How long would I live if I did that – two seconds? Besides, I might shoot Jack by accident. I could slip out the back and wait in the jungle like Rambo. Wait for just the right moment to make my move. But there was no back door. Where was Joe?

I spent a minute doing deep breathing, eyes open and watchful for arachnid boy, focusing on being calm, avoiding looking at Rupert. I tip-toed out of the tent, trying to adopt a look of submission and shame.

Some of Rupert's men were pacing slowly around, looking bored. A couple of them were sitting under trees, asleep by the look of it. Couldn't see Jansen. Unconscious in his tent? Dead, maybe. I hoped so. I shouldn't think like that.

Jack was still tied to the tree. When he saw me, he hung his head, so defeated and exhausted.

The men started to show interest as I strolled across the clearing. One of them walked up to me, speaking harshly, but I had no idea what he was saying.

'Ssh. He's sleeping,' I whispered, my finger to my lips. I put my hands against my cheek to show sleeping and pointed to Rupert's tent.

'Ah,' he said and backed away. He pointed his gun at me and indicated I should sit on a rock and wait.

'Rupert said we could go,' I tried, but he poked me with the gun.

Jack and I looked at each other. His bloody face was so battered. One eye was closed.

He said, 'Are you alright?'

I nodded. 'Are you?'

'Yes.'

I said, 'Have you seen Jansen again?'

He hesitated, said, 'No. Why?'

I asked, loudly, looking around, 'Do any of you guys speak English?'

They all looked at me.

'Rupert's monkey likes to masturbate.'

Blank expressions. Jack said, 'What are you doing?'

I ignored him, speaking to the crowd, 'Cheeta killed your boss.'

Nothing. I looked at Jack. He was staring at me.

'Yes,' I said, still loudly, but with eyes now on Jack. 'It's true. And I've got something of his under my dress.' I looked around again. Most of the blokes had gone back to ignoring me. A couple seemed amused. But mostly, they were bored. Perhaps they often had to sit around while Rupert had afternoon sex with some hooker or hostage and then slept for a couple of hours.

'I need to know what you've got,' said Jack. 'But careful. There are words they'll understand.'

'I've got his … nug.'

He blinked with his one good eye. 'Has it still got the silencer?'

'Yes.' I knew that because I remembered a silencer makes a gun longer, and Rupert's was much longer than my own at home.

'Okay,' he said. He took a deep breath. 'I need to think.'

I waited. After a minute, Jack said in a conversational way, 'Can you kill one of these guys?'

'Sure.' Could I? Geez.

'If you can't, we're dead. You know that, don't you?'

'I know.' Talk about pressure.

The man next to me was now either suspicious or sick of the sound of my voice, because he pushed me and said something that I interpreted as, 'Shut the fuck up, woman.'

Jack said, 'Say you need the toilet.'

The man shouted at Jack.

'Kill the guy who goes with you.'

The man stood, threatening.

'Then shoot my ropes and throw me his gun.' He reminded me, 'You're a good shot.'

The man approached Jack, screaming at him.

'Then run as fast as you can, get away.'

The man swung his machine gun and smashed Jack across the stomach. Jack roared and I stood, shouting, 'I need the toilet!'

The bashing guy moved towards me. I crossed my legs, bounced up and down, pointed to the bushes. 'Toilet?'

As we walked, the guy shoving me along, I tried to remember my gun training with Jack. I'd only ever fired one in a shooting range, but I was good at it. A natural, Jack had said. So that's what I'll do now, I thought. Pretend I'm shooting a paper target. One that looks like a man. An awful man who wants to kill me.

When we got out of sight of the camp, I stopped, put my hand up and pointed to a bush, indicating that I didn't want him to follow. He seemed to think that was fine. He watched me and, as I went to lift my dress, I glared at him. 'I'll tell Rupert you were perving.'

He got the message and turned his back.

I squatted behind a bush and peed (I really did need to go), slipped the gun from my boot and sucked in three deep breaths. *I'm a trained killer, I'm a trained killer.* I stood.

The man's machine gun was slung over his shoulder and he was lighting a cigarette. He was a paper target, that was all. A moving one.

I aimed at his head and held that position. But I waited too long. Doubt filtered through the bravado and froze me. I knew that I could no sooner shoot someone than fly to the moon. The man turned and saw me standing there, feet apart, arms straight and the gun aimed shakily at his face. The cigarette fell from his mouth as he snatched at his swinging machine gun, fumbling with it. The knowledge that I was two seconds away from death caused all thought, reason and doubt to leave me. With eyes shut tight I squeezed the trigger. But nothing happened. The safety was on! I squatted and tried to release it, but my hands were trembling violently now and I could barely hold the gun let alone use it. Why hadn't the guy shot me? Why was there just silence out there?

I dared to peek. Joe was there! He was bent over the guy, who was unmoving on the ground with a spear in his back. I squeaked and ran to Joe.

He held a finger to his lips as he plucked the guy's machine gun from under him.

He whispered, 'We don't have much time.'

'Jack wanted me to shoot his ropes and throw the guy's gun to him.'

'I'll do it.' He pointed to a tree. 'Hide there. I'll come back for you.'

As I hid behind the tree, my heart hammering, I heard a burst of machine gun fire. Then shouting. Lots of shouting and guns. What was happening? I tried to see. Couldn't. Still holding Rupert's gun, I released the safety and crept towards the camp, staying low. When I got close, I peered through the green, saw men charging and shooting. Jack and Joe running, diving, firing. Berringer's men falling. And then Jack was behind a tree, not far from me. Behind him I saw a man raise his gun. I stood. Jack saw me. A scream stuck in my throat and I ran, both arms straight out, gun wobbling. Jack started racing for me. The man shifted his aim. Jack or me. Or him. I fired. My arms jerked up. The man fell back. Jack's eyes were fixed on something behind me. He screamed, 'No!', his hand raised, *stop!* I looked around; saw a warrior man with his bow drawn. And then I was in Jack's arms, clutched against his chest. He twisted, roared, and dropped like a sack of potatoes at my feet.

Joe yelled, 'Hold your fire! Hold your fire!' and raced across the clearing to us, hands empty, arms up in surrender. I looked in my hand for the gun, but it was gone.

CHAPTER 42

*J*ack writhed on the ground, an arrow in his leg, and I
crouched next to him. We were surrounded by warriors
and more were coming. Joe was there with his hands on
his head, a prisoner again. One man's voice rose above all others:
Samson. He moved through the crowd, shoving men out of the way as
he came to stand over us. His face was as contorted with anger as
Jack's was with pain.

Jack roared as he pulled the arrow out of his leg. 'Mother*fucker.*'

It should have been in me.

A WARRIOR HELD me at a distance with a gun at my head while Joe's
and Jack's hands were tied behind them. We were marched in single
file – Jack limping, head hanging – for about twenty minutes, and
arrived at a narrow dirt road where two cars were parked. Samson's
black Hummer and a white van. I saw Samson up ahead, getting into
his Hummer. And Kitty! What was she doing there? She wasn't a
prisoner; she was sitting in the passenger seat of Samson's car. I
didn't imagine he'd be too thrilled about his British mate being
wasted. We'd watched him barge into Berringer's tent and out again,

face red, fury silencing him. I wondered if Jansen was alive and where he was.

In the back of the van, I was seated nearest the door with Joe next to me and Jack on his other side. I went to scramble over Joe so I could sit between them. The guys opposite made a fuss about it, poking me and shouting and causing Jack and Joe to shout back, and I yelled, 'Cool it!'

I pointed to the space between Jack and Joe and said, 'Okay?' They didn't seem to object so I sat there. One of the warriors was quiet in the corner, holding a rag to his shoulder. He was the one I'd shot. He gave me a dirty look. Fair enough. Everyone calmed down.

I leaned into Jack and looked up at him. He kissed my forehead and I thought that if we were still on the run in the jungle, I wouldn't mind eating grubs and raw snake so much.

I whispered, 'Are you alright?' His pants were soaked in blood.

He smiled, but he was very pale. I put my hand on his forehead. Clammy.

'Do you want me to take a look?' I indicated the leg wound.

'No. Nothing you can do.' He looked down at me, 'How are you?'

'I'm fine.' I wriggled closer.

Jack said, 'You were amazing back there.'

'Really?'

'Yes.'

Well. How about that? I sighed, content.

'You were very brave,' said Jack, and Joe agreed. 'But . . . '

'But what?'

He shook his head. 'You were so upset about that leech . . . '

'I know.' I shrugged. 'Ask me if I'd rather face death by firing squad or go swimming with leeches.' I shuddered. 'That's a no brainer. And let's not talk about spiders.' They chuckled and I thought about Gigantor in Rupert's tent. Maybe it'd found its way into Mick Jansen's tent. I hoped so.

The men opposite were scowling. They probably wanted us to be shitting ourselves. And that would have been more appropriate, but I'd be buggered if I was going to give them the satisfaction.

I glanced up at Jack; he was looking at me strangely.

'What?' I said.

'In the tent —'

'Rupert? No, he didn't touch me. Didn't get a chance.'

'Then, how?'

I smiled. I knew I shouldn't be smiling, but I did, anyway. Maybe something had switched in my brain. The switch a person needs to turn them into a cold-hearted killer. I told them what happened. I looked from Jack to Joe. They were staring at me.

'The world's well rid of him,' said Joe.

'He wanted to rule the world,' I said.

Joe scoffed.

'But I can't understand how he planned on using Tupperware to do it.'

The boys glanced at each other over the top of my head.

Jack said, 'You do realise my mission was to kill that bastard.'

'Yeah, sorry to spoil your fun.'

'No need to be sorry,' said Jack. 'Just don't tell anyone.'

'Deal. But I do quite like having something over you. I could bribe you into doing all sorts of things for me.'

'Name it.'

I liked thinking about being home again, safe and sound, bribing Jack. I felt happy. Not thinking about what happened before or what was about to happen soon. Just being in the moment with Jack and Joe, thinking about being home again.

We drove on in silence, our death convoy. I wondered if prisoners of war throughout history had spent time like this. Being content and at peace in the time before dying, laughing even. I bet they had. I rested my head on Jack's shoulder and he leaned more heavily against me. I could tell he wasn't feeling too well with the arrow wound.

'Tell me,' I whispered, 'what would you two be doing right now if I wasn't with you?' I looked from Jack to Joe and they looked at each other over the top of my head. I said, 'You wouldn't be sitting in this van, would you?'

'No,' said Jack.

'I'm holding you back.'

'No. If it weren't for you, Joe and I would be dead. We're a team, Erica.'

IT WAS dark when we arrived at Samson's. As I stumbled out of the van I saw Kitty standing by the Hummer. She gave me a little wave. I gave her a pleading look. Please help?

In a group we walked to the back of the house where I'd climbed the fence the day before. *Just* the day before, but it felt like forever ago. The grounds were floodlit. Jack and Joe were shoved along, their hands tied at their backs, Jack stumbling and falling, fresh blood staining his pants. I tried to go to him, but I was pushed along. We walked past the section of fence I'd climbed and were led along to the part where creatures other than patrolling men and dogs lurked.

'Samson,' said Jack, his voice weak. 'Let her go, please.'

I could hear voices, people talking and shouting, but I was much too busy watching the crocodiles, wondering why Samson had brought us to see them. I stared from Jack to Joe to Samson. Kitty looked worried.

Samson was pointing at the gate in the fence and shouting at one of his men. The man walked to the gate and wrestled with the padlock. And that's when I wet my pants. I felt it running down my legs and I could hear someone whimpering. It might have been me.

I was aware of a sound near the house and everyone turned to look. It was the crunching of car tyres on gravel. A beautiful sound. *Any* sound that distracted Samson from his current mission was a beautiful sound.

Out of a silver SUV stepped Emeline. At first I was beyond thrilled to see her, but then I worried what she'd think when she saw me there at her husband's house. She marched down the sloping ground towards us, murder in her eyes but not for me. I looked at Samson, and his expression reminded me of my own when I'd first seen the crocs.

His voice suddenly had honey in it, and his face was lit with false happiness. He opened his arms, welcoming his wife as he strode towards her. Kitty hid behind one of Samson's men.

Emeline's eyes widened when she took in the scene, in particular the sight of me in my blue sequined dress.

'Erica. My dear friend.'

Her friend! Oh, thank God. 'Emeline. How lovely.' I laughed hysterically.

'What are you doing here, at my dreadful husband's house?' She pointed at Jack and Joe. 'And who are these men?' She turned to her husband. 'Samson!'

He jumped and said something gushy. She pointed at Jack and Joe, speaking angrily. Samson spoke back, his voice regaining some of its authority. They snapped at each other in Portuguese.

Emeline spotted Kitty and narrowed her eyes. 'Do I know you?' she said, and Kitty shrugged, trying to look nonchalant.

Samson was then talking loudly and smiling again, waving his arms around. Trying to push his wife towards the house.

But Emeline batted him away, pointed at Kitty, said to me, 'Is this your friend?'

'My friend?' I said. 'No, never seen her before.' I felt only slightly guilty about that. I didn't want Emeline thinking I was in any way associated with her husband's philandering, and besides, it seemed entirely possible that Kitty would actually enjoy watching me play with the crocodiles. She'd probably like to get in there herself for a game of tag.

Emeline scanned the scene, and if I hadn't been so terrified I would have been fascinated, watching all the big tough guys turn to jelly in front of her.

'Is this your man?' Emeline asked me, pointing to Joe.

'Ah, er, they both are.'

'I beg your pardon?'

'I mean, um . . . ' I pointed to Jack. 'Him.' I hoped Jack didn't think I'd been going around telling people he was 'my man', even though I had.

'And what about this one?' she said, pointing to Joe again.

'Our friend.'

She inspected them again. 'Will he be the best man at your wedding?'

I could feel the blush crawling up my neck and I didn't dare look at Jack. 'Oh, yes, definitely,' I said.

Emeline turned to Samson again and shouted at him. He shouted back this time, and they argued. Samson stormed away towards the house.

Emeline said to me, 'You can go, Erica.'

I squealed and ran to hug her. 'Thank you, thank you!'

'But,' she said, 'I am sorry. My husband will not let the men go and I cannot ask him to do that.'

'No! Oh, please. Jack needs a doctor. *Please*, Emeline.'

She shook her head. 'I am sorry.'

I looked at Jack and Joe in dismay. Jack nodded at me. *Go.* He looked so unwell, swaying where he stood, leaning on Joe.

Emeline said, 'Now, my dear, would you like a lift back to town? I saw a car at the bottom of the driveway. Do you have someone waiting?'

I nodded dumbly, shook my head, said in a small voice, 'I don't know.' But I didn't want to sit in a car with Emeline, making small talk. 'Yes, I think someone's waiting.' I wanted to stay with Jack and Joe, but I knew there was little point. I was of no use to the boys if I was stuck in a cage with them. As long as one of us was free, there was a chance of getting help. But what could I do? Who could help? We were back where we started, but now I had a whole lot more information than I had when I first arrived. Now I *knew* there was no point my being here in Saint Sebastian.

A tear ran down my face. 'Thank you, Emeline, very much. It was so nice of you to help us.'

'I'm sorry I cannot help you more, my dear, but I will ask my husband not to kill your men.' Her eyes cut to Kitty and Kitty shrank away. 'He will want to please me, I think.' She put her arm around me and gave me a squeeze. 'Perhaps I can persuade him to wait a day or two.'

I stared over my shoulder at Jack. He was watching me walk away, nodding. I couldn't help it. I broke away from Emeline and ran to Jack, throwing myself at him, sobbing into his neck. His mouth was at my ear. 'Go straight to the airport. Do you hear?'

'No, no, I'm not leaving you.'

He tried to shoulder me away, but I hung on. And then two pairs of hands pulled me back and pushed me to Emeline. She was waiting for me. I walked past her and didn't look back.

.   .   .

I WALKED down Samson's driveway, numb, wondering if I could take comfort in the fact that I'd at least seen Jack again before he died. Or would I have been better off at home, hearing about it by phone? There was rustling in the trees just near me. Kitty jumped out, shocking me out of my trance. I let out a yell.

'Hello, Erica Jewell,' she said. 'Surprise!'

'What are you doing?'

'Oh,' she said, 'they told me to go. I think Samson's men knew it wasn't good to keep me around. Emeline might have remembered where she's seen me before.' Kitty gave me a wink.

I walked on. Kitty hummed and skipped. I wiped my nose on my arm and wondered how I was going to get back to town. I thought I could probably just start walking and see what happened. Kitty might have some ideas. Maybe she had some clients nearby she could ask for a lift. Actually, I couldn't give a shit what happened. But as we approached the bottom of the driveway, I saw Phil's ute sitting there in exactly the same spot it had been when he dropped us off yesterday. Surely he hadn't waited?

I peered in the window. He swigged his beer. I opened the door and got in, sliding to the centre.

'Have you been waiting here since yesterday?' I said, as Kitty got in next to me and slammed the door.

'Nah. Had to work,' he said.

'Well, thanks for coming back, Phil.' I looked at all the stubbies on the floor at my feet. There didn't seem to be any full ones left.

Phil pulled out slowly and hit his high beams.

We'd been driving about twenty minutes, and I was lost in depressed thought, when Phil said, 'Where's ya bloke?'

I glanced at Kitty. She looked happy, her head back on the head-rest, eyes closed, wind blowing her hair. I wanted whatever she was having.

'It was a bit of a mess,' I said with a big sigh. In monotone I explained what had happened.

Kitty was staring at me.

'What?' I said to her.

'*You* killed Rupert Berringer?'

'It was an accident.'

'Oh, you are the most exciting friend I have ever had.' She laughed brightly.

I remembered then that Berringer was a friend of Phil's and I glanced at him. But his expression hadn't changed – maybe he'd heard about Rupert. Maybe he didn't mind. Maybe he could take over Rupert's Tupperware business or something. Anyway, who cares? Emotion came over me again. A wave of it. A tsunami.

'I don't know what I'm going to do now,' I said, and started to cry.

Phil accelerated a bit and Kitty threw her arms around me.

'*Mon ami – Kitty est là pour vous aider, n'ayez pas peur!*'

I said, in response to whatever she'd just said, 'Thanks, Kitty, but I'll take it from here.'

CHAPTER 44

In the morning, I was on the stool next to Phil at the Bum Crack Bar as soon as it opened. I sipped my beer, waffling on and on about the past couple of days, trying to work out how I could have been more useful, blaming myself for everything that had gone wrong.

'You know what I mean?' I said to Phil but he was staring, fearful, at the fridge. Its reflection contained two warrior guys who were storming in my direction. I spun on my stool as they stood either side of me. They said nothing, just picked me up, stool and all, and walked me out of the bar.

Good, I thought. They're going to kill me. I hoped they'd get it over with quickly. I was marched outside and across the road to where Samson's black Hummer was waiting, its engine running. I felt a grain of hope he was delivering Jack and Joe, but that hope dissolved as the door was opened and I was thrown into the back, next to Samson.

He said something snarly to the men and they shut the door, leaving us alone. I was trembling, but his angry scowl vanished in a flash and he gazed at me with a look of . . . what was it? Desperation?

'You must help me!' he said.

'Ah . . .'

'My wife, she is furious.'

'Um . . .'

'I am afraid she will speak to her family about me.'

'Her family?'

'Yes. They are wealthy, powerful people. Oh, I have been so stupid. How could I think spending time with that *whore* . . .'

'Kitty?'

'You must help me,' he said again, this time clutching my arm. 'You! You have killed my source. They won't work now, with Berringer gone.' He shoved me away, not too hard.

'Who won't work?'

'The thieves. The only chance I had to please her.'

'Emeline?'

'Of course.'

'What can I do?' Was there a chance here? A chance for Jack and Joe?

Samson reached behind him and produced a yellow, dog-eared brochure. I tried to see what it was, but he was clutching it to his chest. He eventually held it out to me.

'This is Emeline's,' he said. 'She got it in Australia many years ago and has kept it always. She asks me every time I travel to your country to bring her some of these items, and I have tried, but it is impossible.'

'I think you have to have a party,' I said, gazing in wonder at the ancient Tupperware catalogue. 'Have you tried ordering online? Or eBay?'

'Oh, yes. But the thieves in this country . . . bah! My order will not pass customs here. Someone steals it always.'

I was pretty surprised about that. Not the thievery, but the cheek of the thieves. 'Um, do they know who they're stealing from?'

He waved his hand in disgust and stared out the window, biting down on his knuckle.

'May I?' I said and held out my hand. He gave me the catalogue, with some hesitation. I opened it.

He flipped the pages to a black and white picture of my mother's special edition lettuce crisper.

'Here.' He pointed. 'This is the one she wants.'

'I can get this for you,' I said.

He leaned closer. 'You can? This exact one?'

'Ah, yes.'

'I would forever be in your debt.'

Samson was so happy. Hope welled inside me. I was afraid to ask, but, 'My friends … are they still alive?'

He turned his head. Looked out the window again. 'Yes,' he said, quietly. 'They are alive.'

'If I get this for you, you'll release them?'

His head snapped back and his body jerked away from me, as though I'd bitten him. 'No! No, I would lose the respect of my colleagues.'

'We'd be very discreet. No one would know. You could tell them you threw us all to the crocodiles. I can get us out of here without anyone knowing. Truly, I can. I will get this lettuce crisper for Emeline!'

Samson regarded me, frowning. He was considering it, I knew.

'Oh, *please*,' I said. And then, in a smaller voice, my eyes cast down, 'I'll do anything.'

I looked up at him and I knew he knew I meant *anything*. And I would have. Of course. If it would save my friends' lives.

He shook his head. 'No. If my wife found out …' He shuddered. 'Very well,' he said. 'You will get this item and I will release your friends.'

'Oh, thank you. Thank you! And,' I ventured, 'you'll take care of them until I can bring the item?'

'Yes, yes,' he waved his hand again. 'Now, you must go. And you must show fear when you leave this vehicle.'

'No worries. I can do that,' I said.

I pushed open the door, setting my expression to one of terror. I even fell from the car onto my hands and knees, letting out a sob. I stood and ran across the road, wailing.

Everyone from the Bum Crack Bar was at the doors and windows, watching me. Even Phil had left his stool. I rushed past them all, shouting, 'I need a phone, I need a phone!'

I knew Lucy would be sleeping – it was late morning in Melbourne and she'd been working night shift. She wouldn't be happy, but that wasn't my problem. My problem was that she didn't pick up the phone. I had no choice but to call Steve and ask him to go around and wake her. There was no point asking Steve to do what I needed done. He just wasn't capable of such treachery.

He was worried about me, asked what was happening. Lucy had told him what I'd done, where I'd gone, even though she shouldn't have. I simply told him I had a chance to rescue Jack, but I needed Lucy's help.

'No worries,' he said, when I told him it was a matter of life or death. He was a little hesitant, though. He and I both knew we were potentially risking *his* life by getting him to wake up Lucy. I said I'd call Lucy again in twenty minutes, and we hung up.

When I called back, she answered the phone with, 'If someone isn't about to die I'll make sure they are.'

When I heard her voice, I felt overwhelmed with emotion. 'Luce…'

'Honey, what's happening?'

'They're going to kill Jack.'

'You found him? Who's going to kill him?'

'It's too much to explain, but I can save him. I need you to get something for me.'

'Of course, hon. What do you need?'

'I need you to go to my parents' house…' I told Lucy she needed to break in, tie them up – I didn't care. She just needed to get Mum's lettuce crisper. The special edition one still in its box. 'It might be in the cupboard on top of Mum's wardrobe – remember where she used to hide the Christmas presents, where we always found them? But you'll need to take Steve and his boltcutters in case it's still in the locked cupboard.'

Lucy said, 'Okaaaaay.'

'I'll call her, try to get them out of the house.'

'Okay, sweetie. I'll go there now.'

'You remember where the spare key is?'

'Of course.'

'Thank you, Lucy, thank you!'

I took some deep breaths and practised my call to Mum. It had to sound convincing. And it had to be something *really* important to get her out immediately. I practised and practised my happy voice. And then I dialled.

'Hi, Mum. It's me!'

'Well, it's nice of you to call your mother for a change. You sound very excited.'

'I am because you'll never guess what happened. Jack proposed to me last night!'

Mum screamed into the phone and started crying. I felt a bit bad.

'I wanted you to be the first to know.'

She was hiccupping and making no sense. She spluttered, 'He proposed on a Sunday. The Good Lord is watching.'

'Mum, listen, I need you to go somewhere right now for me.'

'Now?' she squeaked.

'Yes, it's important. Can you go and choose some wedding stationery for us? Jack wants to get it organised as soon as possible.'

'Oh! Oh! Let me talk to him!'

'No, Mum. He's not here. Can you go now? Please?'

'Well, I have to wake your father – he's snoring – and I need to put some lipstick on.'

'Mum.' I tried to calm my rising voice. 'You can put your lippy on in the car. Please, just go. I don't want Jack to have time to change his mind.'

That did the trick. Mum said goodbye and slammed down the phone.

LUCY PICKED up immediately when I called an hour later.

'God, take your time why don't you?' she said. 'I've been sitting here, staring at the phone for ages.'

'Did you get it?' I said.

'Of course.'

'Oh my God —'

'Steve had to use his boltcutters. We felt really bad about doing that to your parents.'

'So you got the lettuce crisper in the box?'

'Yep.'

'You are the *best* friend.'

She said, 'Now, how the hell am I supposed to get it to you and get enough sleep before I start work tonight?'

'Shit. Shit, shit, shit. Um, okay, you'll have to courier it. High speed, whatever it takes. I'll give you my credit card details.'

'No go, hon. While I was waiting I called all the courier companies. None of them will do it. They can't guarantee it won't get stolen at the other end. In fact, they said, unless you know someone, it *will* get stolen at the other end.'

Remembering my conversation with Samson, I knew that even knowing someone wouldn't guarantee a thing. I deflated. 'Then I don't know what to do.'

'Sweetie, ask around and see what you can come up with, huh? But for now I need more sleep. I'll keep my mobile with me.'

'Okay, Luce. Thanks so much.'

'Love you, babe,' she said.

We hung up and I sat on the bed with my head in my hands. I couldn't cry any more. I was dry. What to do? I looked around the room, which depressed the hell out of me. So I slumped down the stairs and into the bar. I sat next to Phil and told him what had happened with Samson in the car and then with Lucy on the phone. He didn't even look surprised. Just sucked on his beer. He nodded in understanding about my problem with couriers.

He said, 'Ya friend needs to get the thing to Darwin.'

'Why?'

'I can bring it on the barge.'

I stared at Phil for a full five seconds before I threw my arms around him and gave him a big kiss on the cheek. I retreated quickly, not only because it wasn't a very pleasant experience for me, but also because he clearly got a big shock.

CHAPTER 46

*P*hil and I waited in his ute at the wharf, watching the barge pull into the harbour. It was like watching grass grow, except that you're also depending on the grass to grow so you can use it for something important, like saving the life of the man you love. I jiggled in my seat. I couldn't stand it after a while so I got out of the car and stood in the sun instead. Phil got out too and leaned against the bonnet.

When I'd called Lucy and told her what she needed to do – get the lettuce crisper to Darwin that day for the overnight barge – she'd said she'd take it to the airport herself, make sure it got on the plane. Phil had heard from his mates to say it was on board.

I said, 'Good grief, that thing moves slowly.'

'Yip.'

The barge was a great hulking beast, lumbering into position at the concrete ramp, nose first. It shuffled around a bit until the skipper seemed satisfied, and the deckhands moved like arthritic old men, finally getting it tied up. Its great jaw opened, and the ramp was lowered at about one centimetre an hour. I jiggled some more.

'Can I go over there?'

'Nah,' said Phil, glancing around. 'Wait 'n see.' He twisted the top off a stubby.

'What are we waiting for?' I said.

'Customs.'

'Oh. Shit.'

I was about to ask Phil who he thought would have the stuff when I saw, oh my God, Lucy strolling down the ramp! I let out an excited squeak and lurched forward, but Phil snagged my top.

'Not yet,' he said.

Lucy had her handbag over one shoulder and was carrying a plastic bag. A man in uniform approached her and she stopped, dropping everything onto the ground. She opened her handbag and the plastic bag.

'Oh shit, oh shit,' I said and grabbed Phil's arm.

The customs man was checking out her stuff and I saw Lucy hunt around in her handbag. She handed something to the guy and he turned and walked away.

Lucy gave the boys on the barge a big wave, picked up her bags and jogged towards us, yelling, 'Oh my God, your hair!'

I ran to meet her, hugged her tight, squealing with relief and happiness. I stepped back to take in the beautiful sight of her.

'Fuck, it's hot,' she said.

'I can't believe you're here!'

'Did those gang people do this to you?' She ran a hand over my head.

I threw my arms around her again, whispering, 'Thank you, Luce. Thank you, thank you.'

She pushed me gently away, 'Too hot, hon,' and handed me the extra-large Myer bag – the size you get when you buy towels and bed linen – with Mum's special edition lettuce crisper and a celery crisper as well.

'Where did you get the celery one?' I said, shaking it, then opening the lid. 'There's celery in here!'

'I found it in your mum's fridge. Thought it might come in handy.' Lucy shrugged. 'You can get her another one.'

'God, I love you, Lucy. Why did you come?'

'Well, I didn't trust the courier to get it to Darwin on time,' she looked over her shoulder at the wharf, 'and once I got to Darwin and met those thieving bastards, no way could I trust them to deliver.'

I carried the Myer bag and we walked arm in arm to where Phil was waiting by his car. He seemed a bit embarrassed, not knowing where to look.

I introduced them. 'Phil Collins, this is my friend, Lucy Collins.'

'Hey,' said Lucy, 'maybe we're related!'

Phil looked to the left, then right, up, down, then grunted and got into the car. Lucy and I got in next to him, me in the middle, the Tupperware on my lap.

'Geez,' said Lucy, gazing around as we drove. 'What a shithole.'

'Do you want me to take you to my hotel and I'll go get Jack?'

'No, hon. I'm coming with you.'

'Are you sure? These people are dangerous.'

She gave my arm a squeeze. 'I'm sure.'

I squeezed her back, but I admit I was thinking about how we were all going to fit in Phil's ute. The boys could sit in the back of it. I had a sheet to cover them so no one would see us. Jack would need to see a doctor for his leg. Maybe Lucy could have a look at it. After I made the exchange we were going straight back to the barge. Phil had arranged with his mates for us to be taken back to Darwin tonight. It was going to cost, big time, but Jack had lots of money.

As we drove, I asked Lucy about her trip on the barge. The skipper – a mate of Phil's – had given up his bunk for her, so she'd had a good night's sleep, but not until she'd drunk all the crew under the table.

'What did you give the customs guy?' I said.

'Money.'

'Really?'

'Yep. He was pretty happy about it.'

'He obviously was.' I looked at Phil and thought I saw his beard move. Was that a smile?

Phil's ute clattered along. Ahead I could see kids chucking things at each other from either side of the road.

Lucy said, 'Oh, shit, those kids!'

Phil maintained speed.

'What are they doing?' she almost shouted, gripping the dashboard.

I patted her arm as we rattled past. 'It's fine, Luce.' The young men stopped their missile throwing while we went by.

'Where are their parents?' she said, twisting her head to watch them.

Where indeed? Probably at cocktail parties with prostitutes and masturbating monkeys. With cupboards full of guns and Tupperware, and prisoners in cages.

I opened the celery crisper and tossed the celery past Lucy and out the window, wondering briefly if I'd just transported a deadly vegetable virus across the sea that would now mutate and decimate the country's crops. All of them. I wiped the inside of the crisper with a tissue. It still looked used, but there wasn't much I could do about that.

s we approached Samson's driveway, I said to Phil, 'Do you want to wait down here?'

'Nah,' he said and made the turn, grinding the column shift down to climb the hill to the house.

We stopped and two guards approached us.

'Jesus,' said Lucy. 'I feel like we're in a movie.'

I said, 'Wait here,' and climbed out of the car slowly, smiling tentatively.

I held up the bag. 'This is for Samson.'

One of the men approached me and looked in the bag. He gave me a small shove and Lucy yelled, 'Hey!'

I said to Luce, 'Quiet!' Tried again. 'This is a gift for Samson. He's expecting it.'

The guy glared at me. I didn't know what else to do – he didn't understand me – but then the front door of the house opened and Samson strode out.

'Who are you?' he shouted. 'What do you want?'

'It's me, Erica. I've got the thing you wanted.'

Recognition changed his expression in an instant. He stopped, said something to the two men and they walked back to the house, stood by the door.

I glanced at Phil and Lucy in the car. She was ready for a fight, eyes narrowed, fists clenched. Phil was trying to shrink into his seat.

Samson snatched the bag and opened it, his eyes lighting up. 'Ah! This is the very thing she wants.' He pulled the lettuce crisper from its box and inspected it, returned it to the bag. 'And what is this thing?' He held up the celery container.

And then, surprise, surprise, Kitty skipped out of the house.

'Hi,' she said, waving as she ran up and gave me a hug.

'Kitty,' I hissed, 'what the hell are you doing here?'

I looked towards the house, half expecting to see Emeline rush out with a carving knife. So much for Samson never having anything more to do with this "whore".

Kitty peered into the car. 'Hi. Who is this?'

Lucy scowled and they sized each other up. I didn't introduce them.

I said, 'Um, Samson, where are the boys?'

'Boys?' he said, looking up from the Tupperware. He was taking the lid on and off the lettuce crisper.

'You know, my friends? You were going to let them go?'

'Alright,' he said. 'You can have the men. But . . . ' he said with a finger in my face, 'you must leave this country today. If I discover that you have been seen I will find you and kill you all!' He waved his arm angrily to make his point.

'Yes! No! I mean, no problem!'

'One minute,' he said and turned, striding back into his house.He returned with a small bag that he handed to me. 'A gift,' he said.

I opened the bag and pulled a strange object out of it. I had no idea what it was. Something lumpy and grey – about the size of a golf ball – and it was on a thick string. It was the ugliest thing I'd ever seen. Samson took it from me and put the string around my neck.

'Oh,' I said. 'It's a pendant?'

'This will bring you good fortune.'

'Well, um, thanks,' I said.

Samson nodded to his men and walked back into his house without another word. The men headed down the slope to where the boys had been in the cages. Were they back there? I'd thought he might have let Jack and Joe stay in his house. He'd said he'd look after them. I beckoned Lucy and followed the men. Lucy scrambled after me. Phil stayed put. I was feeling sorry for him; he seemed so fearful with his big round eyes under his bushy eyebrows.

Kitty was beside me. She said, 'That is a very special gift, Erica. It is *sico lopes*. Shrunken monkey foetus. Very good luck.'

I stopped dead, scrabbling at the thing to get it off me, but Kitty grabbed my hands and held them still.

She said, 'You must wear it. At least until we leave this house.' The look in her eye suggested I'd be suicidal to do otherwise.

I let the petrified foetus flop back against my chest and walked on, shuddering as it bounced against me. Lucy was now ahead of me, following the two warriors. As we approached the cages I could see Joe sitting in his and I looked for Jack. Where was he? Lucy ran ahead. As I got closer I could see a lumpy form on the bottom of the cage.

I called out, 'Joe!'

He turned his head and stared at me. I ran to his cage. His eyes were red and watery. He was a mess. I wasn't even sure he knew me. 'Joe?' Samson hadn't looked after the boys at all. And Jack wasn't even moving.

I said to Samson's men, 'What's wrong with him?' They ignored me and went about lowering the cages to the ground.

Joe found his gravelly voice. 'Erica. Oh, God.'

Lucy had hold of Jack's cage before it hit the ground. She screamed at the men, 'Get this open now!' I wanted to tell her not to do that, to not scream at them, but my voice wasn't working.

Joe pushed past me, stumbled and pulled Jack's cage door open, dragging him out of it. Jack was unconscious. He looked dead.

'What's wrong with him?' I yelled in case someone had the answer.

Joe knelt, holding Jack's head in his lap and Lucy was all over him.

'He's alive,' she said, and Joe told her to look at the arrow wound.

'It was poisoned,' he said.

Lucy looked up at Joe and said, 'He's septic. We need to go now.'

Joe tried to hoist Jack over his shoulder. It took him a couple of goes with Lucy's help. I stood there, mute. Joe struggled up the hill with Lucy walking next to him, holding his elbow, supporting him. I staggered after them; Kitty skipped along beside me in silence.

Joe lowered Jack into the tray of the ute alongside my backpack and climbed up next to him.

Lucy said to Phil, 'We need to get to the hospital.' And she hopped in the back with the boys. I covered them all with the sheet and sat next to Phil, feeling useless and thoroughly, completely, shocked.

Phil started the car and Kitty stuck her head in the window. 'Where are you going now?' she said.

'Straight to the hospital, Kitty,' I said. 'Move away.'

She held the door and shook her head. 'No. You will die if you go there. Samson will kill you.'

I stared at her and Lucy yelled from the back, 'Let's *go!*' She thumped the car.

Kitty held the door and my stare. 'Wait one minute,' she said and ran into the house, returning in seconds with her bag. She opened the passenger door and shoved me along with her hip. 'I will tell you what you need to do.' She looked past me at Phil. 'Okay, now we can go.'

CHAPTER 48

Phil drove back to Seni in record time and Kitty directed him to her flat.

'Why are we here, Kitty?' I said.

'You will stay here while I get some things from the hospital.'

'But we need to get out of here.'

'He needs medical attention first, my friend. Then you go.'

We got out of the car. I pulled the sheet off the trio in the back, not looking at Jack because I couldn't bear it.

Before Lucy could start yelling and bossing, I said, 'Samson'll find us if we go to the hospital. Kitty's going there now to get what you need and we'll wait here.'

Lucy glared at Kitty. 'Like hell. I'm going with her.'

Kitty took a step back, which is the effect Lucy has on people.

Lucy said, 'What I need isn't available over the counter.'

'We can steal it,' said Kitty, without hesitation. 'I know someone there. A surgeon who owes me a favour.'

'Well, what are we waiting for?' said Luce.

They exchanged a brief look of admiration. We all helped the boys up the stairs to Kitty's flat. Kitty ran ahead to her bedroom to put Cecil in his cage so we wouldn't 'disturb' him. Today Cecil was wearing a blue bow tie around where I supposed his throat was. We stood in silence as she cooed and coaxed Cecil into not strangling her.

Joe lay Jack on the bed and Kitty said, 'Let us go now!'

Phil, Kitty and Lucy left. Joe staggered into the kitchen and returned with a glass of water for Jack, lifting his head gently and carefully tipping it up to his mouth, tiny sips that mostly ran down his face and neck, wetting the bed.

Joe drank and drank himself, and kept trying to give water to Jack.

I said, 'I'll do that, Joe. You look after yourself.' But there didn't seem much point. God knows what had happened to them over the last couple of days. Just left to rot, by the look of it. Joe lay next to his mate and groaned. I sat by Jack and ran my hand through his hair. I went to the bathroom and came back with a damp washer to wipe his face. I didn't know if it was any use, but at least I felt I was doing something.

Joe peered at me through half-closed eyes. 'How are we getting out of here?'

'We're leaving on the barge tonight.'

His head rolled away from me and I could barely hear him when he said, 'Jack won't survive it.'

Won't survive it? But what else could we do? I stared at Joe for a full minute. He closed his eyes, defeated. I paced the room. Should we go to the airport? Risk being caught? How could we get Jack onto a commercial flight? We couldn't. I paced. *Come on, Erica, think.*

Kitty's phone rang. I watched it for a few seconds then picked it up in case it was Kitty. But it was a man's voice, and I didn't understand what he was saying. I hung up and stared at the phone. I picked it up again and dialled Australia.

Celia answered.

'Celia, it's Erica and I need Mr Degraves urgently.'

'He's got the chairman with him —'

'NOW, Celia. Go in there and tell him it's life or death and don't you dare not do this!'

I could hear her hesitation before the phone was quietly placed on her desk. A minute later she said, curtly, 'Putting you through.'

John Degraves sounded annoyed and suspicious when he said, 'What is it, Erica, and where are you?'

'I'm in Saint Sebastian and I've got Jack. He's dying and we need to fly him out of here but we can't go to the airport because a gang is looking for us and will kill us.'

There was silence, then he said, 'And what do you expect of me?'

Rage coursed through me and I sucked in a huge breath. I screamed into the phone, 'You get us out of here NOW or I swear I'll expose you and the Team and anything else I might be able to dig up!'

I was breathing heavily, almost panting. JD knew I could carry out those threats. My job at Dega meant I had contacts in every media outlet across the country.

He didn't say anything for so long. I held my silence and waited.

Finally, he said, 'Call back in ten minutes.' And hung up.

I watched the clock on Kitty's wall. Fifteen seconds before the ten minutes was up, I picked up the phone and called JD's office. Celia answered.

I said, 'It's Erica.'

She said, 'Hang on.'

JD came on the line and said, 'Go to the airport now. The air force will bring you home.'

I put the phone down and gazed down the short passage into the bedroom. Jack and Joe, the elite of the elite, lay side by side, broken. Fallen soldiers. The very best Australia has to offer, sent here to this stinking country for what? Right now I hated John Degraves more than I'd ever hated anyone or anything in my life.

Jack groaned and his head rolled. Joe sat up and put a hand on Jack's shoulder. I rushed to his side.

Joe said, softly, 'Mate.'

Jack's eyelids fluttered and half opened. His face was pointing at me, but I don't know if he saw anything before he closed them again and slept. I wanted to believe this brief moment of consciousness was a good sign. Denial tried hard, but I knew it was more likely the opposite – a fleeting farewell.

· · ·

THE WAIT for Kitty and Lucy seemed interminable, but finally, Lucy rushed back into the bedroom carrying a bag. Joe stood to make room for her. Kitty was in the doorway, watching us. Probably having the time of her life.

I said, 'JD's organised something for us, Luce. We need to get to the airport.'

'Okay,' she said, without looking up. 'I need to sort this first.' She said to Joe, 'Get him undressed,' and to Kitty, 'We need transport.' To me she said, 'Phil had to go.'

Joe stripped off Jack's pants and I helped. The arrow wound on his leg was horrible: red, pussy, swollen, dried blood everywhere. His whole body was a terrible grey colour. I clutched my monkey foetus.

Lucy put a drip in Jack's arm, injected him, washed the wound. 'He might lose his leg,' she said, without emotion, and I felt relieved. If Lucy was talking about him losing a leg, then she must be thinking he would survive.

Kitty said, 'The taxi is here.'

'Five minutes,' said Lucy.

'I will tell the driver,' said Kitty and ran out of the apartment.

I went into the bathroom and threw up.

e carried Jack down the stairs using a blanket as a stretcher. Lucy held the IV bag above him.

'Pretty lady!' said Bruce Willis, looking astonished as he took in the scene. I wasn't surprised to see him there, leaning on the bonnet of his car, smoking. Joe and Lucy loaded Jack into the back. I pulled Kitty into a tight hug.

'Thank you,' I whispered. 'I'll never forget you.'

'I'll never forget you either, my friend.' Her eyes became misty. She handed me something. It was the framed photo of Jack and me. Kitty had nicked it from my backpack. I almost laughed out loud. She turned and ran back up the stairs to her flat.

I clutched Bruce Willis's T-shirt in both fists. He pressed himself into his car, trying to escape the mad woman. I said, 'You take us to the airport and you drive fast! Got it?'

He nodded, ran around to the driver's side. Joe and Lucy sat in the back with Jack draped across them, his legs curled to fit in the car. I wondered how Lucy was breathing with all that dead weight on her. Dead weight.

I sat in the front with Bruce Willis, who was very quiet as he drove. He kept glancing at me, nervous.

'Faster,' I said and he accelerated.

As we approached the airport I could see the rock-throwing kids ahead of us. Some of them were stumbling onto the road as they hurled their missiles. Bruce Willis slowed and I shouted, 'Faster!' leaning across him and hitting the horn, holding my hand on it as we blasted past the kids.

As we approached the airport I said to Bruce, 'We need to go where the Australian military planes are. You know where that is?'

'Yes, lady!' He drove past the terminal to a tall cyclone wire fence that marked the end of the road. A fence that reminded me of crocodiles. But beyond this fence were planes. Beautiful Australian ones. I leapt from the car as a man in uniform trotted over to us.

Joe and Lucy got Jack out of the taxi. Bruce Willis got my backpack from the boot.

The air force man shouted over the aircraft noise, 'Are you the people for urgent transport?'

'That's right!' I shouted back.

'PM said we've got an injured soldier,' he said, looking past me at Jack. He unlocked the gate and swung it open.

'Yes, that's him,' I yelled, pointing. The Prime Minster? JD had come through. But I still hated him.

'Follow me, ma'am. We'll take you on Clarissa over there.' He indicated a Hercules aircraft. Two more soldiers arrived with a stretcher. They transferred Jack and continued on to the plane; Lucy ran alongside them, holding the IV bag high.

I said to Bruce Willis, 'Alright, then. How much do you want?' Which was pointless because I had nothing – no money, no passport, nothing. My bag was probably still at Rupert Berringer's camp, or on its way to Identity Thieves R Us.

He grinned, broadly. 'Free ride today for pretty lady.'

I hugged him. 'Thank you. And I hope your wife gets better.' I ran to catch up to the others, and as we boarded the aircraft, the air force guy said, 'Let's get you folks home.'

It was fascinating inside the giant Hercules and I would have been enthralled if Jack wasn't dying. Joe, Lucy and I were seated along one side of the plane and told to wear the harnesses. Joe showed Lucy and me how to fasten them.

Jack was on a stretcher against the far wall, strapped in with his bag of fluid hanging from a hook above him. Lucy had checked him before we settled in, and given him another injection. I made a mental note to leave all my worldly possessions to Lucy in my will. Except Axle, because hopefully he'd be dead before me.

I said to Luce, 'How is he?'

She took a moment to answer. 'I'm not really sure. He's breathing. His heart's beating.' She shrugged. 'Septicaemia's dangerous. We won't know for a couple of days how badly his organs have been affected. That's the biggest concern.'

I asked her what happened at the hospital in Seni.

'Kitty knows absolutely everyone,' she said. 'There was an Aussie surgeon there and she told me he's one of her clients. I think he was drunk.'

'Was he on duty?'

'Yeah. Kitty told him she'd get Samson to pay him a visit if he didn't do what we wanted.'

'Good old Kitty.'

Lucy nodded. 'Yeah, I liked her.'

The plane took off and I was reminded of Phil's barge. The Hercules was like an airborne version of it – great lumbering beasts, both of them. I thought about Phil and how sad I was that I didn't get to thank him or say goodbye. I could probably send a letter to the Bum Crack Bar.

I also thought about my conversation with John Degraves. I'd now have no jobs at all, I supposed. No job at Dega Oil and no job with the Team. JD might even take out a contract on me, in case I decided to follow through on my threats. I thought maybe I should take some precautions, like writing a letter blaming him in case I turned up dead, and posting it to someone with a note on the envelope that says, 'Open only if Erica Jewell dies'. Maybe he'd hire Jack to do it. Nah. Jack wouldn't kill me. My mother would make his life hell. Then I thought that I shouldn't be focusing so much on my own death in case the Law of Attraction got the wrong idea.

But anyway, I was still angry with JD, sitting there in his cushy office. If JD was able to get the Prime Minister to organise a Hercules, and do it so quickly, why couldn't he have organised some blokes to rescue Jack in the first place? I scowled at the floor. I wasn't so sure I could look JD in the eye after this. It also made me wonder if the PM knows about the Team and just turns a blind eye to it all. If I was the PM, that's what I'd do.

All the way to Darwin, Joe leaned against the wall of the aircraft with his eyes closed. I offered him my shoulder, but he shook his head slowly. Lucy was quiet, watching Jack across the plane. We'd been in the air less than an hour when we started the descent into Darwin airport. The air force guy had told us we'd be taken straight to Darwin Hospital because it was an emergency. And sure enough, as the ramp at the back of the plane lowered, there was an ambulance, lights flashing.

· · ·

ONLY ONE OF us was allowed in the ambulance with Jack and of course that had to be Joe. He probably needed medical attention anyway. Lucy and I said we'd meet them at the hospital.

Joe quietly asked me to bring him something to eat.

I said, 'Oh, God, of course. You poor thing.' The boys hadn't been fed. No food, no water. What was Samson thinking? Maybe he hoped they'd just drop dead and he could throw them into the croc pen? Psycho. He and Kitty were perfect for each other. I wondered what Emeline saw in him and I wondered if Emeline liked her special Tupperware. I was sorry that I didn't get to say goodbye to her either.

In the taxi, Lucy said, 'I'm starving.'

'Me, too,' I said, thinking about the meals at the Bum Crack Bar and how I wouldn't mind one now. 'When did you last eat?'

She shrugged and stared out the window. 'I had toast on the barge this morning. I can't even remember. It seems like such a long time ago.'

At the hospital we went to the cafeteria and bought Joe three sandwiches, plus one each for ourselves. I thought I should probably call Mum at some stage. She would have been trying to get hold of me to tell me about the latest burglary. God, she'd be devastated about her special edition lettuce crisper. I decided to wait. Besides, I had no phone. A great excuse for delaying the inevitable conversation with Mum about my wedding. We went to find Joe.

JACK HAD BEEN TAKEN straight to Intensive Care and Joe was in a private ward. He was sleeping when Lucy and I found him. I stood next to Joe and gave his hand a squeeze. He half-opened his eyes, whispered, 'Kate?'

'It's Erica. I've got you some food.'

He struggled to sit up, took the food and scoffed the first sandwich down.

'Do you want me to call Kate for you?'

He nodded. 'Yeah.'

. . .

KATE STARTED CRYING on the phone. I told her where we were, that Joe was okay, and that Jack wasn't. She told me she'd come as soon as possible.

That afternoon I checked into a motel near the hospital using Lucy's credit card, which she told me to keep and use while I was in Darwin. She flew back to Melbourne after a very emotional farewell from me. That night I went back to the hospital, but I wasn't allowed to see Jack, and Joe was asleep.

I LAY in bed in the motel, staring at nothing until visiting hours started again the following morning. When I arrived at Joe's room, Kate was sitting on his bed, holding his hand. I wanted to feel excited that I finally had proof they were an item, but it kind of didn't matter any more.

Kate and I hugged. She was Jack's doctor so she'd been allowed to see him, and he was stable, she said. But in a coma.

Did that mean he might never wake up? Just lie there on a machine for the rest of his life?

'It's an induced coma,' said Kate. 'Temporary, to keep his body stable.'

They'd operated on his leg, and didn't think he'd lose it. And he was alive.

Kate suggested I go back to Melbourne, that she'd call me if there were any changes and that she'd try to get Jack relocated to Melbourne as soon as they could move him.

I knew I should go home. God, I'd been missing from work for … how long? Well over a week now. But I didn't want to leave Jack. I needed to call Rosalind. I needed to buy a new phone. I needed Jack to wake up. I told Kate I'd come back later and left.

CHAPTER 51

I pushed open the door to Yvonne's hairdressing salon and waited for her to notice me. She was snipping a blonde head, focused on the gossip.

'Won't be a minute,' she called out and glanced in my direction.

I smiled, gave her a little wave.

She put down her scissors and rushed across the room, crushing me in a hug.

'Kitty called me,' she said, shaking her head. 'I can't believe what you've been through.'

'Well, if it wasn't for you and Kitty, I wouldn't have been able to do it.' Bloody Kitty, whom I both loved and hated, with a passion.

She looked me over. 'I'm speechless,' she said.

'I know.' I ran a hand over my head. 'I can't work out how to style it.'

'Not that!' she laughed and glanced back at her client. 'Can you wait ten minutes?' she asked me.

'Sure.'

I took a seat and picked up a magazine. It was a gardening magazine and that made me think of Phil, which gave me an idea.

'Yvonne,' I called out. 'Is there a bookshop near here?'

'Yes, just up the road.' She pointed.

'I'll come back later.'

AT THE BOOKSHOP I found a gardening book for tropical gardens, and on the way back to Yvonne's salon I passed a jewellery shop that had all kinds of gold trinkets in the window, including tiny gold crocodiles, and that gave me another excellent idea. I went in and asked the woman behind the counter if they were able to dip something in gold, and if they could do it straight away.

'If you can drop it in today and come back tomorrow, no problem.'

I caught the bus back to my motel, and then back to the jewellery shop. It took forever, and I was impatient, but I reminded myself that I had nothing to hurry for. I had a new phone now, my old number cancelled, and on the bus I made some calls. All Rosalind could say to me, her voice chilled beyond recognition, was that I clearly didn't value my role at Dega Oil and we'd be discussing my future with the company. I wished I'd called Mum instead. Maybe not.

I plonked the monkey foetus on the jewellery counter and the woman poked it.

'What on earth is it?' she said.

'You probably don't want to know.'

'Okay. Well, we can dip it for you. Don't know why you'd want it, though.' She screwed up her nose. 'It looks like a lumpy golf ball.'

I caught a bus to the wharf. The Saint Sebastian barge was there. I walked up the ramp and caught a guy's attention. I asked him if he would make sure Phil Collins got a parcel, but he pointed over his shoulder and said, 'Give it to 'im yaself if ya want.'

And there was Phil, standing there looking embarrassed. I ran up to him.

'Here you go, Phil. A present.'

He opened the bag and peered in, then quickly looked around to make sure none of his mates were watching. He turned bright red and didn't know which way to look, so I hugged him and whispered in his ear, 'Thank you for everything.' I released him and stepped back. My arms were sore from hugging everyone.

He looked down at his feet. 'How's ya bloke?'

'Alive.'

He looked at me. I shrugged.

'See ya, Phil.'

'Yip. See ya.'

I ran down the ramp and to the bus stop without looking back. I went to Yvonne's and she showed me how to style my hair and it looked fantastic. Well, not really, but it was much better. She wanted to catch up that night, but I just wanted to go to the hospital. Which I did, and I was allowed to see Jack through a window. He lay there with all kinds of things hanging out of him. A tube out of his mouth, needles in his veins, not to mention all the machines beeping and huffing. He looked so sick and vulnerable. But he wasn't dead, and that's what mattered. He was in good care now, recovering, and I knew there was nothing more I could do. I'd done my job, the one I'd set out to do. I'd found the boys and brought them home. And now I needed to resume my life.

I decided that it was time for me to do exactly that.

CHAPTER 52

The following afternoon, as my plane descended bumpily through grey clouds onto the tarmac at Tullamarine, I squeezed the gold monkey foetus for luck, thinking about everything I was about to face. My mother, Rosalind, JD. I wasn't ready. I sighed, wishing once again that I was in Bali instead, frolicking with dolphins and Jack.

At home I took in the cold silence of my house and decided I needed to get Axle straight away – he made me feel better about everything – but also, I knew I needed to see my mother and get that over with. She was expecting a wedding. Holy crapola.

I unpacked my backpack, remembering my confiscated bullets and that I was yet to confess to Jack about what had happened. Maybe I didn't need to. I held up the palm-tree vibrator, wondering what I should do with it. Give it to someone? I propped it in the centre of my bedroom mantel. That would do for now, I decided. A reminder of where I'd been, what I'd been through, and what I thought of the whole business. In fact, sitting there like that, it kind of looked like it was giving me the finger. Good on it.

· · ·

I DROVE to my mother's. I should have called first, to soften the blow, but I knew that whatever she had to say to me on the phone she'd repeat when I saw her, so I thought I'd save her the bother and me the pain.

'Erica!' she screamed as I walked in the door.

Dad was watching telly. He peered at me over the top of his glasses. 'Hi, Dad.' He kept peering. 'It's me, Erica.'

He grunted and turned back to the TV. Axle ran across the room and headbutted my leg. I picked him up and cuddled him, and he purred loudly, rubbing his head on my chin.

Mum said, 'Oh, I don't know what to say to you! You haven't called. What did you do to your hair? I've been trying to get hold of you because you won't believe what happened.'

I followed her to the kitchen and sat at the counter while Mum put the kettle on, telling me that she really needed a new one and maybe she could get it at Myer's homewares sale, or that maybe *I* could get it because it would make a nice gift from a daughter. She gave me a look.

'What happened, Mum?' I said, not wanting to hear about it, but knowing I couldn't avoid it.

'Well, more Tupperware was taken! The cupboard was padlocked, but she came with boltcutters this time.'

'She?' My face grew hot. Mum knew it was Lucy?

'Yes. The police found all the stolen Tupperware in her garage. She's been stealing and hoarding it for years.'

'Wait a minute. Who are you talking about?'

'Mary!'

'Mary up the road?'

'That's right.' Mum opened the cupboard with the shiny new padlock and produced a box. It was a special edition lettuce crisper, the same as hers but even I knew that Mum's didn't have 'Mary Taylor' written on the box. 'She stole the celery one from my fridge, can you believe it?' Mum produced a celery crisper.

And I sat there, mute.

'Close your mouth, dear. You'll catch flies.' Mum continued, 'Mary carried on a treat, saying these things were hers, that she'd had them for years, but of course I know my own Tupperware. The police found these ones in her kitchen. They weren't in the garage with the rest of it.'

'Was she arrested?'

'Oh, yes. All the neighbours have been going through her garage, finding their precious things.'

Shame Dwayne didn't know about Mary. He could've saved his thieves a lot of time and effort.

Mum put a bag on the bench in front of me. 'Now, I think you and Jack will love what I've chosen. Do you have a date yet? But it doesn't matter. I've spoken to Father and he's got plenty of dates available.'

'Ah, Mum —'

'I thought a winter wedding might be nice. Winter white, you know. You can go to the solarium.'

She pulled the wedding stationery from the bag. It had a cross as the watermark, and a cutesy-pie bride and groom in the right hand corner that I suppose was Mum's idea of young and fashionable.

'And here.' She put a pile of magazines in front of me. 'I saved these from when I got married. Bride books! You can have a look and see if there's something that takes your fancy —'

'Mum —'

'Will you have children straight away? Because I've got these knitting books I've been saving —'

'Mum!'

She looked at me. 'Yes, dear?'

I leaned across the counter and gave her hand a squeeze. An action designed to comfort, something I don't think I'd ever done before, even when I'd told her Danny and I were divorcing.

'I …'

'Yes?'

'I got you something.'

I fished the beetroot container from my bag and gave it to her.

She said, 'But I've got one.'

'You said it was stolen.'

'Well, it was found in Mary's garage, of course.'

'Okay, well, I'll keep this one.'

She clutched it to her chest. 'I need two.' She lifted the lid. 'The thing's missing!'

I said, 'I got you something else as well,' and pushed the gold monkey foetus across the counter. 'Sorry it's not wrapped.' How to wrap a golf-ball-sized lump of gold-dipped shrunken foetus? I should have put it in the beetroot container as a surprise.

'It's solid gold!'

'Er ... well ...'

'Oh, how divine! Janice will be so envious.' She rushed from the room, putting it around her neck. I'd had it mounted on a gold chain. I made a mental note to stop using Luce's credit card and work out how much I owed her. I could hear Mum from her bedroom. 'I must call Janice straight away.' She rushed back to the kitchen, the monkey foetus bouncing on her chest, and picked up the phone. 'It's so unusual,' she cried, admiring it as she dialled. 'What is it?'

'It's a ... lucky charm. From Bali.'

'A lucky charm! From Bali!'

'Mum, before you do that,' I reached out and took the phone, returning it to its cradle. 'There's something I have to tell you.'

I WAS twelve years old the last time my mother chased me up the street with a wooden spoon. Back then she was wearing an apron and had a perm. But she could still run fast. I kept calling over my shoulder, 'Mum! I'm thirty-two years old.'

I'd tried to soften the blow as much as I could, starting with the fact that Jack was in a serious condition in hospital, having been bitten on the leg by a shark while rescuing a drowning older lady 'who reminded him of you!' I said he was delirious when he proposed, and took it back later, just like Mr Sheffield did in *The Nanny* and that turned out okay.

Mum had stood there for a while, still and stony-faced, then slowly opened the drawer, took out the wooden spoon and walked around the counter with it. She smacked me across the shoulder and kept doing it until I realised she intended to never stop.

As we raced up the road, she yelled things like, 'It's because you cut your hair! Men like long hair! You need to get a wig!' and 'You must have done something terrible, something to make him take it back!'

I yelled, 'I don't want to marry him anyway, Mum. He was flirting with women in Bali!'

And Mum screeched, 'You *will* marry him, Erica Jewell, if it's the last thing you do!'

CHAPTER 53

The next morning, Friday, I switched on the telly to watch the news while I had breakfast. I was surprised to see that one of the top stories was about Saint Sebastian. I hit the volume and leaned in. It seemed some sort of infighting had broken out, and that the local Australian troops were getting involved, with more being sent over. Well, looks like we got out just in the nick of time. As if it wasn't dangerous enough!

On the train going to work, wondering if I'd be allowed into the building to pack up my things, I got a text from Kate.

He's awake.

I called her straight away, squished against the door of the train, trying to hear her soft voice. She told me he'd woken for just a minute, knew who she was, asked about me and Joe and then fallen asleep. But he was out of the coma, she said.

I asked her what he said about me – most important of course – and she said he just seemed to need to know I was okay. Joe was up and about, and had moved into the motel with Kate. I now felt free to get a bit excited about those two being together. I wondered if they'd keep on hiding it. Maybe we could double date? Yeah, right.

· · ·

I STOOD in front of Rosalind's desk. Would she chase me up the street with her ruler? She sat there po-faced, blinking (can vampires blink?), not saying anything. She didn't ask how my stress levels were now that I'd had a relaxing break.

'Look, Rosalind —'

'Don't speak. I can't look at you. Go away.'

With pleasure. I backed out of her office and sat at my desk, not knowing if I even still had a job. When Marcus had seen me earlier he'd whistled long and low and said, 'Honey, you is in capital T trouble.' He'd given me a hug and said, 'Roger and I'll take you out tonight, yes? I want all the goss.'

'Thanks, but I don't really feel like socialising.' I'd given him a quick smile before entering Rosalind's crypt.

Celia called me. 'JD wants to see you straight away.'

Why not? My life was over anyway. My mother would never speak to me again, Rosalind would fire me, JD would take out a contract on me. I wondered if I should have the annual report file with me. There was no update since the last time.

On the executive floor I passed two guys in dark suits, one sending a text message and the other flipping through a business magazine. They checked me out, but I didn't bother saying hello or anything. I didn't feel like it.

I stood before Celia, cringing. 'Hi,' I said. It had been almost two weeks since I'd last stood in front of her desk, unable to tell Celia why I was there to see her boss. This time, JD had summoned me and, presumably, she still didn't know the reason.

She looked up at me, but didn't smile.

I said, 'Look, I'm sorry about the way I spoke to you on the phone, but it really was life or death.' I gave her a pleading look. I was running out of friends.

She nodded, briefly. 'Okay. I don't know what's going on, but I believe you.'

'Thanks. I'm not feeling very loved at the moment.'

'I like your hair.'

'No one else does.'

She gave me a small smile and thumbed over her shoulder. 'Go on in.'

'Thanks.'

I pushed open JD's door and froze. John Degraves and the Prime Minister were standing there looking official and serious.

'Come in, Erica,' said JD, but it took my feet a few moments to respond.

He pointed to the meeting table. 'Have a seat.'

I aimed for the nearest chair, needing it.

JD and the PM sat also.

The Prime Minister said, 'I'm sure you're surprised.'

I nodded.

'I'll explain,' he said.

Mr Prime Minister went on to tell me that I had intruded on a top-secret mission undertaken by a small team of elite military experts. That is, Jack and Joe. A mission that had been requested by England's PM, who was embarrassed to learn that one of Her Majesty's own military elite – a Mr Rupert Berringer – had turned mega evil. The team's mission had been to apprehend this criminal, who had stolen weapons from the Australian military with the intention of establishing and training a team of terrorists for 'God knows what terrible purpose'.

'Weapons?' was all I managed to say.

'Fortunately, in spite of the potential problems associated with your interference, our team's mission was successful,' the PM went on. 'There are some local issues as a result, but that's something we'll deal with quickly.'

'Interference?'

JD said, 'It's important you understand the confidentiality of this mission.'

I nodded. *Interference?*

PM said, 'We'll need your word on that. We can't have confidentiality agreements floating about.'

'What about the Tupperware?' I said.

JD and PM glanced at each other, eyebrows raised. JD said to me,

'You should probably get some rest, Erica. I'm sure you're very tired.'

JD then made me stand, hold my hand up witness-stand style, and repeat a whole lot of crap that would apparently ensure I never uttered a word about the top-secret mission I'd *interfered* with. And while I did that, I wondered again why JD was involved with an Australian military mission, and the only conclusion I could come to was that the PM knew about the Team and had sought JD's help in having Rupert Berringer quietly eliminated. I decided also that I needed to write that letter in case I disappeared or was found dead under not-very-suspicious circumstances. And let JD know about that letter's existence.

The PM left with his minders, and JD sat at his desk.

I stood opposite him, waiting. There was more, I knew. I still hated him. But now I was back and I kind of needed a job. And I didn't want to be some assassin's target.

'I didn't mean what I said, Mr Degraves.'

He glared at me.

I ventured, 'I would never have carried out those threats, but —'

'I know that,' he snapped.

I nodded, my mouth shut.

'You will never threaten me or my team like that again,' he said, his voice even and calm but laden with ice.

'No. I won't.'

'How dare you.'

'I'm sorry,' I said, my head bowed, but I didn't mean it.

'Rosalind is snowed under,' he said, suddenly, and I looked up. 'She's behind on the annual report production.'

'You mean . . . '

He checked his watch. 'I need a media release ready to go by three this afternoon. That blasted business in Western Australia. Environmentalists are giving us a terrible time. Rosalind has the details, but she doesn't have the time. You'll need to get a draft to me as soon as possible.'

'So, I still have my job?'

'Not if you're going to keep standing there, wasting time.'

'Okay, well, thank you.'
He nodded and I walked to the door, feeling like skipping.
'Oh, and Erica?' he said.
I turned, my hand on the door. 'Yes, Mr Degraves?'
'Good work.'

As soon as I woke on Saturday morning, I called Kate. She told me that Jack had stabilised but was sleeping a lot, which was a good thing. I'd thought about flying to Darwin for the weekend, but she talked me out of it, saying they didn't want him to have visitors. I was a bit miffed. I didn't think I was just a 'visitor'.

Lucy knocked on my door late morning, still in her uniform from work. She was doing double shifts, making up for lost wages.

'Here's your credit card,' I said. 'I'll transfer the money I owe you today.' I actually planned on transferring more than I owed her. How much do you give someone who's saved a life or two?

'Thanks, hon. And, ta-da!' She produced a large plastic bag. 'Here's your Tupperware.'

'Great.' Tupperware. Woo hoo.

Luce emptied the bag on my kitchen bench and we picked through all the colourful items, opening boxes, taking lids on and off things. But I felt sick at the sight of it. It would all be going straight to the Salvos. Or I could give it to my mother to make up for forgetting her order. Or I could save it for Mary for when she comes out of jail.

Lucy said, 'Jack might be moved to Melbourne this weekend.'

I looked at her, surprised. 'Really? Isn't he too sick to move?'

'Darwin needs the beds, and he wants to be here anyway.'

'Right. Well, that's good, isn't it?'

'Yes, for him it is. But not for the people who need the beds in Darwin.'

'What do you mean? What's happened?'

She looked at me like I'd just arrived from Mars. 'Haven't you heard? There's all this fighting in Saint Sebastian and we've got injured troops.'

I'd seen that snippet on the news yesterday, but I'd been too preoccupied to think more of it.

ON SUNDAY MORNING Kate called me to say Jack was coming home. I waited all day, and that evening I got a text from Lucy.

I've got a new patient. He's pretty cute.

I called her. 'Is he going to be alright?'

'Of course. I'm looking after him. Listen, I'm going home for some sleep, but I'll be back in the morning. I need to supervise all these salivating nurses. He's already the talk of the hospital.'

'Can I see him?'

'Tomorrow, hon. He needs rest.'

I DIDN'T THINK he looked too bad. But then, I'd seen Jack when he was almost dead, so anything by comparison was pretty good. It had been an agonising day at work, clock watching until I could leave. I'd raced home, dumped my stuff and sprinted up the road to the hospital.

I said to Lucy, 'I'm glad he came to the Epworth.'

'He asked to come here. Clearly, my reputation precedes me.' She grinned and gave me a nudge.

He was asleep, so I quietly pulled up a chair next to his bed and waited. I didn't care if I had to wait all night, I was just so happy to watch the rise and fall of his chest. I rested my chin on my crossed arms on the bed. In front of my face was his right hip. I moved my arms forward so they were pressing slightly against him. His right arm lay across his middle. There were no tubes in that one, but I checked to see if anyone was watching before I moved it. I took his hand in both of mine and kissed the back of it. I softly stroked each of his fingers, counting them, then I put my head down again, this time resting on three hands.

Lucy woke me. 'Go home to bed, hon. You'll need a chiropractor if you stay like that.'

'How long have I been here?' I stretched my back. Jack was still in the same position, but his hand was across his middle again.

'Couple of hours,' she said. 'He woke while you were sleeping. Just for a minute.'

'He did?' And took his hand back.

'Yeah. I think he was happy to see for himself that you're alive and well.'

'With funny hair.' I could see my reflection in the window. How did it get so mussed up?

'Come on, I'll walk you out.'

When I went back the next evening, in the lift to Jack's floor I thought about the fact that exactly two weeks earlier, I'd been packing for my trip to Saint Sebastian. What if I hadn't gone?

I met Lucy at the nurse's station. She said, 'He's such a tough bastard. Anyone else would have dropped dead.'

We went together to see him. When we walked in, two nurses were rearranging the flowers and fluffing up his pillows. Lucy gave them a look and they scampered. Joe was sitting beside the bed.

Jack smiled at us. Just a small one. Lucy checked his chart and I stood there with a stupid grin that threatened to turn to tears. Floods of them.

Jack held out a hand to Lucy and she took it, standing next to him.

He said to Luce, his voice soft and hoarse, 'This is the second time you've saved my life.'

'I know. I'm good, aren't I?'

'I want to give you something. Anything. Name it.'

'That's alright,' she said. 'I'm sure you'd do the same for me if I was dying in a disgusting cage in some God-awful country.'

'Let's assume that situation won't arise,' he said. 'What can I give you?'

'Well… you could cover my lost wages if you want. I was going to earn a bucket last week on night shift.'

Jack turned to Joe. 'Can you transfer fifty thousand dollars to Lucy's account today?'

In unison, Lucy and I screeched, *'What?'*

'No worries,' said Joe, smiling.

Lucy continued gaping at Jack, for once unable to speak. Something I'd never seen.

I recovered and said on her behalf, 'God, Jack, thank you.'

Lucy left, probably to lie down. Joe stood and said, 'I'll come back later.' He gave me a smile. It was a sad one for some reason. One laced with pity. Or something. Maybe I was imagining it.

I sat beside the bed. Jack didn't hold his hand out for me to take.

We looked at each other.

I said, 'I worked out who the redhead is. Why I thought I recognised him.'

He raised his eyebrows.

'The PM's nephew.'

Jack nodded.

I said, 'Is that why JD wanted you to take him? As a favour to the PM?'

Jack glanced at the door – I probably needed to be a bit quieter – and didn't respond. Anyway, I no longer cared. What else could we talk about? Should I tell him about my mother's wedding plans? No.

'Mum thinks you were attacked by a shark saving a lady who looked like her.'

His eyes smiled.

'I had to tell her something. She thinks we were in Bali.'

He nodded.

'When will you be able to go home?'

'Soon, I hope.'

And when Lucy allows it, I thought. 'So —'

'I'm really tired, Erica. Sorry.'

'Oh. Okay. Well, I'll come back tomorrow.' And I didn't feel like I was being invited to give him a kiss or anything like that, so I just said, 'See you later,' and left, pushing down the hurt, reminding myself that he'd been on death's door, and I really shouldn't expect too much at this stage.

CHAPTER 55

The next evening, straight from work, as I was about to walk in to Jack's room I heard Joe say, 'I won't be a part of it.' He shut up when he saw me, and looked away.

I looked from one to the other. Jack was sitting up, the blanket pulled back from his wounded leg, which was bandaged. He held eye contact with me.

'How are you?' I said to Jack.

'Okay.'

'Joe? How are you?'

He looked up. 'Yeah. I'm good. Not bad.'

I said, 'I'm a bit worried JD's going to take out a contract on me.' It just came out. I hadn't intended saying anything. But I was worried that Joe was being asked to do just that. Sort me out in case I decided to talk.

I watched their reactions. Joe looked at me, startled. Jack frowned. I took a chair and pulled it to the end of the bed so I could see both their faces clearly. 'Well?' I said. 'What do you guys think?'

Jack mumbled, 'Don't be ridiculous.'

'Is it? Is it ridiculous? You tell me.'

They glanced at each other. Joe scoffed slightly. 'Probably not,' he said, then looked at me, all concerned, like he shouldn't have said that.

But I smiled. He smiled back. Not too much smiling, though.

Jack said, 'My guys are keeping an eye on you.'

'So, you've considered it. The possibility of my being taken out.'

He said, annoyed, 'We're not in a movie.' Then he glanced at the door behind me. 'I wish you'd be a bit quieter.'

'Why? So people don't hear that I know what's planned behind my back?'

Jack pushed himself up so he was sitting straighter. He leaned forward and looked right into my eyes. 'It won't happen.'

I sat still for a few moments. Held his gaze.

'Okay. I believe you.'

We all relaxed.

'The PM said I interfered with your mission.'

We all tensed.

'PM's a dick.' That was Joe.

We all relaxed.

The relaxed/tense atmosphere was disrupted suddenly by the arrival of a new visitor. I watched Jack's irritation return as he looked past me at the door. I turned and there, grinning at me, was Dwayne from the plane.

'Well,' he said. 'Here's my girl, alive and well.'

I found that I'd shot out of my chair and was standing there, gawping. Dwayne put his arm around my shoulders and kissed me full on the mouth. I pushed him, but not hard enough to put any space between us. I didn't look at Jack or Joe, but neither said anything.

Dwayne addressed Jack. 'Got a few questions for you boys.'

I moved away from Dwayne, stood at the end of the bed. Dwayne held a card out to Jack, who ignored it. Joe leaned in and took the card. Scoffed. Second time today. He flicked the card and it landed on the floor.

Dwayne said, his accent still American but no longer Texan, 'I need to get a better understanding of your involvement with the black market operation —'

Jack said to Joe, all quiet and threatening, 'This joker needs to leave.'

Joe stood. Dwayne stopped talking.

I said, 'What's going on?'

Everyone ignored me.

Dwayne informed the room, 'CIA, fellas. You don't wanna mess with us.'

Joe took a step towards him.

A nurse bustled in with a clipboard.

Dwayne held up his hands. 'Okay. See we'll need to do this another time.' He turned to me. 'I'll see *you* later, chicken. Dinner?'

'Ah …'

He gave me a warm smile – the warmest I'd seen in a long time – tickled me under the chin and left.

I WASN'T COMPLETELY SURPRISED when Dwayne knocked on my door later that evening. In fact, I think I was now impervious to surprise. He held a bunch of red roses. Maybe he was the one with the contract? I peered into the flowers to see if they were hiding a gun.

As Dwayne had left the hospital room earlier, Joe said loud enough for him to hear, 'Fucking spook' (Joe's language had deteriorated since Sebastian) and Jack had asked me who he was.

I'd shrugged. 'Spook, apparently.'

'How do you know him?'

'Why do you want to know?'

He'd stared at me.

'Well, I'm off,' I'd said while I had the upper hand.

As I left, Jack had called after me, 'Stay away from him.'

Dwayne pushed the flowers into my chest. 'Surprised to see me?' He gave me another big smooch on the mouth.

'Dwayne —'

'Glen.'

'What?'

'Glen Campbell. That's my real name.'

I shook my head. 'What the hell's going on?'

'Let's have a drink,' he said and held up a bottle of red wine.

I discovered in that moment that I no longer drank red wine. The sight of it took me straight back to lunch with Rupert Berringer in the jungle. I swooned. Dwayne put an arm around me and led me down the passageway to my living room. Where was Axle when I needed him?

Dwayne found two wine glasses and poured. He offered me one. I shook my head. He put mine on the coffee table and sat next to me on the sofa.

He said, 'I realised at Samson's party why you were really there.'

'What?'

'I thought you were involved. The Tupperware biz.'

'No, I —'

'But you weren't. You were there to rescue your man.'

I nodded.

'You could do better than him, you know.'

He moved in for a kiss. I slid along the sofa, away from him.

'Dwayne —'

'Glen.'

'Whatever. If you knew why I was really there, why didn't you help me?'

'Sweet thing, I *did* help you.'

'How?'

'There was the matter of a small explosion?'

'That was you?'

'Uh-huh.'

I'd thought it was Kitty. So what did that mean? That Kitty *didn't* help me. Bitch.

He said, 'I came looking for you, but you'd taken off. By the time I reached those cages, there was nothing left but three dead guards and two empty prisons. You kill those guards?'

'No.'

'Sure you didn't.'

'I didn't!'

'Whatever.'

'Dw–Glen, what about the Tupperware?'

'I'm a private investigator. Employed by Tupperware to get to the bottom of the black market operation.'

'I thought you were a spook. CIA,' I corrected.

'Ex.'

'So *did* you get to the bottom of it?'

'I reckon so. Turns out the whole thing was started by Samson, trying to find the right piece of Tupperware for his wife. He wouldn't give up.'

'Makes sense, I suppose.' I asked, 'What about Rupert Berringer?'

'Samson gave him protection and cover for his illegal arms trade and terrorist training camp, and in return Berringer provided thieves and protection for the people bringing in the Tupperware.'

'What will happen to them? People like Phil Collins?'

'Probably nothing. Too hard to prove and, to be honest, I don't give a shit.'

I shook my head. It was like a dream. A nightmare.

Dwayne gave me an admiring look.

'Why are you looking at me like that?' I said.

'You've caused a hell of a ruckus.'

'What? Where?'

He chuckled. '*Where*, she says.' He laughed some more. 'Sebastian, sweetheart. All the fighting.'

'What do you mean?'

'You don't know?'

'Obviously not,' I snapped, losing patience.

'You gave Samson the Tupperware he wanted, which meant he no longer needed Berringer's gang of thieves. With Berringer dead anyway, Samson abandoned them. The men Berringer had been training had no leader, nothing to do, so they got bored and started fighting other gangs.'

My mouth hung open for a long time. With his finger Dwayne/Glen gently closed it and moved closer. He tickled the back of my neck, but I didn't feel much like laughing.

I finally got rid of Glen Campbell, who took substantial convincing, after I let him kiss me again, that Jack really is my boyfriend, which he isn't.

Dwayne said, 'Why are you letting me kiss you if you love him so much?'

A very good question – maybe something to do with the fact that someone was being nice to me. Anyway, he suggested that *he* could be my boyfriend, even though, I discovered as I pushed him out the door, he was heading back to the US the following day.

I poured the red wine down the sink, sat on the sofa again and Axle gave me dirty looks from the kitchen bench.

CHAPTER 56

The next night I visited Jack but just for a short time. Steve was there, and happy to see me, raising his eyebrows at my hair, but Jack kind of ignored me. They were having a good old laugh about something when I walked in.

Steve said, grinning, 'Tigers are back.'

'What? Oh, yeah.' They'd thrashed Carlton last week but I didn't really care.

I left the boys and their football talk, and took myself to a movie in Brighton. It was comforting to know I could do something as innocent as seeing a movie all by myself while Jack was safe and sound in hospital. I chose Brighton not only so I could drive past Jack's house, but because Church Street, Brighton, is about as different from Saint Sebastian as any place could be.

On the way home it started to rain and I slowed my car. The roads were oily, and tram tracks are slippery in the wet. I was in an especially bad mood after the stinking movie, which for some reason made me think about Jack's surliness and everything else that had ever annoyed me. Driving up Swan Street I got stuck behind a tram, right in front of that horrible nightclub. Through the blur of heavy rain and a misting window, I watched the line of kewpie dolls huddled against the wall of the building. A figure emerged from the shadows, trotted to the front of the queue, shook hands and laughed with a security guard at the front door, and walked in. Mick bloody Jansen.

Weirdly and suddenly, some alien force acquired my body and parked my car illegally, pushed me out of it and across the road, past the protesting security guard and into the nightclub, right up to the bar where Mick Jansen stood and where I punched him in the face. He was so shocked he didn't respond right away, which gave me time to punch him again and again and then kick him in the balls. By which time security had caught up with me, grabbed me in a bear hug and hoisted me across the room to a quiet space, away from the delighted crowd, where I was detained while the police were called. The police of course looked bewildered and unconvinced, amused even, but took me into custody anyway because, after all, I had violently assaulted someone for no apparent reason. No reason other than the fact that several witnesses, and I, declared him to be an arsehole. So then I was in the local lock-up. Who to call?

JOE ARRIVED at the police station and presumably dealt with all the paperwork. I didn't know or care if money had to be handed over for my release/bail/whatever – Jack could afford it and Joe had access to Jack's money.

On the way home, Joe, looking pretty sceptical, said, 'Who'd you assault?'

'Mick Jansen.'

He pulled over. Actually, he swerved so abruptly I was surprised we didn't cause an accident. He stared at me, mouth hanging open.

I said, 'Do you want to know why?'

'I'm pretty sure I know *why*, Erica. What I don't understand is how you survived it.'

'I sort of took him by surprise.'

Joe stared at me for a few seconds more then threw his head back and roared with laughter. It made me smile. I'd never seen Joe so delighted.

'It really hurt,' I said, shaking my wrist and flexing the fingers of my right hand. Actually, I'd used both.

'I'll show you how to hit so it doesn't,' he said, still laughing.

'You won't tell Jack, will you?' What the hell would Jack think? What would he say? Gawd.

Joe considered that, gazing through the windscreen. 'No, I won't tell him.' He looked at me.

'Thanks.'

'The reason I won't tell him is because he's already distressed about the danger he's put you in.'

'He hasn't put me in danger.'

'We've talked about this, Erica. If it weren't for Jack, you'd be living a quiet, safe life.'

'Yeah and bored out of my brain. And with no money.'

'Jack doesn't care if you're bored. He just wants you safe.'

'Safe, schmafe.' I huffed.

Joe started driving again.

I sat with my arms crossed, huffing, watching the blurry lights of Richmond glide by. After a while I said, 'Joe, why's Jack being so unfriendly to me? He's hardly spoken two words to me and he's being nice to everyone else.'

Joe didn't answer for a long time. The windscreen wipers squeaked as the rain eased and stopped. Finally, he said, 'He's hoping you'll give up on him.'

'You have *got* to be joking.'

He shook his head. 'I'm not.'

'After all we've been through, as if I'm going to give up on him!'

'You have to remember, Jack doesn't do relationships.'

'I'm not asking for a commitment. I don't want a boyfriend.' Well, I didn't want anyone *else* to be my boyfriend, but I didn't go into that detail. 'I like my job with the Team.'

'Good,' he said. 'I don't want you to give up on him.'

I nodded once. 'Good.'

My car wasn't where I'd left it, and I assumed it'd been towed. I reckoned it'd been blocking the trams. Joe said he'd get it for me tomorrow.

When we pulled up at my house, I asked, 'What do you think will happen to Mick Jansen?'

Joe smirked. 'You don't need to worry about him.'

CHAPTER 57

I went to the hospital the next night. Joe was there.

'I need to tell you something,' said surly-face Jack, 'but I don't want you to be afraid.'

'What could possibly frighten me ever again?'

He said, 'Mick Jansen's been seen. He's back in Melbourne.'

'Really?'

Joe and I exchanged a quick glance.

'He's already been in trouble,' Jack continued. 'Apparently, a woman attacked him last night . . . '

He stopped talking and narrowed his eyes at me. I set my face to innocent. Bambi eyes. I hid my grazed knuckles behind my back and avoided looking at Joe.

'It was probably Lucy,' I said.

He held my gaze, worry clouding his.

'I'm joking,' I said and he relaxed, slightly. 'What will happen to him?'

Jack was looking unconvinced but probably deep down he didn't want to know the truth, anyway. He said, 'We'll sort him. Don't worry.'

'I'll try not to.'

. . .

JACK WAS SENT HOME a couple of days later and I left it a few more days before visiting him. I wanted him to miss me, think about whether he'd like his life without me. But then I worried he might, so after work one night I drove straight to his house. Joe was happy to see me.

At the front door I said, 'How's the patient?'

'In bed.'

'Is he still feeling the same about me?'

Joe nodded. 'Yeah. He's a bit depressed, actually. Kind of angry.'

'Well, he needs to get over himself.' I marched up the stairs, barged into his bedroom. The room was dark except for the light from a bedside lamp. There was no one there.

'Oh,' I said out loud, but then the door to his ensuite opened and there he was, standing in the doorway, backlit by the bathroom light, naked apart from the bandage on his leg. The glow from his bedside lamp was strong enough for me to get a good look, and I did. But then I felt embarrassed, the puffed-up wind knocked out of me. I wasn't sure if I should look away or not as he stood there, making no attempt to cover himself.

He limped across the room and got into bed.

I recovered, puffed myself up again, stomped across to his bedside and propped there, hands on hips. He was full of self-pity, I could see that. He hadn't shaved in a while.

'Can you give me a *good* reason to walk out of your life?'

His frown deepened. 'Obviously —'

'For example,' I interrupted, 'do you find me boring? Or maybe it's because of my hair?'

He shook his head.

'No? Well, are you worried I might have romantic expectations of you?' I thought about what I'd said in front of all the people at Samson's house – that Jack was 'my man' and Joe was to be best man at our wedding.

He didn't respond, so I said, 'Get over yourself, Jones, you're not that good.' (This wasn't exactly true.) 'Yes, I like having sex with you and,' I muttered, 'wouldn't mind doing it again, but,' I held up a finger to emphasise my point, 'I have no expectations.' Even though my mother did.

He didn't say anything.

I said, 'So, you're worried I might get hurt or even killed if I hang around you?'

He mumbled, 'Of course.'

'But you wouldn't care if I'm devastated because you've ended our friendship, and I'm so distracted by the grief I'll walk in front of a bus and get killed. But at least *you* are free of the burden of guilt, because you would have no way of knowing the reason I walked in front of that bus.'

I thought there was a tiny lift at the corner of his mouth. Those tell-tale eyes certainly weren't sulking any more.

I poked the air. 'You're a very selfish man, Jack Jones. You only think of your own heart. Not that you've got one anyway.'

He nodded slightly.

'Well, I'm going,' I said.

He had the decency to hesitate before saying, 'Alright.'

I huffed and left his bedroom, went down the stairs and out the front door. I didn't bother saying goodbye to Joe because I knew I'd be seeing him again, with or without Jack's friendship.

I LAY IN BED, staring at the ceiling, sighing loudly, thinking about moving to America.

Axle heard something before I did. His head popped up, ears twitching, and I was aware of my front gate squeaking as it was pushed open. I was sure I'd locked it. But then, I did know someone who's especially good at picking locks. I smiled because I was happy he was here, and then I was cross because he was so bloody presumptuous.

There was a tap on my bedroom window and he called out, his

voice deep and low and always sexy, 'You'd better be alone in there,' and that pissed me off, too.

When I yanked open the front door, there he was with a look of hope, despair, sadness, happiness all mingled on his gorgeous, freshly shaved face.

Axle dashed up his leg – the good one – and Jack hissed, 'Jesus Christ.' He lifted Axle by the scruff and held him in front of his face. 'You're getting too big for this monkey business.'

Axle didn't respond. I took him and put him on the floor.

Jack looked at me, sheepish, said, 'Joe reckons I'm an idiot.'

'And what do you reckon?'

'I agree with Joe.'

I looked past Jack at the white Mercedes humming by the kerb, Joe behind the wheel. The passenger window was open and I could see his face in the glow from the dash. I said, 'What's he doing?'

'Waiting to see if you'll let me in.'

'Why would I?'

'Because you love me?'

If he wasn't looking so pathetic I would have hit him over the head. I took a breath, ready with an onslaught of, well, not abuse exactly, but maybe a whole lot of information about what I thought he should know about himself. But there was no fight left in me and besides, I did love him. And I hated him.

He said, 'So, can I come in?'

'What's in it for me?'

'My friendship.'

'Maybe that's not enough. You're a pretty crappy friend.'

'Money?'

'How much?'

'Ten thousand dollars.'

'You gave Lucy fifty thousand!'

'Alright. Fifty thousand. A hundred thousand.'

I nodded slowly. 'Hmm.'

'You could renovate your house.'

'I can afford that without you,' I said. 'What else?'

'Really dirty sex.'

'And sweaty?'

'Of course.'

'Well, okay.' I stepped back and swung the door wide.

Jack gave Joe the thumbs up.

I could see Joe's broad smile. With a wave he drove away and Jack limped through the door. He put one arm tightly around my shoulders, drawing me close. He said, 'I'm sorry.'

'Good.'

'It's just, I couldn't bear it if you were hurt, especially —'

'I know.'

He kissed me, softly. 'Thank you for rescuing us.'

'You're welcome.'

Together we walked into my bedroom. He kicked off his shoes and flopped heavily onto the bed, groaning.

Axle sat on his stomach and I lay beside him, my head on his shoulder, my arm draped across his chest. I played with his earlobe and twirled my fingers in his hair. He squeezed me very hard for a long time.

Finally, he said, 'I lied. I don't think I can.'

'Then let's sleep.' I pushed Axle gently away and knelt beside Jack, carefully pulling off his jeans.

He sat up, lifting his T-shirt over his head, and said, 'Is that what I think it is?' He was checking out the palm tree vibrator on my mantel.

'Probably.'

'What's it doing there?'

'Long story.' I pulled the doona over us both, kissed his cheek and we held hands as I lay there watching him until he relaxed into a peaceful sleep. Axle settled between our feet and I turned off the bedside lamp, listening to a glorious duet of soft snoring and thunderous purring.

After a few hours, Jack's breathing changed and he stirred.

I whispered, 'Are you awake?'

'I am.'

'How are you feeling?'

'Sensational.'

Well, I did what any self-respecting girl in my situation would do. I sat on him, my hands on his chest. Light from the street glowed through the blind. I could see his smile.

'Do you like my hair?' I said.

'Yes.'

'You're just saying that because you want sex.'

He chuckled and ran his hands up my arms. 'I suspect I'll get that with or without compliments.'

'True.'

'Actually,' he said, reaching up and pushing his fingers through my hair, 'I was thinking you look like that actress —'

'Halle Berry?'

'Yes, but better.'

'Better!'

'Yes.' With a hand behind my head, he pulled me into a deep, delicious kiss. 'Watch the leg,' he murmured, and kissed my nose, my chin.

'Don't you worry, Jack Jones.' Like a cat in the sun, I stretched out along his hot, hard body. 'You're in safe hands with me.'

ABOUT THE AUTHOR

In 2005 Kathryn Ledson took a deep breath (whispered a prayer) and left her secure, 25+ year career as a PA in the stuffy, high-stress corporate arena which, admittedly, included a few exciting breaks to travel overseas, work on a tropical island, and tour with famous people like Peter Ustinov and rock bands Dire Straits and AC/DC.

Kathryn returned to study with relief and a great sense of home-coming, and what emerged from that professional writing and editing course was a huge surprise in the form of hapless heroine Erica Jewell, lead character in Kathryn's series of funny, romantic, action-packed novels, which so far includes *Rough Diamond*, *Monkey Business* and *Grand Slam*.

If you enjoyed this book and have a spare moment, please leave an online review. Reviews are of great help to authors.

http://kathrynledson.com/

ACKNOWLEDGMENTS

With thanks to my publishing house, Pilyara Press – in particular Jennifer Scoullar, Sydney Smith and Kate Belle – without whom *Monkey Business* would not have travelled globally.

I am still and will always be grateful to those who made the original edition of this novel possible.